ONE DOWN . . . SIX TO GO.

Pallafox did what he was told. He threw carefully, wisely putting the ball just where he wanted to, despite the icy grip in the pit of his gut.

He gave up just enough fat pitches to throw the game away. He walked to the showers feeling like a loser in more ways than one.

Two things mattered to Pallafox: baseball and his little girl. He might be throwing away his big-league career pitch by pitch—
but at least his little girl was still alive.

Maybe.

The 7th GAME

DON KOWET

A DELL BOOK

Published by
Dell Publishing Co., Inc.
1 Dag Hammarskjold Plaza
New York, New York 10017

Dell ® TM 681510, Dell Publishing Co., Inc.

ISBN: 0-440-17669-7

Printed in the United States of America

First printing—September 1977

THE 7th GAME

1

A sudden hush fell over the Oakland Coliseum. The Oakland Golds and the St. Louis Cardinals were tied at two games apiece in the National League championship play-offs. Now, with two out in the ninth inning of the final game, the Cardinals had scored three times, reducing the Golds' lead to a single run. Vendors stopped hawking bags of peanuts and steaming hot dogs and cups of cold beer, as the Golds' pudgy manager, Danny Oswalski, slowly trudged from the dugout to the pitcher's mound to confer with Marcus Hayes, the Golds' catcher, and with Spider Johnson, the Golds' starting pitcher. The manager's squinty eyes darted from the Cardinal runner at third base to the Cardinal runner at first. Then Oswalski waved to his pitching coach.

"Now pitching for Oakland," the public-address announcer boomed, "number fifteen, Jim Pallafox."

The hometown crowd howled its approval.

In the visitors' dugout, the Cardinals' manager began restlessly pacing back and forth, watching the new pitcher jog in from the Oakland bull pen.

Moments later, Jim Pallafox reached the pitcher's mound. He gazed into Spider Johnson's weary black face. He wondered what he could say to soothe the pain, to soften his roommate's disappointment. To be removed at this decisive instant was embarrassment enough. To be replaced by Pallafox, Spider's rookie protégé, was vinegar rubbed into a raw wound. Pallafox was still searching for words that would console without seeming arrogant, when Spider slapped the baseball into his hand and angrily strode off toward the Oakland dugout.

Manager Oswalski reminded Pallafox to hold the base runners close, wished him luck (gruffly), and followed Spider. Marcus Hayes reviewed with Pallafox the signs he would flash to call for different pitches, then trotted back to his position behind home plate.

Pallafox took off his cap. He ran his fingers through his fiery red hair, then put his cap back on. He knew his teammates on the field were shouting words of encouragement. He knew his opponents in the Cardinals' dugout were trying to unnerve him and shatter his concentration. But all he could actually hear was the voice of the crowd—so dense, so unyielding, he felt he could almost reach out and touch it.

He took only five warm-up pitches. It didn't matter that after thirty regular-season victories in this, his rookie year, his legs were getting stiff, the elbow of his left arm—his pitching arm—feeling arthritic. It didn't matter that he had already started and won a game in this championship play-off. Suddenly, all that mattered was that irresistible psychic energy radiating from the stands. Suddenly, he felt free of the problem that had been tormenting him.

With two outs, the Cardinal hitter stepped into the batter's box. Pallafox leaned forward, bending toward the ground. Then he reared back, his six-foot, three-inch body drawn like a taut bow, and released the ball—a fuzzy blur, streaking inside and high, thudding against the catcher's mitt only inches from the batter's jaw.

The batter flinched. As Marcus Hayes tossed the ball back, Pallafox noticed that the hitter was moving a few inches farther away from the plate. A few inches too far: Pallafox's second pitch was also a fastball, but this time low and over the outside corner. One ball, one strike.

On the third pitch—another fastball, another strike—the runner on first sprinted to second base. Marcus Hayes didn't even bluff a throw. He was sure Pallafox had wanted the runner on first to steal second. Pallafox wanted the hitter to know he didn't care. Pallafox wanted to tell that Cardinal batter he was going to strike him out, end the ball game, and give the National League championship to Oakland.

The count was one ball, two strikes. Pallafox felt sharp now, his legs supple, his pitching arm limber—and lethal. The dilemma that had been troubling him seemed distant, unreal. The only fact was *now,* this instant, this pitch. He bent down, his glove hand resting on his right thigh. Hayes crouched behind the plate.

Pallafox stared deep into the Cardinal batter's eyes. The batter stared back; he was smiling, anticipating the fastball, tensing every muscle to explode against it. Pallafox smiled, too. He was going to throw the fastball, he knew the batter was waiting for it. It would be one-against-one, his strength, speed, and accuracy against the batter's. Then he leaned back, kicking his right leg high, snapping his left wrist fiercely as he threw. . . .

Even before the batter finished his futile swing, even before the umpire signaled the third strike, Pallafox was running toward the Oakland dugout, dodging teammates sprinting to embrace him, and ecstatic Oakland fans leaping the metal railing to mob him.

Fifteen minutes later, the Golds' locker room was in pandemonium: ballplayers charging stark naked out of the showers, then gingerly sidestepping the scan of TV and movie cameras; smells of sweat and rubbing alcohol and dead flashbulbs. From time to time, someone would dart out of the manager's office and douse a teammate with champagne. Or a jet of beer would squirt into a reporter's face.

The crush of bodies was suffocating. Already the print journalists—newspaper and magazine writers—were beginning to complain. They were, as usual, having to wait, cramped into a third of the locker room, while half a dozen TV technicians littered the rest with cables and cameras. Between the TV crew and the newspapermen, crouching on top of the trainer's tables, were the cameramen, their equipment whining, whirring, adding an eerie, irritating buzz to the babble of questions and complaints from newsmen, the pithy and often unprintable replies from naked ballplayers frolicking in front of their lockers.

Jim Pallafox sat on a stool, surrounded by TV cameras and the coils of cable that snaked all around him. He was naked except for a blue towel draped carelessly across his middle. His long, thin face was perspiring under the hot TV lights. His face looked tired, it looked tense.

"How much longer?" he asked one of the TV technicians, his deep voice polite, but strained.

"Now, Jim," the technician replied.

Joe Garibaldi, the ex-major leaguer who had handled the network color commentary, thrust a microphone inches away from Pallafox's face. "Folks, they don't give an MVP award for the outstanding player in the play-offs," he told his nationwide audience, "but if they did, this sure is the guy who'd deserve it." Then he said to Pallafox: "Hey, Jim, people are sayin' you're the best left-handed pitcher in the history of baseball—better even than Sandy Koufax."

Pallafox had been staring at his large bony knuckles. He looked up, blinking into the blinding lights. "Koufax was one helluva pitcher," he replied quietly, then dropped his eyes to his knuckles again.

"Sure was, sure was," Garibaldi agreed. "But one thing, Jim—Koufax woulda never let that guy steal second base. Why didn't you bother holdin' the runner on first tight? If he'da scored, it woulda been a real big run."

"I don't know, I can't remember why," Pallafox mumbled, his voice barely audible.

"Sure, you were just concentratin' so hard on the batter, right?" Garibaldi went on, becoming more and more effusive as Pallafox became more and more withdrawn.

"That's it," Pallafox said softly. "You could say I had a lot of things on my mind—more important things than whether he was going to steal second base."

There was a bitter edge to Pallafox's voice that made Garibaldi back off. He changed the topic. "Too bad about your roomie, Spider Johnson," he said. "I guess finishin' this game woulda meant a heckuva lot to him, after the year he had."

Pallafox glanced across the room. Spider was sitting in front of his locker—alone, forgotten. His eyes met Spider's, and it was Pallafox who lowered his gaze. "Spider didn't need this game," he spat, surprised by the intensity of his denial. "Spider will be back again next year. He'll win twenty again next year."

Out of the corner of his eye, Pallafox could still see Spider—on his stool, casually sipping beer from a can and pretending he hadn't heard a thing. Their relationship had become so ambivalent, Pallafox couldn't be sure whether Spider would resent his defending him or feel grateful.

Anyway, Pallafox decided, he didn't have time to worry about Spider's troubles. He had too many damn problems of his own—the symbol and substance of them soon to be winging into Oakland on a Boeing 727.

He stood up, keeping the towel around his waist. "Sorry," he told Garibaldi, "but unless I get my pitching arm in some ice, it's going to stiffen up. And then," he added, forcing his face to smile, "Mr. Kelly is going to get a stiff arm, too—a sudden attack of palsy, so he can't get his hand out of his pocket when I ask him for a raise."

Garibaldi was laughing—out of relief that the interview had ended, Pallafox mused, as he pushed past reporters, toward the trainer's office. He had deliberately given the broadcaster an opportunity to end the interview on an upbeat note.

"Those lefties," he heard Garibaldi tell his TV audience. "Who says lefties aren't all flakes?"

At that moment, Pallafox happened to turn around. A TV camera zoomed in for a close-up, and millions of Americans were left with a troubling image: a face touched by neither elation nor ecstasy. A face full of suffering.

Three thousand miles away, Phil Hanson was sitting in front of a large TV console, studying the pained expression on Jim Pallafox's face.

"You know," Hanson said, "anyone who hadn't seen the game might have thought Jim Pallafox was the losing pitcher."

The game was just over, and the offices of *Action Sports* magazine in midtown Manhattan were in turmoil. The typesetter in Philadelphia was already shipping sections of the magazine to the printing plant in Ohio; as usual, the magazine was going to bed late. Editorial assistants, their arms stacked with type layouts and proofs and galleys, were scurrying up and down the long, softly lit corridors.

In the miniuniverse of *Action Sports,* the edit assistants were minor satellites, constantly in the grip of someone else's gravity. Phil Hanson, the editor in chief of *Action Sports,* was the dazzling sun, his office bedecked with original prints, a mahogany desk once owned by Harry Truman, a color TV console, a conference table, an enormous green suede couch that blossomed into a bed, and a thick, plush-pile carpet. The managing and senior editors orbited in the editor in chief's glamorous glow, their offices one on each side of Hanson's. Their floors were covered with a less costly carpet, while the edit assistants inhabited cubicles in a cold, carpetless region at the far end of the corridor.

As he watched Jim Pallafox's careworn face, frozen momentarily on the TV screen, Hanson was talking to his managing editor, Jennifer Cohn, a petite, auburn-haired woman in her early twenties, and to a free-lance writer named Rick Holman—in his early thirties, of medium height, with a stocky build and thick black curly hair. Hanson was wearing a blue sport jacket, with pocketless gray slacks, and a tie. Jenny Cohn had on a smart, if conservative, brown pants suit. The free lance, Rick Holman, was dressed in blue jeans, a worn blue sweater, and scruffy white tennis shoes.

"Dammit," Hanson said, getting up from the green suede couch to shut off the TV, "somehow I've got to find a cover story to sell our World Series issue—or else Bela is going to put me through hell."

"Bela" was Arthur Wormwood—the magazine's advertising director. The staff of *Action Sports* called him

"Bela Lugosi," because of his cold, deadly demeanor, and his habit of dressing, day in, day out, in funereal black.

Rick listened to Hanson, then smiled. "If you have to go to hell," he said, "you couldn't find a more knowledgeable guide." He knew why Hanson was worried. Bela had started in the magazine business at the old *Saturday Evening Post,* in the days when the Post covers were red and green every time it carried a red and green ad from its prime advertiser, Wrigley's chewing gum. For Bela, the editorial text in any magazine was merely incidental—glue to bind together its advertisements. Bela was one reason why Rick had quit the magazine a year ago to free-lance. Phil Hanson was the other.

"Ad revenues are down, so Bela's after your ass?" Rick said.

Jenny Cohn started coughing, covering her mouth with her hand, so that Hanson wouldn't see her smile. Ad revenues *were* down.

"Since when do you know anything about ad revenues?" Hanson replied, his voice flippant and mocking.

Rick hated that satirical tone.

When he had worked for Hanson, during those three years as managing editor, Rick had been on a dizzying seesaw, alternately charmed, then appalled. Once upon a time, Hanson had been a "boy wonder" newspaper columnist; beneath Hanson's meticulously combed silvering hair was a first-class intelligence. Gradually, though, over the years, he had opted more and more for style over content, in his craft and in his life. Now, at forty, Hanson's writing had become shallow, relying on cheap anecdotes at the expense of insight. Two years ago, he had shed his wife of twenty years to marry the daughter of a prominent Hollywood television talent agent. Not long after, he had become editor in chief of *Action Sports* as well as a TV sportscaster. Even when Rick was with him, in person, Hanson's face seemed no more substantial than those subliminally shifting dots flashing across a color TV.

"All right," Hanson said, changing gears, "you're leaving next Monday for the World Series' opener in

Oakland on Wednesday. You've got your five-hundred-dollar expense advance. I'll pay you the usual fee—two thousand dollars for the story. All we have to decide is what story I'm paying you to do. I need something to spice up this crappy issue," he added. "I need a cover story for Bela."

Rick glanced at Jenny. Jenny met his glance, then shrugged her shoulders helplessly. "But Pallafox *is* the story," Rick said. "A twenty-four-year-old rookie. A rookie who's won thirty games—the first pitcher to win thirty since Denny McLain. The Golds won the National League championship play-offs with him, and they can't win the World Series without him. He'll pitch the opener, game four—and, if there is one, the seventh and deciding game. The Golds really don't have much pitching apart from Pallafox, either—Spider Johnson pitched lousy this year. So if Pallafox doesn't win, the Golds don't have a chance. The Patriots will wipe them out."

"Terrific cover story," Hanson said sarcastically. "Jim Pallafox. And just what do we put on the cover? Wait, I can see it now. We send a photographer to Egypt. He shoots the Sphinx. Then we superimpose Pallafox's stony face."

"And for a coverline?" Jenny said, amused by the squabbling.

"We don't use a coverline," Hanson replied. "We won't even need a story. We can just title the piece, 'The Wit and Wisdom of James Pallafox,' and run three absolutely blank pages."

"Okay, okay," Rick said, holding up his hand like a traffic cop. "So the guy hasn't said much about himself."

"He hasn't said *much*," Hanson replied. "Now, that is what I call understatement. The fact is, he has only one thing to say ever—that he's not going to say *anything*—no print interviews, no TV, nothing." Hanson launched into a passable imitation of the pitcher: soft monotone: " 'That pitch to Reggie Jackson? A slider. Over the inside corner. Low.' "

Rick smiled. "'I still think he's a good cover story."

"That," said Hanson dryly, "is why you no longer work here."

Jenny saw Rick's face flush. She knew the danger signal, had seen it flash often, just before Rick and Hanson had engaged in one of their shouting matches—like the one Rick had ended with: "I quit this goddamn job," leaving a vacuum which she had filled.

But Rick had done more than create an opportunity for her. He had pulled her into the job as he was leaving it. She had been the ally he needed in those debates with Hanson, the pawn the knight needed to checkmate the king—but still, she was grateful. Rick had taken her, an edit assistant fresh out of college, and had force-fed her everything that a managing editor should know.

Jenny felt gratitude toward Rick . . . and, she admitted to herself grudgingly, something more. She had grown to admire him. His blunt directness, as opposed to Phil Hanson's cute evasiveness. Rick's conviction that sports were a mirror for society, as opposed to Hanson's conviction that pro sports were merely a substitute sandbox, where grown men were paid absurd sums of money to carouse like boys. She admired Rick's courage, too—he was the only member of a staff of forty who, in his own phrase, had refused to "kiss Hanson's ass." She liked the profanity itself—she didn't swear, she didn't drink, but held those who did in awe.

Most of all, Jenny admired the fact that Rick felt for the ballplayers he wrote about, that he identified with the underdog. She had always considered herself an underdog—not half as pretty as most of the women she met. Rick had made it clear from the start that he was helping her in order to gain an ally against Hanson, but behind his tough exterior, she had always sensed he was rooting for her because she was a woman in a world that smelled of jock-itch lotions and liniment.

"Look," Jenny said, "I hate to break up all this bickering, but there is one angle on Pallafox that we've all overlooked. Maybe I'm paranoid, maybe I'm suspicious over nothing, but it's always seemed to me that Pallafox has to be hiding something."

There was silence for a moment.

"That's it, damn it," Rick blurted. "Jenny's right. Here's a rookie, a fantastic pitcher, the best left-hander maybe since Sandy Koufax. Good-looking, educated. A bachelor, with no wife or kids to tie him down. He has everything going for him, and he obviously likes money, 'cause he's trying to renegotiate his contract with Wally Kelly. He should be capitalizing on all the good things that are happening to him this year. He should be giving interviews left and right, because the interviews are going to get him endorsements, and fat banquet fees in the off-season."

"Mike Marshall, the Atlanta Braves pitcher, didn't like reporters, either," Hanson said. "He wasn't trying to hide anything, not even his bad manners."

"But this guy is usually polite to reporters," Rick replied. "Just says he doesn't want to talk about himself. Finds talking about himself boring. Can you believe that? Have you ever met a pro athlete, a pitcher—a *lefty* pitcher—who didn't know in his heart of hearts that he was the greatest damn sensation that ever walked the earth? You don't win thirty games with no ego. You know that."

"I don't know that," said Hanson. "Maybe he gets his kicks out of saying, 'Aw, shucks, folks, it waren't nothin'.'"

"Maybe," said Jenny. "Or maybe he *is* hiding something."

Hanson thought for a moment. "All right, suppose Holman here does angle the story that way," he said to Jenny. "What happens if this sphinx doesn't have a riddle, or if Rick can't solve the riddle in less than three thousand words?"

"Then," Jenny replied coolly, "we ask our readers to solve the riddle."

Rick and Phil looked at her, astonished.

"Rick interviews everyone around Pallafox," she went on, enjoying herself now. "He gets as close to Pallafox as he can, spends as much time with him as he can. Then, in his story, he lays out all the elements of the 'mystery.' He offers his explanation . . . then tells the readers to send in theirs. What is the answer to this riddle: Why does Jim Pallafox refuse to talk?"

Hanson sat back, staring at Jenny. He was drumming on his desk with a pencil. "And then we pick the best ideas. We run them in the 'Letters to the Editor' column."

Jenny nodded. "The readers will be writing their own endings to the story."

"It might be one helluva hook," Hanson admitted.

"And I'm sure Bela would be overjoyed with the idea," Jenny added, "if, say, we ask him to get his advertisers involved—by offering a couple of small prizes."

"Not bad," Hanson said, "not bad at all."

"Hey," Rick said to Jenny, "do I have to give you the ten percent I usually give my agent?"

Jenny smiled at him for the first time that afternoon. She *was* plain—small, with a good, curvy figure—but still plain, except, Rick decided, when her face glowed with that special smile. There were beautiful women who turned ugly when they smiled; their smiles were cheap junk-jewelry. Jenny wasn't beautiful *until* she smiled. And then, Rick thought, you could set her smile on a velvet pillow, you could exhibit it at Tiffany's.

By five o'clock that afternoon, the reporters milling in the Golds' locker room were satisfied that they had captured the glory and drama of today's Oakland victory. They began to elbow past the throng of well-wishers blocking the locker room door, turning left down a long gray corridor, till they reached the Golds' hospitality suite.

During the play-offs, and later during the World Series itself, the home ball club was responsible for the care and feeding of the press. The practice was a carry-over from the regular season, when the writers who covered each club were fed lunch or dinner at the ball club's expense. Depending on the ball club, and the philanthropy of its owner, the fare varied from sumptuous

to simpering, from incomparable to downright inedible.
In St. Louis, the press had feasted on sirloin steak and
Rioja wine. But the buffet in Oakland had been as unpredictable as the Golds' owner, Wally O. Kelly. One
day lobster flown in fresh from Maine, the next day,
soggy hash. The only invariable was chocolate chip
cookies. Chocolate chip cookies were Wally Kelly's favorites.

Now, approximately one hour after the Oakland
Golds had won the National League pennant, and thus
the right to meet the New York Patriots, champions of
the American League, in sports' ultimate event, the
World Series, reporters were awaiting the appearance of
the benefactor who had provided today's rather dismal
fare of cold cuts and warm beer. In front of a dais decorated with gold tinsel was a coterie of baseball writers
from New York newspapers, led by Ray Fowler, in his
hallmark black-and-white checked sport jacket. At
that moment there was a commotion at the far end of
the room, near the entrance: a buzzing, the mumbling
"busy noise" bit players make in college drama produc-
tions. Then, as the murmur of the reporters near the
door grew, so did another sound. Ray Fowler stopped
talking. He listened, then remarked, "The sound of
thundering hoofbeats. It's a bird . . . it's a plane . . .
it's the Wally O.s, man and mule."

Just then, the tanned, beetle-browed visage of Wally
O. Kelly peered into the hospitality suite. "Greetings,"
the Golds' owner bellowed, as he entered. In his right
hand, he was holding a sign that proclaimed, "We're
Going to Whip Those Patriots!" With his left hand, he
was leading a mule by the halter. The mule was Wally's
mascot—the symbol of his own obstinacy. Across its
back, it carried a blanket with "Wally O." in large letters.

Kelly led the mule down a path cleared by reporters,
toward the dais. When he spied Fowler, Kelly stopped.
"Ray Fowler," he roared, "I want to see what happens
when a Kentucky mule is confronted by a New York
ass! Those lies you wrote about me trying to break up

my team, so fans would stop coming out to my ball park, and I could break my ball-park lease using that minimum attendance clause—that's all they were, lies and calumny.

"You'll see," Kelly hissed, waving the sign around menacingly. "This team I'm supposed to be trying to destroy is going to *massacre* Fred Hartwood's gang of pin-striped pin heads. After my Golds get done with them, people won't call them the 'Patriots,' they'll call them the 'Patsies.'"

Fowler was staring at Kelly incredulously, his lips locked in a dazed smile. Just then, Wally tugged at the mule's halter. The Wally O.s, mule and man, edged forward; the mule's tail brushed Fowler's hand, spilling his cup of beer, staining the writer's checked sport jacket in sickly brown streaks.

"Goddamn you, you blundering buffoon," Fowler yelled, "you're gonna get a bill for this!" Then the writer turned on his heels and marched out of the room.

Wally watched him leave, a bemused smile on his lips. Wally considered all newspaper sportswriters hypocrites. He manipulated them shamelessly, turning them, whenever possible, into compliant spokesmen for his ball club's PR department. Wally fed them those free meals at the ball park; access to morsels of information also depended, to a large extent, on whether the newsmen criticized the franchise, or were subservient. Wally regarded magazine writers with slightly more respect; they were more difficult to control. They moved from city to city, they owed no allegiance to any particular club. They could hit and run.

Although his assault on Fowler had been premeditated, Wally knew that the press, Fowler included, would interpret the incident as one more proof of his epic eccentricity. "I have the worst sense of public relations of any businessman I know," Wally was fond of telling people. And few were perceptive enough to see that this disarming candor was the most effective public-relations ploy of all. Fowler would rant and rage ounces of printer's ink in tomorrow's column, but he would think twice about maligning Wally's motives—his loyalty to Oakland—again.

Wally turned the mule over to an assistant. He mounted the dais. "Gentlemen," he said, uttering the word with undisguised contempt, "are there any questions?"

"Is this your way of imposing censorship— embarrassing anyone who writes a piece you don't like?" a New York reporter grumbled.

"I mean *baseball* questions," Wally snapped.

"What's wrong with Pallafox?" another reporter asked.

"It seems you weren't at the ball game," Wally said icily.

"I don't mean his pitching," the reporter replied, "I mean his personality. When we talked to him in the locker room, he acted like he's been acting for weeks now—upset, unhappy. He sure didn't seem like a rookie who had just given his team the National League title."

"And, naturally, you think I'm the irritant," Wally responded.

"He's trying to renegotiate his contract, isn't he?" someone else said.

"You know my dictum," Wally answered, turning on his charm. "If they play, they stay; if they want more dough, they go."

Some reporters burst out laughing.

"No, really, I don't know what's bothering him," Wally added, shifting to soft sell now. "I think it's simply that he doesn't like dealing with the press. He doesn't know how to deal with the press. Don't forget— a year ago he was an unknown, in the minor leagues. I think in time he'll learn to handle you gentlemen the way I did. He'll stop ignoring you, and start boring you."

His audience laughed again. Then an Oakland reporter asked, "But why won't he say anything about his personal life—what's the point? Most young guys coming into the league want to tell everything, 'cause they suddenly discover everyone thinks the silliest thing they've done is the most important thing in the world."

Wally stared at the questioner for a moment. Then he furrowed his broad forehead, lifting his eyebrows ominously. "Look, if I've told you people once, I've told you a thousand times," he said. "I don't want anyone snooping into my private life, and I don't snoop into my ballplayers' lives, either. If Pallafox wants to preserve some privacy for himself, if he can get away with it—more power to him. I don't get involved with my players' personal lives, I don't think it's any of my damn business, or, for that matter, any of yours. I pay them to play, not say. The more you get involved in a player's personal life, the more problems you get," he added.

Wally parried the rest of the questions flawlessly. But his own thoughts remained impaled on the dilemma the Oakland reporter had raised, which he had disposed of so easily. In fact, early in the season he had been just as disturbed as the press at Pallafox's reluctance to divulge anything but name, rank, and serial number. At first, he had figured that Pallafox felt trapped. After all, in many ways Pallafox was a prisoner—an idealist who had always played for love, an amateur who suddenly found himself an entertainer, featured in a multimillion-dollar major-league extravaganza.

Wally had spoken to Pallafox more than once. He had lectured his young pitcher, telling him that providing personal grist for the press's mill could be to his own advantage—Pallafox would get financial feedback. Later, there had been one stormy (though private) confrontation after another, with Pallafox arguing that his private life was nobody's damn business, and Wally shouting back that as long as Pallafox wore a Golds' uniform, he would do what Wally O. Kelly told him to do. Eventually, Wally had decided that Pallafox was acting reclusive out of spite—to spite Wally. Then, only a fortnight ago, Wally had finally stumbled onto Pallafox's secret.

Over the past week, Pallafox had become more and more reluctant to talk to the press, and this, in Wally's mind, spelled trouble. Pallafox was, if unconsciously, sending out not-so-subtle distress signals. That was not very good, Wally was thinking, as he kept providing routine answers to the reporters' routine questions. It was absolutely essential, for the success of Wally's plan, that Pallafox's "secret" remain one.

2

The stampede across the bridge from San Francisco to Oakland had already begun. They came in herds of freshly polished compact sedans and station wagons, their bumpers plastered with stickers displaying their favorite team's insignia, their radio antennas flying their team's pennant.

That afternoon, some of these bleacherites and grandstanders would telephone San Francisco's poshest nightclubs seeking reservations, only to be informed by condescending voices with foreign accents that every table, everywhere, was booked till long after midnight. ("Perhaps somewhere else . . . in Oakland . . . across ze bay?") The choicest tables in San Francisco (there were no choice tables in Oakland), those directly at ringside, had already been reserved for the same select group that was destined to watch the Series from one of the forty stadium suites that ringed the uppermost deck of the newly remodeled Coliseum. The tables behind them had been reserved for a lower rank of television executives, and columnists from the large metropolitan dailies. Sportswriters from provincial newspapers had been banished to the rear, near the kitchen, quarantined from the rich and the powerful.

The pecking order would prevail throughout the week—World Series week—in San Francisco/Oakland and then in New York, where the Series would move for games three and four. Being a celebrity was best. But being snubbed by a celebrity conferred a certain status, too: better to be snubbed than mistaken for someone who had arrived in a compact sedan, with a bumper sticker and a team pennant flapping, and a motel reservation on the wrong side of the Bay.

But now, at 10:00 A.M. on Tuesday morning, with less than thirty-six hours to go before the Series opener, NBC roustabouts were already fighting a chill wind howling in off the Bay and over the Coliseum, home of the National League champion Oakland Golds. Outside the Coliseum, a three-hundred-foot canvas had been stretched, to provide an enormous candy-striped tent, into which crates of beluga caviar and Fortnum-Mason link sausages and Dom Perignon champagne were being stacked. Meanwhile, nearby, a crew of NBC technicians was grunting beneath the weight of the thick cables that sprawled like entrails from the bellies of five 20-ton Kenworth trucks.

All the hotels and motor inns in Oakland and San Francisco had been booked—some of them over-booked—for weeks now. At the exclusive San Francisco Shelby Hotel, a towering plate-glass-and-poured-concrete structure famous for the revolving restaurant on its roof, a group of young men, mostly in their twenties, stood waiting to register. Some were white, dressed in natty blue blazers and charcoal black slacks, with bare heads revealing hair trimmed right above the ears; others were black, wearing the same blazers and slacks. A few sported rakish felt hats with broad, floppy brims. But no Afros. The New York Patriots' owner, Fred Hartwood, did not allow his players to wear Afro haircuts, or hair below their ears.

Other guests—even the ones who had arrived from Beverly Hills in sleek, chauffeured limousines, who wore diamonds that gleamed from their fists, and $85 shirts, and $400 suits and $1000 denim dresses—gaped at the Patriot ballplayers, champions of the American League. This much these guests shared in common with the NBC roustabouts outside the Oakland Coliseum and even ma-and-pa-and-the-kids lodged in cramped, seedy motel rooms: a sense of awe, a special feeling of anticipation, that presentiment of things possible only a World Series can arouse.

Though it was still morning, and Rick Holman had

eaten breakfast scarcely half an hour ago, he was sitting in the hotel bar, off the main lobby. With him, at a round table in one corner, were a couple of baseball writers from New York, including Ray Fowler. Fowler, "dean of the New York scribes," as his own paper liked to describe him, was airing his pet peeve: TV sportscasters who refuse to give all the scores of every game every day. Fowler, Rick knew, was directing his comments, in a veiled way, at Phil Hanson, the only New York sportscaster who refused to recite that litany of daily scores. But Rick preferred not to lift the veil. He was in no mood to defend Phil Hanson, something he would feel obligated to do, since Hanson was paying his expenses at one of San Francisco's plushest hotels.

Instead, he left the bar and headed for his room on the sixteenth floor. He had to call Jim Pallafox, to try to set up an interview. He would telephone the pitcher at home, this afternoon, after the Golds' practice. Then he would cab out to the Oakland Coliseum to pick up his World Series credentials. When he reached his room, he found a letter on his desk, apparently delivered by the bell captain. An invitation. From Wally O. Kelly. Rick's name was typed onto the printed invitation which read:

> Dear Rick:
>   In anticipation of my Oakland Golds' inevitable victory, I am inviting about 30 of my most obnoxious enemies, and both of my friends, to a celebratory bacchanal at my home, on Thursday night, after the second Series game. Herb Hannelly, my publicity director, will inform you of time and place immediately following the Series opener—if, that is, Herb Hannelly is still my publicity director after the Series opener.
>
> > Cordially yours,
> > Walter O. Kelly

Rick laughed aloud—imagine the gall: a victory celebration after the second game of a best-of-seven Series.

* * *

By the time Rick Holman got his invitation, the author of that petition was safely tucked in the back seat of his limousine. The chauffeur guided the black Cadillac limo through San Francisco's midday traffic, toward the bridge that led across the Bay to Oakland, and the Oakland Coliseum. Meanwhile, Wally Kelly was dialing a number on the telephone built into the back of the chauffeur's seat. As he dialed, he depressed a button. A thick, soundproofed glass partition rose out of a slot, separating Kelly from the driver. A moment before, at Kelly's instructions, the chauffeur had raised the volume of the car radio to a hysterical pitch. Now Kelly shut off the rear speakers. He was surrounded by total silence. He lowered the venetian blinds over all three windows, and flipped on the light switch.

"Let me speak to Harry," he said into the telephone. "Harry? How are things in Vegas, you old whoremonger. This is Wally."

"Wally," the voice on the other end of the line responded. "Hey, I was just on my way out of here. Herb sent me those tickets—they look good, right behind first base." The voice had a distinct Sicilian shuffle to it. Wally smiled. Why, he thought to himself, do men with names like Vito Genaro choose to call themselves Harry Walters when they go "legitimate"?

"Harry, I don't know why the hell you want those peasant tickets anyway," Wally told him. "I've told you a hundred times, there's always a place for you in my stadium suite."

"You know me, pal," Harry answered. "Gotta stay near the action."

"I think it's because your eyes are going bad, Harry," Wally said, smiling to himself again. "My box is too high up and far away from the scoreboard. You don't feel comfortable unless you can see the pitchers' numbers from every game around the league—even when the game you're at is the only game being played. You have a million bucks, but you still can't stop betting five bills on twenty different games a day."

Harry laughed, a deep dry cackle that scraped Wally's eardrums like sandpaper. "That's how I got my money," he replied. "On five-bill lulus."

"Listen, Harry," Wally said, his voice sobering. "I want you to do me a favor."

"Anything, pal. You call it."

"I want to place a bet."

"Wally, even for a friend—I'm no small-time book-maker anymore."

"Harry, I mean a very substantial wager. One that requires tact—and secrecy."

There was silence at the other end of the line. Then Harry's voice, hard-edged but smoother now, saying, "Go ahead, Wally, I'm listening."

"I want to wager five hundred thousand on the World Series."

"What kind of collateral?" Harry asked.

"No collateral," Wally replied. "I am talking about five hundred thousand cash."

Harry whistled. "That's a big bundle, Wally. Only the big boys will handle that kind of bundle. And if you lose, and you don't come up with it, all of it, they'll drain the blood out of your body and sell it to make up the difference. Look, Wally, take some advice. Your Golds are strong with Pallafox pitching, but no one's that strong in a Series when one team can get lucky, win four straight, and take it all. You got inside dope? Something wrong with the Patriots?"

"Harry, I see I didn't make myself clear," Kelly replied softly. "At whatever odds you can get—I don't really care—I want you to place five hundred thousand on the Oakland Golds to *lose*."

Harry Walters put down the telephone and walked over to the window that looked out on his casino. He was a small, bantam rooster of a man, with straight brown hair, flecked with gray; dark, swarthy skin, a large nose, and powerful arms too long for his thin, frail-looking torso. Harry stared out the window. He nervously twisted the massive diamond ring on one finger. His office was located on the fourth floor of the casino he owned in partnership with some of "the big boys"—

the Shazaam, in the pulsating heart of Las Vegas's famous Strip. Below, there were twenty-four tables—
roulette, craps, blackjack, poker, everything, with customers jammed shoulder to shoulder, even now, at midday. Then he raised his eyes. High above the gaming
tables, the space was filled with carnival madness. The
Astounding Astronauticas, a high-wire trapeze act, were
leaping off towers, linking together in midair to form
swinging human chains. Periodically, one of them
would fall, intentionally, to be scooped up by the safety
net only a few feet above the blackjack tables.

But his favorite was down below—his freak show, he
liked to call it. He pressed a button, and a section of the
floor rolled back, revealing a·pane of one-way glass.
Harry lowered himself onto a floor cushion, kneeling
carefully to avoid creasing his $140 Johnson-Murphy
shoes just below the toes, and stared with fascination at
the craps table below, where a mouse was climbing over
a stack of markers while the customers waited breathlessly. The variation had been introduced by Pappy
Smith, at Harold's Club in Reno back in the late 1930s.
The idea was to let the mouse wander around the table,
establishing each number by crawling down a numbered
hole. Watching the mouse crawl hesitantly around the
board, sniffing here and there, Harry decided that he
and Wally O. Kelly were brothers under the skin, kin to
that mouse. Like the mouse, he and Wally were a different breed from everyone around them, men who
marched to their own drummers with their own stubborn logic; one of the problems of this kind of craps
was that sometimes the mouse refused to go down any
hole at all. And, he thought, Wally and he were capable
of doing what the craps' mice often did to each other.
Casino staff often had to send out for replacements,
since some of the mice had cannibalistic tendencies.

Wally would understand that, Harry reflected, watching the tall, blonde lady-dealer—Norma—open a con-
tainer and release another mouse, preparing to start another round. Unlike Norma, Wally would understand
that it was a mouse-eat-mouse world they lived in.

Harry picked up the telephone receiver. "Tell Norma

I want to speak to her when she gets off this afternoon," he said.

Spider Johnson opened the door to the house he shared with Jim Pallafox. He waited until his two companions entered, then shut the door behind him. The first floor of the house was dark, except for a shaft of light that penetrated from the den.

"Roll us a couple of joints, Willie," Spider said quietly, raising the canvas shades that hid the living room windows.

Willie Richardson, the Oakland Golds' center fielder, was a tall, broad-shouldered black, identifiable instantly on TV screens by the bushy Afro that peeped from under his baseball cap in a profusion of tangled curls. "Now, you don't mind smokin' a little grass, do you, Mamma?" he said to the young white girl.

"I think I should go," she said suddenly, clutching her pocketbook with both hands. "I don't like it here."

She tried to turn toward the door, but Willie's thick arm stopped her. "Hey, we're gonna have a little fun, that's all," he said, cooing the words into her ear. "A smoke, a dance—nothin' to get uptight about."

"But you guys told me I'd be able to meet Pallafox," she whined, no longer resisting as Willie steered her toward the center of the room. "You told me he was Pallafox's roommate," she added, pointing at Spider.

Willie sat down on a black Naugahyde couch. "She's scared," he sneered, licking a cigarette paper, folding it, then twisting the loose fold at one end. "Wasn't scared down at the ball park, though. Runnin' up and down askin' every ballplayer, 'Hey, you seen Jim Pallafox? I just *gotta* meet Jimmy Pallafox.' "

Spider was kneeling in front of a stereo rig. He was pulling out tape cassettes. "I gotta put on somethin' sad and soulful," he said more to himself than to Willie or the girl. "Man, do I need some mournin' music."

"C'mon, man," Willie exclaimed, getting up off the couch and gyrating his body fiercely. "This ain't no funeral. Put somethin' on we can boogie to . . . 'cause I feel like gettin' it on."

Spider, on his haunches, turned to stare at Willie, then the girl. The groupie, he reckoned, couldn't be older than sixteen. "Look," he said soberly, "this was all your idea. I still don't like it. Can't you see she's jailbait, man?"

Willie sauntered over to the girl. He stuck his hand down the girl's dress. "Listen, man," he said to Spider, "she's got good tits. At one o'clock in the afternoon, I don't expect no Lola Falana."

Spider shrugged. This had been Willie's idea— picking up the girl at the ball park. Normally, neither he nor Willie would have wasted even a glance on her— long, stringy brown hair, hooked nose, startled eyes, and breasts no bigger than clenched fists. But these weren't "normal" times. This was the day before the World Series started, and Spider—a ten-year vet, a Cy Young Award winner—wasn't even sure he would be called on to pitch a single game. The tension that had been building in him all season long was now becoming unbearable. That's why he'd gone along with Willie's con— using Pallafox as bait. He had needed some escapade to distract his thoughts, to tranquilize the gnawing pain, to sugarcoat his disappointment at his own performance.

"Shee-*it*," Willie yelled, grabbing the reluctant girl by the hand, pulling her toward him, then slipping his hands up behind her, releasing the catch of her bra, "let's get this here party goin' now, brother. Let's get it on and *boogie*."

Spider set a tape into the cassette deck and turned up the volume, spilling a cataract of sound out of the massive speakers.

The door from the den was flung open. Pallafox stepped out, dressed only in a pair of blue walking shorts. "How the hell am I supposed to concentrate on this stuff with all the noise!" he shouted, waving a sheaf of papers in front of his face.

"Pallafox! It's Jim Pallafox," the girl swooned, breaking away from Willie, lunging for the pitcher, and, inadvertently, knocking the sheaf of papers out of Pallafox's hand, onto the floor.

"Hey, dummy, look out," Willie said to her, stooping down to pick up the papers scattered over the floor.

Pallafox shoved Willie aside. "Keep your goddamn hands off," he said.

Willie stood up. "Just tryin' to help, dude. You don't have to get all tight over a bunch of papers," he added, his voice hurt and indignant. "Anyway, what is all that mess—why you readin' that legal mumbo jumbo?"

"None of your business, man," Pallafox replied, scooping up the documents. "Just clear out. I have work to do."

Willie was getting angry. "You ain't the only one who lives here," he said, nodding at Spider.

"Yeh," Spider said, "I still pay half the rent—even though everybody calls this place 'Pallafox's house.' "

Pallafox opened his mouth, then censored the words before they poured from his lips. He took a deep breath. "Okay, you still pay half the rent," he replied in a subdued voice. "I'm sorry. I blew my cool."

"You sure did," Spider hissed. "You think you're the greatest show on earth. Number one, Mister Perfection. But to me you're still the same snot-nosed kid who couldn't find his way to the john six months ago without old Spider leading him by the hand."

Spider and Pallafox stared at each other appraisingly, their jaws jutting, their fingers clenched into fists. Then Spider's body went limp. Those legal documents in Pallafox's fist—the sight of them was turning his resentment into remorse. He said to Willie: "Go on, man, leave. And take that jailbait with you."

Pallafox went back into the den, slamming the door behind him.

An hour later, Spider was sitting in the living room, distributing playing cards on a small, velvet-covered table, when the door to the den opened.

"It's my *man*," Spider called out, pulling two cards off the table and setting them aside.

"Christ," said Pallafox, "you even cheat at solitaire?"

Spider laughed, and Pallafox was grateful, glad the tension between them was gone.

Pallafox left the room. He returned with a pot of

steaming coffee and two cups. Spider watched him lay
the coffeepot and cups on the floor, then sit down on
the black Naugahyde couch. Dressed, Pallafox looked
heavier than 180 pounds, Spider decided, 'cause he was
so tall, so broad at the shoulder. He looked heavier—
and older, too. The less skin he exposed, the less you
noticed the kid freckles dappled over his body. He had
a good build for a pitcher, though. A lean six-feet-
three—what the scouts called a "Steve Carlton" body,
long and supple and loose.

Suddenly, Pallafox leaped up. "Hell," he said, "what
time is it?"

"Be cool, brother," Spider said, sipping at his coffee.
"You got three-quarters of an hour before we leave for
the airport."

Pallafox relaxed. He sat down on the couch again. "I
just don't want any foul-ups," he said, "not today." He
leaned back and tucked his T-shirt, with the decal
promoting a rock group called The Grateful Dead, into
his faded jeans. He was about to apologize to Spider for
losing his temper in front of Willie and the groupie,
when the telephone rang.

"Spider," the black pitcher purred into the receiver.

Pallafox could tell it was a reporter. He could tell by
the way Spider's narrow, feline face hardened, the skin
drawn tight over the cheekbones. "Uh-huh, uh-huh,"
Spider said into the mouthpiece. "I don't know when
you can talk to him. He don't like to talk to no reporters the day before he pitches." Then he covered the
mouthpiece with his hand. "Some dude named Rick
Holman," he told Pallafox. "Says he's from *Action
Sports*. Out here to do a piece on you—a cover story."

"Tell him I'll be around after I pitch the opener tomorrow. I'll be meeting the press after the game."

Spider relayed the message, listened, then covered the
receiver again. "The dude says he don't give a damn
about the game. Says if he had traveled almost four
thousand miles just to see you pitch, he would have
been better off stayin' at home, watchin' on TV. Says he
needs more than that. He needs personal stuff, what
you're like, how you live, et cetera. He says if there's a

riddle, he's gonna solve it, whatever that's supposed to mean. Hey, you want me to hang up on this dude?"

Hell, Pallafox thought. This was exactly what he didn't need. A writer from a magazine. Christ, why did this guy have to come snooping around now? Pallafox reflected for a moment. "No," he told Spider. "Don't hang up on the guy. Invite him up to that little party we're having tonight. He can get his inside, on-the-spot, bird's-eye view. That should satisfy him."

"I'll get him some fox," Spider added. "His nose can't be in two places at the same time, dig?"

"Hey, Rick, man," Spider said into the telephone. "Pallafox says come on out tonight, man. We're gonna have a few friends in. We're gonna do some pre-World Series partying."

Spider gave Rick Holman the address, then put down the phone. "That's the way to handle them high-powered dudes," he said. "That's the way I used to do it. When I was havin' my good years with the Golds. Give 'em somethin' to write about. So they don't write about what you don't want 'em to."

Pallafox stood up. He left the room and deposited his coffee cup in the kitchen sink. It bothered him when Spider talked about himself as a has-been, referring to his "good years" with the Golds as if they were trophies in some musty sports museum. That, he knew, was exactly why, at least once a day, Spider found some excuse to refer to his good years as gone years.

Rick could see that the cabdriver was getting a little nervous. He had been suspiciously eager to ferry Rick from the hotel in San Francisco all the way to Oakland, and now, as the meter clicked past the $25 mark, Rick realized why. At this point, however, the cabdriver was plainly anxious to get rid of him.

"Are you sure about that address?" the cabby asked for at least the fourth time.

Rick was beginning to share the driver's concern. He hadn't been too surprised to learn from Spider Johnson that Pallafox lived across the Bay in Oakland. Many of the Golds lived near the ball park, finding the commute from San Francisco too tiresome. Pallafox, furthermore, was a UCLA graduate. According to the little Rick had been able to dig up, he still frequented the student cafés and coffeehouses near the Berkeley campus, about a half hour away from the Coliseum, on the Oakland side of the Bay. But for the last fifteen minutes or so, the cab had been plunging deeper and deeper into the heart of Oakland's sprawling black ghetto—full of rickety clapboard houses with peeling paint and an occasional boarded-up window—ominous, all of it, in the shadowy twilight.

The cabby suddenly swerved to the curb and halted. "This is it," he said.

Rick peered out into the deepening night. The house was a two-story brownstone. Scaffolding attached to the front showed that someone was remodeling it. The house, Rick reflected, could take all the remodeling anyone wanted to give it. A post between the roof and floor of the front porch was listing perilously to one side. The rotted stairs leading up to the porch were covered with loose planks of unstained wood. He couldn't believe that Pallafox, with his $300,000 bonus fresh from college a few years back, and the salary that he was trying to renegotiate right now with Wally Kelly, would choose to live in an outright slum. But then, he had to believe it. The front door opened, the porch light went on—and Jim Pallafox strode out the door and down the steps.

"Dr. Holman, I presume," Pallafox said, extending his large left hand. "Welcome to civilization."

Inside, Rick did step into another world. There were the ex-athletes, black and white, coasting comfortably into middle age. A few Rick recognized, ex-superstars now into broadcasting or insurance or car dealerships, looking fat and flush, and others, also ex-ballplayers, many of them just as fat, but less flush, wearing natty outfits, but with, perhaps, the shirt cuffs slightly frayed. Besides the ballplayers-past, there were the ballplayers-present; you could spot them by the women who clung to them. Stunning, dazzling women. White, black, Oriental—a groin-tingling spectrum of pulchritude, draped in sheer silks and clinging pants suits. In the center of one clump of partygoers, Rick recognized Willie Richardson, the Golds' center fielder. A tall, slim black woman, with hair cascading past her waist, was snuggling against him. Rick had interviewed Willie for a piece in *Action Sports* a few years ago. Now, over in one corner, he spotted Willie's wife, Doris. She was a pretty lady—an ex-airline stewardess. Rick had written the piece just after Willie and Doris had gotten married. He had asked Willie how marriage was changing his life. "Now," Willie had bragged, "I just gotta hide my datebook." Rick caught Doris's eye for a second. She glanced at her husband, then back at Rick, shrugged her shoulders, and turned back to her conversation with some other women, who, Rick supposed, were ballplayers' wives, too.

"How about this for an opening?" a voice muttered in Rick's ear. He turned. It was Pallafox. His Grateful Dead T-shirt was stained with beer. He was swaying a little. Rick hadn't realized it when Pallafox guided him in from the street, but the pitcher was a little drunk. "Start the article like this," Pallafox continued, his good-looking, hawklike face bobbing down toward Rick's. "Sportswriters and renegade athletes have already chronicled the impact of expansion and inflation on pro sports. A few, like Jim Bouton and Wilt Chamerlain, have even given us earthy insights into the sexual revolution that has made, for the first time," and Pallafox wagged an unsteady finger in Rick's face, "a pro athlete's life qualitatively different from yours and mine. But no one, till this intrepid reporter, that is," he added, tapping Rick on the shoulder, "has scrutinized the pro athletes' sex lives. While mapping the spaces between our pro athletes' ears, sportswriters still refuse to fill in the blanks between their legs."

"If they did," Rick replied sharply, "they would find that most jocks spend more time in bed than on the ball field, care more about women than about winning, and put in more hours balling than batting. They'd learn that pro athletes pursue sexual encounters like junkies in search of a fix," he added, the banter leaving his voice.

"That's pretty good," Pallafox said. "Not bad at all. You sure have filled in some of those blanks."

"But not enough," Rick replied carefully. "You're still a puzzle."

"What's that supposed to mean?" Pallafox asked.

"That maybe you're deliberately erasing a part of your life, censoring it from public view, 'cause you're hiding something."

It might have been an effect of light from the pink paper Chinese lantern hanging overhead, or the result of one beer too many, but Pallafox's face suddenly turned pale. "I don't know what in hell you're driving at," he said quickly.

At that moment, a couple of ballplayers, with two women trailing in their wake, descended on Pallafox, dragging him off toward the dining room. Rick stood staring, slightly shaken by the encounter. Rick had never played organized baseball, except as a teen-ager, on school playgrounds in the suburb of Boston where he grew up. But now, after talking to Pallafox—an inebriated Pallafox?—he knew how it felt to stand in the batter's box, with Pallafox leaning in, mean off the pitcher's mound. Pallafox, the aggressor, the competitor. He wasn't content to excel at pitching baseballs. He had gone out of his way to prove he could throw verbal curves, too. He had gone out of his way to demonstrate to a writer, whom he had never met before, that there was far more to him than any box score could insinuate. Yet, when pinned down, he'd crawled back into his shell, becoming monosyllabic and obstinate.

An hour later, Rick was sitting on the floor in the living room—a jumble of nondescript couches and chairs and coffee tables. A girl who said she was Selma was sitting on Rick's lap. That was just fine, he was thinking, as he and Selma clinked glasses for perhaps the fifth time. Perhaps. He had lost count. Selma, who said she was a friend of Spider's, had been plying him with drink like some horny high-school senior working over the class virgin the night of the prom. She was obviously trying to keep him away from Pallafox, but hell, he no longer cared. She had blonde hair, full lips, and smelled of a sultry, musk scent.

He had, at least, met Pallafox, had exchanged a few hundred words with him, even if the topic, sex among pro athletes, had nothing to do with the piece Phil Hanson was paying him two thousand dollars to write. Pallafox had a brain, though who, knowing Pallafox had been a dean's list student at UCLA, had ever doubted that? But where *was* Pallafox? He hadn't seen the pitcher for at least a half hour.

Rick stood up, dumping musky Selma from her perch on his lap. He staggered off down the hall, up the stairs to the second floor. There he heard a voice. He moved unsteadily down the hallway, then halted, peering into a room. A tall, thin black man was sitting on a couch, his back turned toward the door. He was talking on the telephone.

"Right, Mr. Kelly," the man said, in a voice Rick recognized as Spider's. "I know Jimmy's gotta pitch tomorrow. Right, Mr. Kelly, believe me. He's in bed already. Tucked him in myself. Right next door here. Been in bed this last half hour, I swear. . . . Uh-huh, uh-huh, okay," Spider added, "I'll pick it up later tonight. I'll make sure Harry gets the package. No, don't worry, I won't tell nobody. . . ."

It figured, Rick thought, tiptoeing slowly back and away from the door. Wally Kelly calling to tell his starting pitcher to get the hell to sleep, making Spider Johnson pay for his losing season by turning him into a combination baby-sitter and errand boy.

Spider put down the receiver. Rick ducked into the shadows. "Hey, Willie," Spider yelled, bounding past Rick and down the stairs, "where'd you hide all that tasty dope?"

Rick was debating what to do. Downstairs, someone had turned up the stereo. He could hear furniture being moved, then the *scuff scuff squeak* of shoes gliding and pivoting and shuffling to a torrid disco beat. He could envision Selma downstairs—the smear of red lipstick, the alluring perfume, the soft, curvy essence of her.

. . . And then he thought of Phil Hanson—a chilling image that numbed every erotic urge. Dammit, he didn't want to snoop, but he did want a story. He wanted to write a good story about Pallafox, just because Phil Hanson had insisted so stubbornly there was no story. So he walked back toward the room with the telephone. Within, he saw a door. Rick approached it. He turned the brass doorknob slowly, cautiously. Then he took a deep breath. He flung the door open.

"Sorry," he started to say, slurring deliberately, acting drunk, "I thought the bathroom was somewhere . . ."

He stopped in midsentence, his mouth agape. There, on a king-size bed, was Jim Pallafox, lying on his stomach, fully clothed, his body propped up on one elbow, with his other arm flung tenderly across the sleeping form beside him. "Jesus Christ," Rick blurted in astonishment, staring bewilderedly at the cute little redhead whose face was pressing the pillow next to Pallafox's. "Jesus Christ," he repeated.

At the sound of Rick's voice, Pallafox had spun around. Rick began to back out of the room. Cat-quick, Pallafox sprang out of bed and grabbed Rick by the arm. "If you breathe a word of this, I'll kill you," Pallafox hissed.

"Hell," Rick kept saying, staring past Pallafox at the sleeping child, "I'm no prude, but this kid can't be more than three years old. You must be out of your *mind*."

All of a sudden Pallafox's grip on Rick's arm went slack. "You don't understand," he said in a subdued voice. "This is Kathy. My daughter."

"Your *daughter?*" Rick said incredulously. "You'd go to all this trouble just to keep the world from knowing you have a *daughter?*"

Pallafox shrugged his broad shoulders, the gesture conveying not only resignation, but relief. "Come into the other room," he whispered, in a dull, almost bored voice, as he walked over to the sleeping child and patted the blankets firmly into place around her. "I'll tell you the whole story."

Pallafox had met Norma Windsor during his sopho-

more year at UCLA. She was a cheerleader, tall and
blonde and slim and beautiful. He was already the star
athlete, a letterman in basketball, football, and, of
course, baseball. He and Norma gravitated toward each
other, Pallafox told Rick, pulled together as much by
friends as by mutual attraction. Norma and Jimmy—the
cheerleader and the athlete. Both beautiful people, both
honor students—philosophy majors, when most cheerleaders still majored in home economics and most athletes in physical education. "Oh, Norma and Jimmy—
they're just *made* for each other," friends would say.

"Soon," said Pallafox, "Norma and I found ourselves
saying it, too."

They were inseparable during their junior and senior
years, the "campus couple," always strolling arm in
arm, or sitting next to each other in the library, his right
thigh, say, straining against her left one, as their minds
strained to absorb the thought of Descartes and Kant
and Nietzsche. Afterward, in the snack bar, especially
during their senior year, they would talk of marriage.
He would go on to graduate school, and study to be a
lawyer. She would train as an accountant—she had a
phenomenal memory for numbers—and would help
him in his career, while cleaning the house and mother-
ing their kids. She had long ago convinced Pallafox that
a career in pro sports was a dead end. She hated baseball because she feared the uncertainty of a pro athlete's
life, of being a pro athlete's wife. Those dog years struggling down in the minors. An apprenticeship that often
turned into a life sentence. She had computed the prob-
abilities. She had decided, she said, that the odds were
heavily stacked against him. Pallafox would most likely
be one of the many who failed, instead of the handful
who succeeded in carving out a major-league career. In
fact, though, Pallafox told Rick, what she really feared
was the possibility he might become an utter and instant
success. She had heard about the women ballplayers
kept in every town, a new face in every strange bed. Pro
ballplayers' wives aged early.

Gradually, without even realizing it, Pallafox had ab-
sorbed her outlook, made it his own. Even when, mid-

way through his senior year, he was selected first in the baseball college draft, by the Oakland Golds, he insisted he wanted to pass up baseball and pursue a career in law. Then, just before graduation day—the day, in fact, after Norma and he had set their wedding date—he was sitting in his room at the dormitory when there was a loud, peremptory rapping. Pallafox opened the door and stood face to face with the Golds' owner, Wally O. Kelly. One hour later, Kelly departed with Jim Pallafox's signature on an Oakland Golds' contract.

Norma was hurt. She felt betrayed. Worse, she felt embittered. More so, when, two weeks later, she found out that she was pregnant. Pallafox pleaded with her to marry him. She heard his plea with a grim mouth; her answer was stony silence. Then, he admitted to Rick, he had made a clumsy mistake. He offered to pay for an abortion. Norma became hysterical. She vowed never to speak to him or see him again. The next day she disappeared from the campus. She didn't even bother to attend her own graduation.

"She went ahead and had your child," Rick said.

"Yeh," Pallafox replied. "She had Kathy. Out of spite, I guess."

"When did you find out?" Rick asked.

"About a year ago," Pallafox answered. "Spider Johnson, my roommate, spends a lot of time over in Vegas. He likes to gamble, and there's this casino owner, Harry Walters—an ex-gambler with mob connections—who's a big fan of Spider's, has been for years. He always puts Spider up at his hotel for free and gives him chips to play with—all so he can tell everybody how tight he is with Spider, I guess. Well, I met Spider when I was up at spring training, two years after I signed with the Golds, before they sent me down to the minors for my second full year of seasoning. Spider told me he'd met my ex-girlfriend—Walters told him— she was a dealer in Walters' casino, working a gimmick craps table, where a mouse runs down a hole.

"I couldn't believe it was Norma—the cheerleader, the philosophy major? I knew it had to be someone else, maybe someone I'd dated sometime, who was just putting Walters on. I was a little less skeptical, though, when Spider told me the woman had this little daughter, a little red-haired daughter.

"Still, I told myself it couldn't be Norma. I decided to settle all doubts. I showed Spider a photograph. 'That's the same lady,' he said. He was absolutely positive."

"She went from cheerleader and numbers whiz to craps dealer, all in a little over three years?" Rick said incredulously.

"I still can't believe it myself," said Pallafox. "There's got to be some explanation, but I'll be damned if I can figure it out."

"Did you contact her—to try to find out what happened to her, to try to see your daughter?"

"Sure I did," Pallafox answered, "but she wouldn't have anything to do with me. That," he added, "is when I got a lawyer."

"A lawyer?"

"Yeh, a lawyer. To get custody of Kathy. A year ago, when I was pitching in the minors. If it had happened now, it would have been headlines. But back then, nobody gave a damn. Except Norma. She would have taken it to the press long before this," he added, "but she's afraid of what all the publicity would do to the kid's head. And, whatever she is, this much I do know: she would never do anything to hurt Kathy. She couldn't have changed that much."

"I still don't understand," Rick said. "Why the need for a lawyer—and why the need for all this damn secrecy?"

"Look," Pallafox replied, patiently. "Maybe I've been acting crazy. But this kid, right now, is illegitimate, born out of wedlock, as they put it. Now, I know she's my kid, but I can't prove she's my kid. Her blood type and mine match—but about eighty percent of everyone in this country have O-positive, too. So I have to adopt her if I want to get her out of that rotten environment Norma was bringing her up in. And I'm a bachelor, twenty-four years old, in the public eye, in a profession that's not known for its saints.

"So, I've been trying to keep the kid out of the public eye till I could legally give her my name. And I've been trying to keep as little of my life as possible from becoming public gossip. The more you give the press, the more they demand. The less I tell reporters, the less they can misrepresent and misinterpret me. I don't want some officer of the court reading something that would spoil my chances of giving Kathy a good life."

"What does Norma think about your adopting Kathy?"

"She's been fighting it all the way," Pallafox replied, a little sadly.

"And where has the child been staying?" Rick asked.

"Since I got custody, with my parents," Pallafox said. "When my dad retired, they moved from L.A. to Fargo, North Dakota, so the old man could hunt and fish."

Rick was quiet for a moment. "I wish now I'd never found out," he said glumly.

"I understand," said Pallafox. " 'Cause now that you know, you gotta print it, right? What a crazy deal," he added. "All I needed was a little more time. My lawyer tells me that the final adoption papers will be ready in just a few days." Then he was silent, brooding. "I shouldn't have brought the kid here, I know it," he said, fighting back the emotion in his throat. "But . . . it's crazy . . . I just missed her so goddamn much. People wouldn't understand. How Kathy's the only one in this whole scene," and he gestured at the partygoers below, "who isn't trying to *use* me."

While Pallafox was talking, Rick had been thinking, hard. "Look," he said, "I have an idea. This is a scoop for me—I'm not going to pretend it isn't. I'm getting paid to do a story, and I'm going to do that story. But if all that's involved is one or two days—I'll keep your secret until you give me the okay."

Pallafox brightened. "Fabulous," he said. "Fabulous. 'Cause once the proceedings are finalized, damn it, I *want* to tell the world about this beautiful little kid of mine. I'll give you an exclusive story. Every bit of it. For free. . . ." Pallafox leaped up and grabbed Rick in a bone-crunching bear hug.

"Wait a minute, wait one minute," Rick pleaded, laughing away the little breath he had left. "When I walked into your room, and saw you with your arm around Kathy, I thought to myself, My God, this guy's some kind of pervert. You explained that one. But how," he said, as he freed himself from Pallafox's exuberant embrace, "if someone walks into this room right now, are we going to explain us dancing cheek to cheek?"

Rick arrived back at his hotel at 2:00 A.M. As soon as he reached his room, he dialed Phil Hanson's home number, but Hanson was out. He waited for Phil's taped voice to finish reciting the instructions for messages, then he said: "Phil, this is Rick. I've solved the riddle of the sphinx." He hung up, the first real smile of the evening splitting his face. That, Rick thought maliciously, was enough to keep Phil Hanson tossing and turning all night long. Then Rick spread his opening-game press credentials on the night table. At this point, he reflected, they were more valuable than the traveler's checks he had deposited in the hotel vault when he'd left his room that evening. He stripped down to his underwear and turned on his bedside clock radio. He searched until he found a funky, hard-driving jazz trio—bass, electric guitar, and organ. He fell asleep thinking about organs. His own. Selma's.

The noise awakened Rick. He glanced bleary-eyed at the clock radio. Eight A.M. Damn it, he thought drowsily, he didn't remember having set it. He reached over and tried to turn the alarm off, but it was already off. He rolled around till he could reach the telephone on the other night table.

"Phil?" he said.

"This is Pallafox, you goddamned liar," a voice shouted at him. "You said you weren't going to tell anybody!"

"What are you talking about?" Rick replied, suddenly awake. "What's happened?"

"What's *happened?* Oh, nothing important. Just an

even bigger scoop for you, something you're gonna love. *Somebody's kidnapped my daughter!"*

"Are you sure?" Rick said helplessly.

"Am I sure, he asks," Pallafox spat back, behind an ugly laugh. "I'm not sure about anything—except that I have a kidnap note right here in my sweaty hand and Kathy's no goddamned where in sight."

"I'll be right over," Rick said, already out of bed and slipping on a pair of jeans.

"You had better be, mister," Pallafox replied, his voice growing suddenly more calm, and more menacing. " 'Cause if you're not over here in twenty minutes, I am coming over there. To strangle you. *Who did you tell!"* he shouted, slamming down the phone.

Rick reached Pallafox's house in less than twenty minutes. He was surprised that Pallafox was alone: no gaggle of squawking TV broadcasters, no ant army of newspapermen, no wolf pack of vicious, snapping photographers. Not even the police.

It took him the best part of an hour to convince Pallafox that he wouldn't risk forfeiting his own scoop by imparting what he had learned about little Kathy to the hyenas of the press who prowled the hotel bar. "I didn't see Ray Fowler—in fact, I didn't say a word to anybody, honest to God. I just went back to my hotel, left word at my boss's home that I had some info, but I didn't say what info I had. Honest to God, Jimmy, I'm telling the truth."

At last Pallafox's anger evaporated, leaving only a hard core of despair. "All right, I believe you, I believe you," he murmured. His face was ashen white. His fingers were trembling uncontrollably. Pallafox looked down at his hands, then said, "I hope to hell the manager doesn't notice this."

"Are you crazy?" Rick said. "You can't pitch today. You're in no condition to do anything. You have to call the police. You need help."

Pallafox turned away from him. He went into another room. He returned with a sheet of paper in his hand. "I shouldn't show you this," he said, "but damn it, I gotta tell somebody."

He handed the sheet of paper to Rick—typing paper. Rick read it, his throat tightening with each word. It said:

> We have your daughter. If you want to see her alive again, do three things:
>
> 1. pitch every Series game you are supposed to pitch—numbers one and four and, if necessary, number seven.
>
> 2. tell no one that your daughter has been kidnapped. Her life depends on you shutting your mouth.
>
> 3. lose every Series game you pitch.
>
> Remember, if you tell the police, your daughter will die.
>
> Slowly.

Jenny Cohn instinctively raised her hand to shield her eyes. When she had left New York, the sky had been gray, overcast, a chill wind blowing through the streets of Manhattan—an icy, lecherous wind, full of New York mischief.

Now, as she stood in front of the airport terminal in Oakland, there was no wind at all, not even a breeze. It was the kind of California day she had always fantasized about: warm and sunny in mid-October. None of that fabled smog she had always heard about back East. Just a brilliant, brittle, red-orange glare midway across the vault of the sky. It had blinded her for an instant, but now that her eyes were adjusting, how crystalline clear the light sculpted everything. She stared at the men and women strolling in shorts and T-shirts, and sandals that flapped on the pavement in a hundred competing rhythms. She felt suddenly dizzy—the way she felt on the High Holidays after two glasses of Passover wine.

A cab pulled up at the curb and Jenny slid onto the back seat. The contrast between the gloomy New York she had left behind and the bright, invigorating California climate made her feel suddenly glamorous. She unbuttoned the jacket of her beige suit and settled back for the ride to the Coliseum.

The thought had the chilling touch of a gust of New York wind. She had never seen Phil Hanson so impatient—or so surly—as he had been when he'd stormed into her office that morning, screaming that she had two hours to get home, get packed, and "get the hell out to Oakland." Pacing her office wildly, he'd gone on spluttering about sphinxes and riddles and goddamn, sonuvabitch writers until, finally, he'd stood stock-still and shouted:

"I am going to hold the presses open in Ohio. I am going to hold the presses, and I am going to have the cover redone to include one word—in flaming red, across the picture of Pallafox: Scoop! This magazine is going to hit the newsstands one week late, but with the biggest story of the year. That idiot has stumbled onto something out there, and I want it. If you don't get it out of him," he added fiercely, "don't come back here. Go straight to your nearest employment agency!"

She stared out the window. Why did Rick always have to complicate things? By being stubborn when he should be flexible? By turning matters of convenience into moral absolutes? If another free lance had promised a scoop, then backed off, Hanson immediately would have supposed the writer was trying to peddle his story to a better market than *Action Sports*—perhaps *Sports Illustrated*. And he would have been right. But not Rick. No. Rick would be impaled on the horns of some quixotic dilemma—a conflict between his assignment and his altruism. That, Barbara Holman once told her, shortly after she had divorced Rick, was why she had decided to end their marriage.

"Saviors are nice people to spend a weekend with," Barbara had said in that cool, distant way of hers, "but they're murder at the breakfast table."

Jenny had seen the breakup coming in her early days at *Action,* when Rick would have her and three or four other staff members over to his apartment in Greenwich Village—a three-bedroom duplex that Barbara was always nagging him to trade in for a house in Westchester. Mount Holyoke-bred Barbara. She had the icy sophistication Jenny had always envied. A kind of inbred contempt for anyone who couldn't ride a horse or play a sizzling game of tennis. "You do all your shopping at Bloomingdales?" she had said to Jenny once. "That's very nice, *very* nice, dear." Her voice had left no doubt that Bloomingdales was a step up for Jenny, but would be a giant step down, from Saks, for her. And then,

liberated by half an ounce of Scotch, sometime during
the evening Rick would begin to talk about UFOs and
parallel universes and Von Däniken and Nazca draw-
ings on Peruvian plateaus. Once in a while, when something interrupted Jenny's spellbound reverie, she would
glance at Barbara—engrossed in buffing her nails, or
chatting with a guest.

That day, after the divorce a few years back, when
Jenny had met Barbara—in Bloomingdales—Barbara
had described what she called Rick's "pathology," cat-
aloging, over coffee (espresso for Barbara), every
symptom. How Rick had graduated from Columbia,
earned a master's degree in economics, regressing then
to become an airline reservation agent, a cheese-cutter
in Macy's imported foods department, a caseworker for
the New York Human Resources Administration, and
finally, when he had discovered there was nothing else
left, an editor, then a writer.

Barbara despised his random route into writing, the
obsessiveness and obstinacy with which he clung to such
a fragile vocation. "Making money didn't help, either,"
Barbara had told Jenny that day. "There was something
morbid about his being a writer."

Later, in the office one day, Rick told her: "Barbara
had always been taught that money was the ultimate
panacea. But our marriage was one terminal disease
even money couldn't cure."

Just then, a panacea was exactly what Rick needed—
a cure-all that would at once dispel his guilt over with-
holding Pallafox's story from Phil Hanson, and his anxiety over the fate of the pitcher's daughter. He had tried
a couple of Scotch sours, and that hadn't worked. Having failed to anesthetize his mind, he was taking the cir-
cuitous route, working up from his stomach toward his
frayed nerves. On his white paper plate, he was piling a
bubbly hillock of beluga caviar, next to which lay three
Fortnum-Mason link sausages.

The NBC tent occupied half a parking lot, and
touched the stadium wall. A canopied tunnel led from
the tent right to the press gate, so that the media—both

print and broadcast—could stroll into the stadium after their pregame snack unsoiled by the envious eyes of bleacher bums. Within the tent, a feast had been laid. Every day, two hours before game time, in Oakland and, later, in New York, the flap over the main entrance would rise, admitting a menagerie of World Series free-loaders. There was, of course, the king himself—the producer of network sports, with his retinue of broadcasters and program planners and statisticians and the ex-jocks who served as "color" commentators. Then came the courtiers—print journalists like Rick, and photographers, and celebrities from Hollywood and New York. Finally, ranking below the courtiers were the courtesans—groups of pretty airline stewardesses, all looking as if they'd been assembled in the same Barbie doll factory; and the girlfriends of ballplayers, those thoroughbreds bred purely for sex, as different from the airline stewardesses as a Derby-bound mare is from a rented nag at a second-rate stables.

Rick shook his head irritably and stuffed a crackerful of caviar into his mouth, then felt someone tugging at the sleeve of his sport jacket.

"Some spread," said Ray Fowler.

Rick was surprised he hadn't noticed Fowler before. In place of the writer's habitual black-and-white checked jacket—stained in the confrontation with Wally Kelly—the newsman was wearing an electric sport coat, an abstract pattern that looked, Rick thought, as if Jackson Pollock had been fooling around with a wet Peter Max.

"It's my backup. Got it in Hawaii," Fowler said, laughing. "I can't decide whether to wear it or frame it or burn it."

"Your wife's idea?" Rick said.

"Who else?" Fowler replied, raising his plastic glass in a mock toast to the absent Mrs. Fowler, then downing its contents in one gulp. "Hey, by the way," Fowler added, "there's someone around here who's looking for you. A girl. Says she's from *Action Sports*. She's the managing editor, I think."

Christ, Rick thought, Hanson had sent Jenny out after him. "Where'd you see her?"

"Go straight past steak street," Fowler said, "turn right at roast beef row, take another left at pâté place, and she should be right there. And if you hear anybody talking about baseball, or about the World Series opener," Fowler added, "report him immediately. Once in a while some of the rabble get in—you know, *people,* honest-to-God fans who think that there's going to be a game played today, and that it means something."

Rick chuckled, then moved off in search of Jenny. He understood what Fowler meant. No one standing in this tent had had to pay for a ticket to the Series. Few really even gave a damn about baseball. For most, they themselves, not the Series, were the event. The games were only an enforced intermission from partying and making business contacts and getting laid. The games were an entertainment designed for the amusement of the media, especially the broadcast media, without whose millions pro sports would still be played in the back lots of starch factories, for the delight of a handful of gamblers and hardhats.

He found Jenny at the junction of mousse mews and asparagus avenue. "I have mixed emotions about seeing you," he said.

"Better me than Phil," she replied, as they sat down at a table away from the babble and tinkling glass and clatter of silverware. "Phil says, and I quote, 'If Holman doesn't call me with the story by the end of the Series, I am going to snip his . . . prick off with a rusty pair of scissors.' "

Rick had to smile . . . not at Hanson's threat, which was no empty one, but at the way Jenny—tough, practical Jenny—had had to pause before uttering that word. Good little Jewish girl. Moral, upright, and efficient. But not quite grown up yet. Nevertheless, he made a decision. He would confide in her—in fact, it was impossible not to confide in her. Too easy to confide in her, he thought. It had always troubled him that he had, one day, told Jenny how he felt about Barbara—even before he had told himself.

Rick reviewed the events leading up to Kathy's kidnapping, and the kidnap note itself. How he and Pallafox had agreed that, for the time being, the pitcher shouldn't notify the police.

"One thing," Rick said, "he's pretty damn sure that someone close to him either arranged it, or is part of it, because very few people even know that Kathy exists. It's got to be someone who knows him well, and who's around the Series. Otherwise, even if they knew about the kid, they wouldn't have known she was coming in from Fargo. Personally," he added, "I think it must be the kid's mother, Pallafox's ex-girlfriend. She's a dealer in Las Vegas, and it sounds like she was pretty determined not to let him get custody of the kid. I'll bet she's probably run into a few characters in Vegas who wouldn't be afraid of stealing the kid out from under Pallafox's nose."

"And that kidnap note?" Jenny asked, tilting her head to one side the way she always did when he was convinced of something, and she was just as convinced that he was dead wrong.

"So she writes a phony note—to try to scare Pallafox off."

Again, Jenny tilted her head. "It doesn't work," she said. "First, why make Pallafox lose games? If you're right, she could have left that whole part out, and still scared him plenty. Second, a mother who would write that 'die slowly' bit is a mother who wouldn't want her kid back in the first place. That's sick, it's sadistic, it's terrifying. Maybe I'm naive, but I can't believe she'd write that."

"Look," Rick said irritably, "there are other mothers in the world besides Jewish mothers. There are *crazy* mothers. *Desperate* mothers. Even *sadistic* mothers. Y'know—they don't go to temple in Brooklyn on Friday nights, so maybe you don't meet them, but I'm telling you they're out there."

She shook her head vehemently. "They may be out there," she said, "but I don't feel it in *here*," and she patted her chest, right over her heart. "What does Pallafox say about your theory?"

Rick looked away. "He says what you say. That Norma isn't like that. That she wouldn't write anything like that. It isn't in her."

"You're outvoted," Jenny replied. There was an authoritative tone in her voice Rick had never noticed before. Perhaps it was because she was out from under Phil Hanson's shadow for the first time. Or perhaps, Rick suddenly realized, there was a lot about Jenny that he had just never noticed.

"Okay," he said. "Go ahead. I showed you my theory, now you show me yours."

"Listen," she said quietly. "It's as plain as the nose on your face that someone is trying to fix the World Series."

"What? Are you crazy?" Rick replied. "They may want to embarrass Pallafox—but fix the World Series? You can't fix a World Series, everybody knows that."

"Everybody knew that in 1919," she replied firmly. "Everybody, except some of the Chicago White Sox, and the gamblers who paid them off for losing to Cincinnati."

"That was different," Rick argued. "Ballplayers didn't make any money in those days. Gamblers flitted around locker rooms like flies. They could buy seven or eight ballplayers for a couple of thousand bucks. In fact, that's just about what happened. Now," he added, "it's different. I don't think you could buy a ball club for five or six million. These guys have too much at stake to risk getting into something like that."

"But you don't have to buy a ball club," Jenny replied. "You don't have to buy anyone."

The angrier he got, the calmer she became; it infuriated Rick. "Hey," he said, "will you cut this cat-and-mouse crap and tell me what you're driving at?"

She smiled at him. It wasn't often she got the upper hand. "Suppose I put an enormous sum of money on the Oakland Golds to lose," she said.

"That," he interrupted impatiently, "would be a stupid bet. Everyone knows the Oakland Golds are heavily favored to win."

"Why?" she asked.

"Why? You know why. 'Cause they have Pallafox, and the Patriots don't, and in a short series, pitching counts."

"And what happens if Pallafox goes out to lose, not to win?"

"Then . . ." Rick stopped. Suddenly, he saw it.

"Basketball's a five-man game," Jenny went on. "If 'Dr. J.,' Julius Erving, decided, for some reason, to throw the ball over the backboard all night, instead of into the basket, two things would happen. First, the offense would shift to someone else. Second, Erving would sit down for the rest of the game. In football," she added before Rick could interrupt, "if you have the quarterback in your pocket, you have a big plus, but you may not be able to decide the outcome of the game. The quarterback can throw interceptions, but once he's thrown an interception, it's out of his hands. The defensive unit comes onto the field, and the other team may not be able to score against them. In hockey, one player has a crucial role—the goalie. A goalie may be willing to let goals get by him into his nets—but his defensemen can still make it impossible for the other team to score.

"Baseball is different," she announced, a glint of triumph in her eyes. "In baseball, the pitcher *is* the game—especially in a short series. You said that yourself. He can put men on base. Then, with one pitch— the home-run ball—he can give the other team runs. And he doesn't need any help from anybody. In fact, he can fix a game and still look as if he's in top form. He doesn't have to throw badly; all he has to do is throw the right pitch to the right batter. When the pitcher throws that perfect pitch—say, the high inside fastball right up a Reggie Jackson's power alley—a power hitter like Jackson will blast it out of the ball park just about every time."

"I get it," Rick said reluctantly. "You're right. The pitcher can change the outcome of a game in an instant, and no one would be the wiser, 'cause the mistake he made—throwing the pitch high inside, say, when the catcher called for it three inches lower—is made every day by pitchers at the top of their form, pitchers who win a lot of ball games."

"A lot of good pitchers—Fergie Jenkins, Catfish Hunter—have a habit of giving up a lot of home runs over the course of a season," she said. "Pallafox could set up three men on base, then allow a home-run ball, giving the other team four runs in about five minutes. And, as you said, no one would be the wiser."

"But he may have to pitch three games—games one and four and, if it goes that far, game seven," Rick said. "It's gonna look awful strange if he loses all three."

"He doesn't have to make himself look bad," she replied, "he can make someone else look great. Jerry Gabriel of the Patriots won the American League home-run crown this year, right? What would people say if Gabriel hit three, even four home runs—or maybe two home runs, a triple, and a double—off Pallafox, in three games?"

"Okay, I give up," Rick said. "They'd say, 'Gee, Gabriel sure had the rookie's number this time around.' "

"And they'd say, 'Wait till next year. Pallafox won't be so nervous as he was playing in his first World Series.' "

"And Pallafox himself would say, 'Hey, that Jerry Gabriel is one helluva hitter. He sure taught me something.' And guys like Ray Fowler would walk away saying, 'Hey, that kid Pallafox's got class, he's a real good loser.' "

"A good loser," Jenny said dryly. "A pitcher as good as Pallafox and as smart as Pallafox could definitely be a good loser."

"Christ," said Rick, "I wonder what he's going to do? He sure didn't tell me anything like this."

Jenny couldn't resist it. "Maybe," she said with a broad smile, "he didn't think you'd understand the technicalities."

Rick should have been annoyed. But he couldn't be angry. Not now. Not when she was smiling that Tiffany's smile. And dammit, Jenny knew.

*   *   *

"The worst thing," Artie Gibbons was saying, "is to give your class-A performance the first time out, see? Then there's no way to go but down." It was an hour before game time. The Oakland Golds were straggling into their locker room, buried deep in the bowels of the Oakland Coliseum. "Still, one of the best things in the world is to have a great night—and then never see her again." Gibbons was standing in the middle of the Golds' locker room, idly scratching the thin blond curls that sprouted in patches on his massive chest. Pallafox, slumped on a stool in front of his locker, watched the muscles in Gibbons's right arm: how they popped up in knots, first bicep, then tricep, as Artie flexed his fingers against his chest. Gibbons was a loudmouth, a braggart, and everybody hated him. But he was the Golds' power, the only authentic longball threat on a team of slashers and sprinters and slappers. Besides, he was one of Wally's pets. "It's a one-night stand, 'cause you know you could never equal it again, and what's the point of dragging the thing on?" Gibbons concluded, his bullfrog voice leaping off the lockers. "You'd probably just end up fighting and ruin the whole thing anyway."

Marcus Hayes, the Golds' black catcher, leaned over from his stool in front of the locker next to Pallafox's. "I hear it's an automatic five-hundred-dollar fine from Wally O. for anybody who belts Gibbons in the mouth," he whispered.

But Pallafox didn't laugh. Today, he couldn't take a joke. He couldn't take Artie Gibbons, his boasting about how many women he screwed. Pallafox had heard too much of it, from too many mouths, throughout his first season. Rick Holman was right: too many pro ballplayers talked like Artie Gibbons, as if a woman were nothing more than a patch of artificial turf: all surface, tricky to maneuver on, but definitely there to be trampled.

"Why don't you shut up?" he suddenly yelled at Gibbons, startled by the venomous sound of his own voice.

Gibbons froze. Everyone else in the locker room became quiet. The white ballplayers stopped whatever they were doing and primed themselves for action—most, Pallafox knew instinctively, in his defense.

"Why the hell should I?" Gibbons roared back.

Pallafox stood up. He uncoiled. All six-feet-three of him. Lanky, but lethal in his anger as a rattlesnake. Gibbons looked around the room, seeking support. The eyes of the white ballplayers mirrored Pallafox's hostility; Gibbons scored with more women than almost all of them, and they resented it. They also resented the fact that he was Wally Kelly's pet. Besides, Pallafox was their meal ticket in the Series. If he damaged his arm in some stupid fight, it might cost each of them about $25,000—the winners' shares. Gibbons didn't bother to make eye contact with the black ballplayers. They were ignoring the entire confrontation now—combing out their Afros, snapping soul-music tapes into their portable cassette decks. Two white boys breaking each other's heads wasn't their damn business.

At that moment, Spider Johnson walked into the locker room. He looked at Pallafox, trembling with pent-up rage, and a few feet away, Artie Gibbons, with an uncertain, but belligerent, half-smile glued to his broad face. Cat-quick, Spider sprang at Gibbons, slapped him once across the face; when Gibbons turned away from the force of that chop, Spider spun him around, clasping his hands under Gibbons's armpits, locking them behind Gibbons's neck. Using the momentum from that unexpected charge, he drove Gibbons straight ahead, into the shower, only releasing him after he had turned the shower heads on full blast. "You lay a hand on Pallafox and Kelly will get your ass, you stupid fool!" Spider shouted at Gibbons. Sopping wet, Gibbons stormed back at Spider, but now the rules had changed. Willie Richardson stepped up, blocking Gibbons's path. Other black ballplayers started to move toward Gibbons. Reluctantly, some of the white ballplayers moved forward, too, to come to Gibbons's defense. Then someone from the far end of the locker room yelled, "Press!"

It was as if they had been rehearsing a scene on some Hollywood sound-lot, Pallafox thought. By the time the first newsman entered the locker room, what might have been an ugly brawl had dissolved into a friendly tête-à-tête, whites and blacks milling aimlessly with paper smiles pinned to their faces. "Hey, something happening here?" Pallafox heard Ray Fowler ask Artie Gibbons. "Aw, just a little pep rally," Gibbons replied, toweling himself off.

"Looks like I came just in time," Spider whispered to Pallafox, before the tide of reporters washed over them.

"Too bad you couldn't have arrived in time last night," Pallafox replied. "You might have saved more than my ass. Maybe even my daughter."

"I told you, man. When I came up to bed, I took the kid and put her in my room, so she'd be comfortable. Then Selma came up. We played around on the couch in the spare room for a while, then I drove her home. When I got back, I checked the kid; she was sleepin' fine. Then, I got that phone call. I coulda sworn it was Sam, Wally's chauffeur. He told me there'd been an accident, that Wally was hurt. He needed me down there right away."

"But it wasn't Sam, was it? And when you got there, there was no accident, no Sam, no Wally."

Spider looked into the rookie's eyes and saw the distrust blazing there. Maybe that's the way it always is, he thought bitterly. Maybe no one knows the victim of a mugging better than the mugger himself. But he couldn't tell Pallafox where he had really gone. If he told Pallafox that, on Kelly's orders, he had delivered a package to Harry Walters, then he would have to tell Pallafox what Walters told him the package contained: the $500,000 Wally had bet on the Golds. To lose. And he knew what conclusion Pallafox would draw from that.

The first game of the World Series actually began long before the ballplayers from either team donned their uniforms that day. In the minds of the thousands of spectators who had managed to purchase a prized ticket, it began the moment they woke up that morning, and got the kids dressed, and chose their wardrobe, and, as a family, started anticipating the drama that lay ahead. In the minds of the few hundred television and radio technicians, the game was well under way hours before the first image or play-by-play account was broadcast. The print journalists were stoking up their creative fires in the NBC tent long before the Golds and the Patriots arrived at the ball park. The grounds crew had started making their contribution to the game early that morning, combing the bumps out of the mound, making last-minute repairs on the artificial turf, so that bouncing balls wouldn't hop up at the Golds' infielders in erratic trajectories.

A quarter hour before the World Series officially began, the spectators and technicians and journalists and grounds crew were already nearly exhausted. And then the opening-game ceremonies finally got under way. While millions of spectators inched closer to their TV sets, and the thousands lucky enough to witness the game in person inched forward in their seats, the public-address announcer began a roll call of the players on each team.

The Patriots lined up along the first-base path. Overall, they received, as each one of them stood forward and politely tipped his cap, more boos than cheers, except for Jerry Gabriel, the reigning American League home-run champion, and Gary Humboldt, the Patriots' only twenty-game winner that year. Humboldt, in fact, got the loudest applause of all. The fans were grateful that a minor injury had sidelined him. Otherwise, it was he who would have been pitching this opener against Jim Pallafox.

Then, it was the Golds' turn. They lined up alongside the third-base path. The roar for them was so deafening, it was impossible to hear the names of the players as they were introduced. In particular, "Big Dog" Garcia, the shortstop; Artie Gibbons, the slugging right fielder; Marcus Hayes; Spider Johnson; and Willie Richardson, the Afroed center fielder—they were the ones the crowd singled out for special vocal commendation.

But the biggest cheer of all was reserved for someone warming up in front of the dugout. The great white hope. The man responsible for luring an average of ten thousand extra fans into Wally Kelly's ball park every time he pitched. The phenomenal rookie left-hander, Jim Pallafox.

After all the introductions had been made, Marcus Hayes strolled over to a box seat behind the batter's box, a gaggle of photographers clucking and clicking behind him. The Vice President of the United States stood up, acknowledged the cheers, shook hands with the presidents of the American and National Leagues and the commissioner of baseball, then threw the ritual first ball to Marcus Hayes. Hayes and the Vice President then tossed the ball back and forth three times, before the still-photographers were satisfied that they had perfectly recorded the ritual opening of the Series.

Moments later, Jim Pallafox was strolling out from the Oakland dugout toward the pitcher's mound, slowly, a swimmer attempting to navigate against the current of cheers and encouragement pouring from the throats of a stadium full of fans. And moments after that, he threw the real first pitch of the Series—a fastball-strike that thudded loudly against Marcus Hayes's glove, igniting a holocaust of sound from the spectators unequaled up to then.

He struck that first batter out. The second Patriot hitter popped out to Hector "Big Dog" Garcia, at shortstop. The third Patriot lofted a fly ball to Willie Richardson, in center field. Willie took it with a casual one-hand stab, sending the fans into ecstasy. The first half of the first inning was over. The Patriots had been retired, one-two-three.

The Golds failed to get on base in the last of the first inning, then Pallafox held the Patriots hitless in the top of the second. It looked like a scoreless pitching duel was developing, till, in the bottom of the second, Artie Gibbons, the Golds' blond, bullish slugger, changed all that. Willie Richardson, batting fourth, led off with a single to left field. Then Gibbons stepped up. He blasted the first pitch into the right-field bleachers, giving the Golds a 2–0 lead.

Now, it was the first half of the third inning. Pallafox stood on the mound, sweat streaming in rivulets from under his cap, trickling down past his ears, and soaking the collar of his shirt. For the fifth time in three innings, Marcus Hayes had called time, and was trotting out to the pitcher's mound.

Pallafox turned his back. He walked off the mound. He bent down and picked up some dirt. He had never noticed the crowds before, they had never bothered him. After his first major-league game, he had never thought about the thousands of people sitting in the stands, swilling beer, yelling incoherently, stuffing hot dogs and hamburgers and peanuts into their faces. On the road, he was only aware of them when things were going badly; then the crowd became a hydra-headed monster luring him to defeat by the sheer force of its psychic malevolence. At home, the fans were an ally. You orchestrated their boos by jawing with an umpire over a close call. They tripped the hammer in your veins that sent your adrenalin exploding.

But not today. Today, for the first time ever, he caught himself looking at individual faces: maybe that one, the bald guy waving the pennant behind home plate. Or the man in the red shirt halfway down the first-base line.

He'd been lucky so far—lucky or unlucky. When he came out, he had intended to put the ball exactly where the Patriots could hit it—being cute and clever, but every once in a while making a pitch that was *too* good. The funny thing was, though, no one had been able to hit him. The two men he had put on base this inning— one on a scratch hit, the other on a walk—were the first Patriot base runners of the game. The left-handers were bailing out—shying away from his inside pitches, afraid of the crippling power of his devastating fastball. The right-handers were reaching for pitches outside and away from the plate. And since everybody was expect-

ing and fearing fastballs, every time he blooped a fat
floater in, guys swung a second too early.

But he knew they would catch on to him soon. The
only time any of these guys had seen him pitch before
was for a couple of innings at the All-Star game. Any
time now, they would figure out that he was acting
scared, not cute. They would stop swinging at the bad
ones. They would start popping the good ones. Pallafox
couldn't wait until they did.

"What's happenin', man?" Hayes said, reaching the
mound and placing his arm around Pallafox's shoulder,
their backs toward home plate. "You sick or somethin'?
I gave you one finger for the fastball, and you threw me
a big fat curve. That dude can hit the ball, man," he
added, jamming his thumb back over his shoulder toward the Patriot slugger, Jerry Gabriel, standing at the
plate. "Only thing that saved you that time was the
dude on second base stole my sign and flashed it to Gabriel. Gabriel was lookin' for the fastball. Don't cross
me up, man," he said, " 'cause this Gabriel will park
your ball in the street." Hayes paused. "Hey, you look
sick. You want me to tell Oswalski?"

"Naw," Pallafox replied, brushing sweat off his forehead with the back of his glove. "Just nerves. I'll settle
down."

"World Series jitters," Hayes said, patting Pallafox
on the rump. "Happens to everybody first time out.
Don't worry about it. Just go on. Pitch your game. And
hold the dude on second base close. Don't let him get
any kind of jump."

Pallafox watched Hayes jog back toward home plate.
The umpire lowered his arms, signaling the end of time-
out. Gabriel dug in, his eyes on Pallafox, his shoulders
hunched, his bat waving in a menacing arc above his
head. Pallafox straddled the pitcher's mound, facing
first base. He read the sign from Hayes: one finger—a
fastball. Marcus was holding his glove outside and low.
Pallafox lifted his arms forehead-high, then lowered
them just below his chest, the ball hidden in his glove.
He looked at the batter. He glanced over at the Patriot

dancing off second base. Then he kicked his right leg up and back, wheeled and threw.

The ball streaked toward the plate, but an inch inside and nearly three inches higher than Hayes had called for. Gabriel swung. Pallafox could tell by the sound that he'd sliced it off the fat part of the bat. He turned around, watching the ball glide high over center field. Willie Richardson, in center field, didn't even move. Gabriel had undercut the ball slightly, and it was still climbing, right above Willie's head. But Willie had lost it in the sun's glare. He just stood there, squinting. By the time he flicked his sunglasses down off his forehead, it was too late. The ball bounced behind him and rolled to the wall, allowing the two Patriots on base to score, and the batter, Gabriel, to reach third base on a triple.

The next hitter lofted a fly ball that brought Gabriel home. It was Patriots 3, Golds 2.

Before another Patriot batter could step up to the plate, the Golds' manager, Danny Oswalski, came chugging out of the dugout. Even as he reached the mound, he was signaling to the bull pen for a right-handed pitcher.

Pallafox watched him approach, feeling grateful that Oswalski was taking him out of the game. The kind of gratitude a mortally wounded soldier feels toward a comrade who is about to put him out of his misery.

Pallafox was stepping out of the shower when he heard his teammates' metal spikes clacking in the corridor. As soon as he saw their faces, he knew the Golds had lost. Their eyes were downcast, their shoulders stooped. There was none of the usual jive-banter that bubbled out in the flush of a victory. Not that any of them were really disheartened; after all, this was only the first game of a best-of-seven series. Even Willie Richardson—the goat of today's game—winked and flashed a quick grin as he passed Pallafox, before turning his mouth grim and his face penitent again. It was all a sham, Pallafox reflected. No matter what they felt, ballplayers knew they were supposed to act contrite after

he lefties kill the third one off. Both Pallafox
won their first five games. Spider won one,
d got two no-decisions. Later, Freddy White
r a losing streak himself, but by that time
long been banished to the bull pen.

s attributed his early-season slump to the
ear of ten years in the major leagues. At
they argued with the dispassionate logic of
vouldn't have to retire till their sixties, he was
ill. Finished. Spider hadn't seen it that way.
t having an off year, he said. He had always
on finesse, not power, and control pitchers
lf did suffer periodic lapses from perfection.
ppened to him in the past. That's why, he told
ho might listen, he had had five 20-game sea-
ead of ten. The problem was, no one *would*
ntally, the reporters covering the club had al-
tired his number. They kidded with him,
im politely, but it was obvious that even if he
o Wally Kelly's future plans, he didn't fit into

, Spider had to admit, had been very support-
much he owed the owner. He kept telling Spi-
as soon as he showed signs of regaining his old
ss, he would be back in the starting rotation.
en that didn't happen, when Spider was consist-
consistent in relief, Wally had come to him with
stion. Wally knew a hypnotist, someone named
Allen. Allen, Wally insisted, might be able to help
regain both his self-confidence and his control.
irst, Spider rejected the idea outright. He had a
idea. If Lady Luck had deserted him, he would
court her. What better place to resurrect his love
with fame and fortune than the casinos of Las
?

ek after week, during Oakland home stands, he
fly off to spend a day or two at Harry Walters's
am Casino. Walters was as shrewd a businessman
was a fanatic Golds' loyalist. He enjoyed rubbing
ders with a sports celebrity of the caliber of Spider
son. More important, his guests and clients did,

every loss. If the coaches didn't see glum looks on their
players' faces, they might suspect them of the ultimate
heresy—not taking baseball seriously, not ascribing to
the Vince Lombardi football credo that winning was the
only thing.

So, today no one turned on his tape deck. No one
kidded anyone else about a girlfriend whose legs resembled redwood stumps. The funereal quiet was only interrupted by water splattering against naked bodies in the
showers.

Then, Wally Kelly burst into the locker room, his jaw
jutting aggressively, his lips set in an angry overbite.
Without a glance at the players, he stormed into Oswalski's office, slamming the door behind him. It didn't
matter. His rage was such that his shouts rang out as if
the door were wide open.

"Why the hell did you lift Pallafox?" Kelly started
screaming.

" 'Cause he was throwin' grapefruits," Oswalski yelled
back.

"I'll tell you when I want Pallafox to pitch," Kelly
replied, "and I'll tell you when I want him to stop pitching!"

The door opened, and Wally barged out of the locker
room.

Pallafox kept on dressing, avoiding his teammates'
eyes. He felt guilty; fortunately for him, though, his
teammates thought he only felt embarrassed. Everyone
pretended that no one had heard the argument between
the owner and the manager. Everyone, that is, except
Artie Gibbons. Gibbons caught Pallafox's eye and
sneered triumphantly.

Just as Pallafox was zipping up the small duffel bag
he always brought to the ball park, ready to leave, Oswalski came out of his office and approached him.
"Don't worry, kid," he said. Oswalski was gruff, plump,
and powerless. He knew the Golds all knew that Wally
Kelly ran this team by telephone. "It wasn't your fault
we lost. You didn't have your good stuff, but I could

see you were pitchin' your heart out. If Willie coulda caught that ball . . ."

Pallafox bit down on his lip. He turned away. He felt like crying.

to let two of
and White
lost two, an
would suffe
Spider had

The pre
wear and
thirty-two,
men who
over the h
He was ju
depended
like hims
It had ha
anyone w
sons, ins
listen. M
ready re
treated
fitted in
theirs.

Wally
ive; tha
der tha
sharpne
And wh
ently i
a sugg
Alvin
Spider

At
better
go an
affair
Vega

We
woul
Shaza
as he
shou
John

4

It was an hour before the secoi
the Golds' locker room, Rich N
porters. Miller had started last s
land pitching rotation, right behi
was a four-year vet—right-hand
slow, Spider was thinking, you a
to swing at his pitches twice. Go
reflected bitterly, as he watched
into their uniforms before battin
of world was it where he, Spider
second fiddle to a dude who co
miles per hour without a jet assist!

The pitching rotation last seasor
and immutable as the heavens—Sp
Swanson, and Freddy White, pitchin
work, each with four days' rest bet
Then, this year at spring training, th
verse had collapsed. Pallafox had sho
the rookie. Pallafox, the goddamn left
three left-handers (Pallafox, Spider, an
on a pitching staff that only needed tw
rotation. Pallafox and Freddy White
and blazing fastballs on their side. Sp
many games as he'd won the previous s
Golds had finished third in their divisi
was thirty-two years old, and his contrac
end of the current season.

In typical fashion, before the season
Kelly had announced that the Golds wou
five-man pitching rotation, including a
handers. The idea, he told his ballplayers

too. Walters furnished Spider with free room and board. By the end of September, Spider had lost six more games than he had won—and $20,000 more than he could pay. His mood had turned black. His Vegas credit-line had turned a fiery red.

Spider became terrified. He owed money, and if he didn't regain his pitching form soon, he wouldn't remain in the major leagues long enough to pay it back. He decided to take Wally's advice. He agreed to see Alvin Allen. Even if the hypnotist couldn't help him—and Spider was convinced he couldn't—by cooperating, he might be able to get Wally to pay off his Vegas gambling debts.

Miraculously, the hypnotist had helped. On Allen's recommendation, Kelly had inserted Spider into the lineup during a crucial game near the end of the season, and Spider, to the astonishment of the press, had pitched a marvelous three-hitter, handcuffing the Dodgers' batters completely. With that showing, Spider had won his starting assignment in the last game of the championship play-offs, against the Cardinals. Again, he had pitched well—until Pallafox had had to bail him out with two out in the ninth inning. Spider had hoped to start one game of the Series, probably in place of Miller, who was the weakest link in the Golds' starting four. And now, there Miller was, the focus of every reporter's attention, while Spider stood alone, forgotten in the excitement.

He was feeling resentful, feeling alienated. It was no longer his team; he no longer shared in the camaraderie. To an outsider it might seem juvenile, a silly detail—but, dammit, no one had put itching powder in his underwear or set his socks on fire for months now. He knew he shouldn't blame Pallafox, but hell, he *was* the new ingredient, the time bomb who'd exploded on the scene this year, blasting Spider into the desolate regions haunted by aging ballplayers. No future. Nothing to talk about but the past. A past that fades all too quickly.

Suddenly, Spider felt someone tugging at his arm. It was Oswalski, the portly manager, a cigar stuck between his lips, his face wearing that perpetually harassed look. "Hurry up and get your warm-ups going," he told Spider. "Don't ask no questions, 'cause I ain't got the answers. Wally called. He said you're starting to-day's game and Miller's taking a trip to the bull pen." The manager coughed, avoiding Spider's eyes when he added, "That hypnotist guy—that Alvin Allen—this genius about baseball has convinced Wally that you're ready to go."

By the ninth inning, it was evident that the Golds were about to record their first victory, against one defeat, in the World Series. Behind Spider's six-hit pitching, the Golds were leading, 4–1. Willie Richardson had atoned for his mischance the day before by hitting a bases-loaded triple in the sixth inning to give the Golds their commanding lead. Now, with two outs and no one on base, Spider Johnson was leaning back, he was tossing a soft, subtle curve. When the Patriot batter swung and missed for a game-ending third strike, fans started leaping over the protective barriers, mobbing their players, tearing at the turf for souvenirs.

But in the press box high above the stadium there was no ecstasy, no joy. Instead of an outpouring of emotion, the final out set off an explosion of energy, as the print journalists began feverishly pounding away at their typewriters. Within ten or fifteen minutes, they would write three hundred or so words, summing up the glory and drama of the Golds' victory. Telex machines would transmit their copy all over the country in time for the morning editions. Jenny and Rick folded up their stat sheets and complimentary programs. They fought the crowd clogging the upper mezzanine, searching for the elevators that would carry them to the street level.

"That was a strange move," Rick was commenting, "starting Spider Johnson, a guy with a one-and-seven regular season record, over Rich Miller, a guy who's won sixteen games."

"That's how Kelly earned his reputation as a genius," Jenny said as they elbowed their way into a packed elevator, careful to protect their vital organs against the thrust of broadcasting executives and working press and assorted freeloaders who were piling in after them. "Spider pitched—and Spider won."

"Right," Rick whispered. "And if Spider keeps pitching, and keeps winning, whoever sent our friend that nasty note is going to be very, very upset."

Decked out in the brown Cardin suit he reserved for special occasions, with a red Bill Blass shirt, and brown silk tie, Rick was ready for Wally Kelly's late-night gala at half-past eleven. Before he left his room to call for Jenny, however, he dialed Pallafox's number again. Yesterday, the pitcher had showered, dressed, and departed from the locker room before Rick had had a chance to talk to him. Rick had spent most of last night, and all his free time today, telephoning him, but no one had answered.

This time, Spider picked up the telephone. He sounded elated—the victory, Rick thought, had restored the wry, bantering patter Spider had been known for, a bubbling upbeat humor which had gone flat during his dogged losing streak. Finally, he managed to cork Spider's gushing enthusiasm long enough to inquire about Pallafox.

"Pallafox has split, man," Spider said. "He told Wally he was tired. Wally gave him the day off today. He gave him permission to catch up with the team tomorrow night in New York. Tomorrow's a traveling day," Spider added.

"I'm surprised Wally let him go on his own," Rick said.

"Wally thinks the pressure of the Big Series is bugging my man," Spider said.

"Where'd he go?" Rick asked. The image of a distraught Pallafox cruising aimlessly over California freeways, his eyes glazed, his foot heavy on the accelerator, was disturbing.

Spider's reply was cautious. "I really couldn't say, man."

"Look," Rick said, hoping his bluff would work, "if you don't tell me, I am going to blow this whole story sky-high."

"Okay, okay," Spider said. "No skin off my butt, after all. He's gone looking for the scout that discovered him at UCLA, a guy named Hardrock Harrison."

"At a time like this? Why would he bother wasting precious time on some baseball scout?"

Spider paused, then said, "This Hardrock Harrison isn't just some ordinary baseball scout, see? He's a part-time scout for the Golds—and a full-time cop for the San Francisco P.D., get it? A *detective* type cop, dig?"

Wally O. Kelly was giving his guests, Rick and Jenny among them, a guided tour of his thirty-room mansion, located in a plush suburb of San Francisco. The tour had begun under the stars, on the front lawn, with the Olympic-size swimming pool and the steam bath, and the set of colored fountains that spurted water, seven shades of blue, seven stories high at the press of a button.

"It's the largest privately owned fountain in the world," Wally bragged. "I just love fountains."

It seemed likely that Kelly loved the color blue, too. He was wearing a blue herringbone suit, blue pin-striped shirt, blue patterned tie, and sapphire cuff links.

"They say that blue is Kelly's wife's favorite color," Rick whispered to Jenny, who was also wearing her most chic outfit: a clinging yellow pants suit, covered with handpainted flowers. "And it was Mrs. K. who loved fountains," he added.

" 'Was'? Is Kelly's wife dead?" Jenny asked.

"As far as Wally's concerned she is," Rick replied. "If the rumors are true, she's about to become the ex-Mrs. Kelly."

Juanita Kelly, a Mexican, was, Rick explained, noto-rious for her quick wit and sharp tongue, a successful real-estate agent in her own right, whom Wally married after his first wife had died. Juanita was fiercely inde-pendent, and just as stubborn as Wally. Once, when Wally decided to raise the American flag outside their home, Juanita had flown the Mexican flag, on a separate, but equal, flagpole, alongside it. Now, Rick reminded Jenny, that second flagpole was bare.

The tour moved into the large house, built in the early 1920s as a replica of some forgotten French château. The guests—press, a few of the Golds' ballplayers (including Spider Johnson) and their wives or mistresses or girlfriends, plus show business and broadcasting personalities—were escorted through room after room, while Wally intoned a roll call of his most prized possessions: a bizarre pastiche of artifacts collected on whirlwind carpetbagging expeditions, during which he scavenged for unusual antiques. In one bedroom, a brass bed with a guillotine for a headboard; in another, a prim wooden couch, whose velvet cushions concealed a hinged bottom—an ancient toilet. ("Open your mouth wide, Commissioner Anson," he said as he lifted the board beneath the cushions—alluding to the commissioner of baseball, whom Kelly considered a villain and a lunatic.) There was an ornately gilted Chinese dresser with hidden drawers, all of them fake; a mirror set into the wall and framed with curtains to look like a window; a dressing table and chair set facing a wall, beneath a window that looked like a mirror—Kelly had a fetish for objects that seemed to be what they weren't, or weren't what they seemed.

The final stop was a long hall on the third floor, Kelly's art gallery, where the guests gaped, awestruck, at the three paintings currently on display, each in an exquisitely carved frame. Kelly approached the first. "A Van Gogh," he announced. "A Degas," he said, pointing at another, "and, of course," he added, nodding toward the third, "a Picasso. All of them perfect fakes—the most perfect fakes, perhaps, in art history. Didn't any of you wonder what happened to all those glorious paintings the great museums buy with such pomp and circumstance—only to find out they're frauds, painted by some disreputable seventeenth-century hack? This is what happens to the best of them," he continued. "They wind up here. They give me great pleasure. Every time I look at them, I can picture those overeducated art-farts who run our museums—I can see them squirming."

"Oh, God," Ray Fowler mumbled. "Don't tell me we're going to get the rags-to-riches story again." Kelly, Fowler told Rick, wore his humble origins like a coat of arms. "Everyone who spends any time with him has to hear the story of how he made his money ten times."

Rick had been surprised to see Fowler, after Kelly had humiliated the reporter so brutally in the postgame press conference the week before. But on second thought, he realized, it was consistent with Kelly's unpredictable behavior to invite to his home someone he had brutally humiliated. And it was consistent with Fowler's flabby principles to accept.

This time, however, Kelly spared his guests his Horatio Alger story. Rick was disappointed. He was curious about how Kelly had made all that money. So, as their host led them downstairs, out back where a barbecue spread was being laid out by ten or fifteen flunkies costumed in white coats and white chef hats, Rick asked Fowler for the details. He guessed, correctly, that if Fowler had heard Kelly's story ten times, he himself had told it to others at least twenty times. In New York, any inside gossip a reporter could provide about a celebrity was worth a free drink from someone.

"C'mon," Fowler said to Rick and Jenny, leading them over to a long table, where a bartender was mixing drinks.

"Thanks, but I don't drink," Jenny told Fowler. She looked prettier tonight than usual, Rick thought. He was glad now that she had come out from New York.

"Maybe you don't drink," Fowler replied, "but you sure as hell can read." He handed each of them a cocktail napkin. "Read that," he said.

In the dim light from naked bulbs strung overhead, Rick had to squint to make out the pink letters printed on the white frilly napkin:

> Of all God's creatures on earth,
> Like an oyster there's none so fine.
> Who else would donate his home
> In order for me to build mine?

"He started off in the early fifties, with five thousand dollars capital—almost all of it borrowed," Fowler explained. "He used that money to start Kelly Pharmaceuticals. He was the only owner, and the only employee. The first product he put on the market was called Cambin. Kelly claimed it would cure an illness he called 'common fatigue.' He bottled some standard ingredients —I don't know what—into pills, in his cellar. Then he started calling on doctors. He'd barge right past the receptionist, corner the cowering medico in his office, and start giving the guy his spiel. 'Now, Doctor, I have *just* the thing to rid your patients of that toxicity they're suffering from,' he'd spout. 'It's called Cambin. It contains *vitamins* and *choline* and *mositol* and *methionine*—three *lisotropics* that will detoxify the upper tract.'

"Naturally, Kelly didn't know what the hell he was talking about," Fowler added, "but neither did the doctor. Anyway, before the doctor could cough up a protest, Kelly would plunge his hand into his detail bag and yank out a bottle of enormous yellow pills. 'Yes, Doctor, I *know* they look big,' he'd continue breathlessly. 'They *have* to be big to hold all those ingredients, but they go down *easy*, 'cause they're *shaped like a football*.' Then he would pop that enormous pill into his mouth. He'd swallow it without water, the whole time keeping a big, blissful smile on his face.

"The problem was," Fowler concluded, "Wally couldn't use that trick as often as he would have liked. Maybe Cambin did cure common fatigue, maybe it didn't. But it sure was one helluva laxative."

Both Jenny and Rick were laughing. Pallafox had said it had only taken Kelly a few hours to make him change the course of his whole life, giving up a career in law for a career in baseball. Now Rick understood just how persuasive Kelly could be.

"But where do the oysters come in?" Jenny asked. She was enjoying the visit to Kelly's house. For the first time in Rick's memory, she was holding in her hand a paper cup full of wine.

"Well, while Cambin was going strong," Fowler said, "Kelly heard about a bone specialist in Minneapolis who claimed his patients with broken bones mended faster when they took daily doses of ground oyster shells, which have a lot of calcium. Now, almost every other doctor said that calcium taken in that form wouldn't help heal broken bones, but that didn't stop Wally. He telephoned some guy in Mississippi, who ran an oyster-packing plant. This guy was only too happy to sell Wally his oyster shells; up to then, he'd been dumping them as garbage. Wally had the shells ground up. He made pills out of the powder. And did those pills sell?" Fowler pointed at the verse printed on the cocktail napkins.

"What's he worth now?" Rick asked.

"Oh, I'd say, right now, anywhere between twenty and thirty million," Fowler replied. "But in a month, after his wife gets done dragging him through divorce court, he'll be lucky if he's worth half that much."

"A tough lady," Rick said.

"A bitch. A five-star general in the bitch army. They'll be fighting down to the very last dollar. Wally," he added, "has said she'll never get one damn penny."

Almost twelve hours before the first guests had arrived at Wally Kelly's mansion, Jim Pallafox was driving through the desert, the afternoon sun big above like a miner's blinding lamplight glaring in his eyes.

He hadn't intended to be driving to El Paso, Texas. When he'd left the locker room after losing yesterday's game, he hadn't intended to go anywhere but home. Then, a few hours later, some astonishing part of him had said good-bye to Spider, telling him he was going into San Francisco to look up Hardrock Harrison; he had obtained Wally Kelly's grudging permission to catch up with the team again on Friday night, in New York, before the third Series game on Saturday. The Golds' reputation for loose discipline was such that the press wouldn't think his absence during the second game extraordinary.

Hardrock's wife, Alice, had told him Hardrock had taken a couple of sick days to do some scouting in El Paso for the Golds. On the spur of the moment, Pallafox had driven to the airport, caught a flight to Phoenix, and rented a car. He had spent the night in a motel outside of Tucson, and this morning, he had headed south, toward El Paso, on a road that sliced through the desert for five hundred miles, with mountains forever suspended in the distance like heavy gray mist. Still, he refused to admit to himself that he was running away.

On all sides, amid the sagebrush and the rattlesnakes and the cactus and the roadrunners, the minitornadoes called "devil dusters" spiraled up from the desert like the ghosts of prospectors who had struck death instead of gold. He passed the San Pedro River—in October, still parched, a dry, barren area that remained much as it had been when Pancho Villa used it as a highway, galloping in from the border to raid the local mining settlements. Once this was Apache country, with Geronimo and Cochise swooping down from their mountain fortresses to attack white settlers. Now, Pallafox reflected, Pancho Villa would have to show his entry permit at the border or slip in by dead of night clinging to the axle of a truck full of farming tools. The Apaches had been corraled into reservations. The mine shafts had been surrendered to the rattlesnakes. The only prospector within a hundred miles was Jim Pallafox, at the wheel of his rented Ford Pinto, traveling all the way from San Francisco to El Paso to pan a vein, that, if odds held, would prove to be only more fool's gold. After college, Pallafox had played two years with El Paso, in the Texas League. Hardrock Harrison, the San Francisco cop who had scouted him, had been like a father to him there. He needed a father right now.

Yes, he admitted to himself finally, he was running scared, running home, escaping into nostalgia, to a time when he'd been a kid right out of college, with his bright future still hovering just beyond his outstretched fingertips. He didn't want to think of the World Series now. He didn't even want to think of Kathy, scooped up out of her innocence, steamrollered by his own runaway fate.

Hardrock's wife, Alice, had told Pallafox where to find her husband, scouting for the Golds at the El Paso high-school championship game. Pallafox reached the high school at 3:00 P.M. He parked the car behind the gymnasium and strolled toward the half-empty stands, thankful that, caught up in their partisan passions, none of the hundred or so teen-agers even gave him a second glance. He found Hardrock sitting a few rows up behind home plate, in the company of a Dodgers' scout and a local high-school baseball coach.

At a glance, he thought, the two scouts could have passed for retired clerks: the tall, balding, fatherly looking gent with the enormous bag of peanuts on his lap, the wiry guy with the French poodle sleeping at his feet. Except that the man with the bag of peanuts, Hardrock, and the wiry guy with the poodle, Lefty Wilson, both balanced small notebooks on their knees. And in their pockets, both carried the stopwatches symbolic of their calling.

Pallafox sprinted over the wooden benches. "Hell, I don't think I can believe my eyes," Lefty Wilson, the Dodger scout, exclaimed, looking up. "What the hell you doin' down here?"

Pallafox was about to fabricate an answer when Hardrock lifted up his enormous bag of peanuts, offered it to him, and said, "Jimmy's down here to take a look at a piece of land I told him about. Three hundred acres, with a hundred head of Angus. Fancies himself a sort of cowboy, California-style, what with all that money he's makin' and no place to invest it up in Oakland. He'll be flyin' on to New York tomorrow, ain't that right, Jimmy?"

Pallafox nodded, took some peanuts, and sat down next to Hardrock. Same old Hardrock, he was thinking. Folksy, talkative—and, underneath it all, one hundred percent cop. Hardrock had himself once been a promising pitcher. He'd come off a hardscrabble farm in Texas and starred in the Texas League, before World War II had turned him into a tail gunner. His B-17 had been shot down, and he'd suffered a wound in his arm, the deathblow to a promising pitching career. After the war, he had drifted to San Francisco. He had become a cop. He had risen through the ranks to chief of homicide detectives. But he had never lost his love for baseball; he had never stopped scouting part-time for the Golds. He had never lost that folksy twang, that down-home earthiness that disguised a sharp, street-wise mind and a gut instinct for the heart of the matter. There was, of course, no "piece of land" for Pallafox to look over. Hardrock had had no forewarning that Pallafox was going to show up. But leave it to Hardrock to sense when there was trouble.

Pallafox looked now at the kid on the mound, tall and gangly and aggressive—a throwback to himself, eight years ago. The kid's fingers looked right—long and thin, enveloping the ball like the tentacles of an octopus. But something else was wrong. Pallafox could tell by Hardrock's face. Vic, the high-school coach who served as Hardrock's bird dog in El Paso, could tell, too. He was worried. If the kid signed an Oakland contract, Vic would get $500. If the kid reached Triple-A, he'd get another $500. If the kid made it to the big leagues someday, Vic would get another $1000.

"The kid's coach doesn't know what he's doing," Vic whispered to Hardrock and Lefty. "He refuses to pitch the kid more often than every other game, so how can the kid build up stamina? I'm not making excuses for the kid, you know that."

But Pallafox and Lefty and Hardrock knew Vic was making excuses. After holding a 2–0 lead for five innings, in the top of the sixth, the kid was starting to get hit. He was still throwing hard, but he couldn't keep his fastball low anymore. It was becoming more obvious that his control was what had made him effective in the earlier innings, not his velocity.

Hardrock smiled at Vic, keeping his tone light. "He's a bulldog, Vic," he said.

"Yeh," said Lefty, "the kid's a bulldog."

"A real tough competitor and he takes instruction real good, too," Vic added, like an auto salesman clutching at the coattails of a customer who has decided to buy elsewhere.

By the ninth inning, the kid was losing; no Seaver, no Sutton, no Pallafox—just a medium-sized fish in a very small pond. He was getting hit, he was getting wild. He was aiming the ball. Too often the target he hit was the fat part of someone's bat.

An hour later, Pallafox and Lefty and Hardrock were sitting in a cantina near the Mexican border in downtown El Paso. Sawdust on the floor, splintery wooden tables, posters of bullfights, and a jukebox blaring the despondent moan of some country singer who had lost his true love in a wrecked pickup truck. Maria's hadn't changed at all, Pallafox thought, except that now, in the off-season, it was no longer a hangout for El Paso's minor-league baseball players.

Pallafox had spent many nights in Maria's during those two years in El Paso, sipping margaritas and listening as the dreams of his teammates grew more detailed and more improbable, as alcohol fueled their private fantasies. This was what he wanted to escape into, he realized now, feeling the salty margarita burning his tongue. From baseball's transcendental moment—the World Series—to its most trivial: the shop talk in a dingy cantina, the gripes about having to change in the bus on the way to ball parks, about uniforms two sizes too big, and big leaguers whom you played with last year in the minors, and whom you knew weren't good enough to carry your bat. There was nothing more calculated to spoil success faster than success itself, Pallafox was thinking. When the dream becomes reality, as it had for him, what was there left to dream?

Meanwhile, Hardrock and Lefty were jawing about the good old days of scouting.

"I used to turn up at the senior prom, around midnight," Hardrock was saying, "when the kid's head would be a little light from firewater and close dancing. I'd flash my police shield in his face and drag him off, in his Sunday suit. I'd book him into a motel and stay up with him all night, till I got that signature."

Scouting, Hardrock and Lefty both lamented, would never be the same. The baseball draft—held twice a year, in January and in June—prevented a dollar war among the major-league clubs. The penetration of pro baseball into every rural backwater meant that no good prospect was overlooked. Kids today, prodded by their coaches, wherever they lived, were only a stone's throw away from some major-league tryout camp. If the scout didn't find them, they'd find the scout. Meanwhile, in the background, hovered the specter of the computer— the Blesto V scouting organization and all the other electronic pigeonholers.

"But you can't program forty years' experience into a computer," Hardrock argued. "Whether it's police work, or scouting, a computer can come up with general standards, but it takes a man to apply them."

Pallafox loved to hear their banter. It brought back memories of raucous evenings spent during his two years' apprenticeship in El Paso. When the team was playing at home, he had come to Maria's almost every night. Something about this dingy little café had held a special attraction for him, as had Maria herself—her black hair knotted behind the neck in a neat bun, the fat mole on her fat cheek, the way her hands always smelled of olive oil and chili when she served him his ritual margarita. In a sense, he thought, he wished he could have played for El Paso forever. . . .

He had always been fond of Maria's, perhaps because it reminded him of another Mexican-style café that served as a student hangout near the UCLA campus, the one he had taken Norma to on the night they first met. While Hardrock and Lefty rambled on about hot prospects, and budding stars who were doomed to supernova prematurely, images began to skitter past Pallafox's eyes like a tatty filmstrip and he saw . . . himself . . . the face even thinner, the mouth slightly less grim. It was a cool night in June, in his sophomore year, the night of the gala celebration for his team's victory in the Western Athletic Conference baseball championship. Dressed in a scruffy T-shirt and faded blue jeans, Jim Pallafox, the sophomore pitching sensation, strolled toward the team party being held in one of the girls' dormitories.

He paused at the doorway a moment, watching, overhead, tinsel streamers undulating like a woman's hips. Then he entered, besieged immediately by slaps on the back, congratulations shouted in his ear, his teammates leaning in with beer on their breath.

Then he noticed her—the cheerleader called Norma Windsor. Not so effusive as the others; he knew that, as a rule, she didn't date athletes. He had seen her in his classes—she was a philosophy major, too—but had never spoken to her, neither in the classrooms nor on the playing field. Someone had told him she didn't give a damn about athletics. She had become a cheerleader because she took modern dance, and in her mind there was some connection between the two. She had intrigued him, but not enough for him to make the effort to speak to her. He felt a kind of resentment emanating from her. Somehow, she seemed to be saying with her eyes, it wasn't fair for him to be a star athlete *and* an honor student, living proof that not every athlete was all brawn and no brain.

"Hi," he said to her, after the well-wishers had drifted off to other corners of the room.

She was about five-feet-seven, with blonde hair that tumbled past her shoulders, and large blue eyes that seemed perpetually searching. "I'm Norma," she replied, with a smile that was warm, quick, and captivating.

"Jim," he said, "Jim . . ."

"I know," she replied, a bemused smile on her lips. "Pallafox—the guy who everyone says I should be dating, because," she added, her tone turning mocking, "we'd be such a perfect couple."

"You don't think much of athletes," he said.

"I don't think much of jocks," she said.

"I don't think much of groupie cheerleaders, either."

They stared at each other, appraisingly. Then, simultaneously, they both burst out laughing.

Norma and Jim left that party in the girls' dormitory. They drove, in the 1965 Ford convertible that Pallafox had purchased thirdhand the previous summer, to a nearby student café. The same splintery tables as Maria's, the same sawdust an inch thick on the floor, the same bullfight posters, yellowing with age. Over tacos and enchiladas and mugs of beer, they talked and talked.

"I got a call from John this afternoon," she said at one point. "He said he called to find out if I needed money for clothes, but he really wanted to know if I was adjusting this year, *adapting*."

Whoever John was, Jim could see his point—about the clothes. In those days, Norma wore baggy skirts and loose blouses straight out of the 1950s. She didn't care about clothes then; she didn't wear makeup, either. "Who's John?" he said, transferring chili sauce from his upper lip to the back of his hand.

"John's my father," she replied, sipping a Coke and coolly scrutinizing him.

"John?" he said. "You call your father by his first name?"

"When my mother was carrying me," she said, "when they were first married, John wanted her to have an abortion. He wanted to let some butcher plunge a rusty wire hanger into me. My mother told me about it after they got divorced. I decided that if he didn't want me, if he was so weak, he didn't deserve to be my father. I decided to call him 'John.' "

"That must hurt," he said. "I could never call my father 'Harry.' "

"He never tried to kill you," she said. "Anyway, John always has someone around to call him daddy. Sugar daddy. He got married again a few weeks ago— he's always either getting married or divorced—to a dancer this time. She's only nineteen. She does bumpy belly dances at a little bistro in Manhattan where they serve horrible Greek food. And I think they're going to be very happy. Jane has big breasts. John loves big breasts."

"What does he do for a living?"

"He's a psychiatrist, what else?" she said, with contempt. Then she smiled, and became naive and unblemished and irresistible again.

Jim sat there, nibbling at his enchilada. He wondered how Harry and Gladys—reared in an Irish Catholic ghetto, weaned on the Depression—would react if they knew his athletic scholarship was paying a dividend aside from a potential career as a pro—his falling in love, with an Episcopalian, whose father, the psychiatrist she called John, was wed to a teen-age Salome.

They had driven for hours that night, laughing and talking, with the convertible top down, and the breeze tousling Norma's silky hair. Though he couldn't remember where they'd gone, he remembered how he'd felt. He felt . . . skin like vellum paper, when his fingers snuggled into the nest she made by cupping her hand on the seat. And he remembered singing, in his crackling, quaking baritone that set her laughter peeling. He threw his head back. He flung the melody at Alpha Centauri. Only her slim, smooth fingers anchored his soul.

The black convertible sped onward, the wind whipping Norma's blonde hair across her face. "I love you," he said suddenly, squeezing her hand.

"What?" she called out, tears of laughter on her cheeks. "I can't hear you, 'cause of the wind."

"I said I love you!" he shouted furiously.

But again the wind intervened, snatching his voice away. Norma kept holding his hand and staring at the star-studded sky and laughing—her laughter climbing, falling, touching his heart. . . .

Now, five years and an eternity of painful experience later, Lefty Wilson's voice was shattering his reverie. "I was sayin' . . . it's been good seein' you."

Pallafox blinked. It took an effort, but he managed to wrench his thoughts away from the past, to the present, where he was sitting next to Hardrock, in Maria's cantina in El Paso, with Lefty hovering in front of him, his poodle suspended under one arm, the other extended, waiting for Pallafox to shake his hand. "I was daydreaming," Pallafox admitted sheepishly, taking Lefty's hand and pumping it.

"Good luck up in New York," Lefty said. "I gotta get back on the road now."

Lefty walked off, out of the cantina. Pallafox turned to Hardrock, who was watching him through squinting eyes, sizing him up the way he had years ago, the first time Pallafox had stepped toward the mound in a college uniform. "Thanks, Hardrock," Pallafox said quietly.

"Thanks? Thanks for what, kid?" Hardrock's face was a mask of innocence.

"For telling that little white lie about me being down here to buy property," Pallafox replied.

Hardrock regarded Pallafox for a moment. Then he said, "I saw you pitch them two games on TV, Jimmy, the last play-off and the Series opener, and I know somethin's eatin' at your guts. I know it's somethin' big, and not that World Series jitters horse manure they're pushin' in the newspapers. I says to myself, 'Not the kid, not Jimmy. He's a hard-on-type pitcher, a hang-tough type pitcher. To get at his guts, you gotta stick a knife in him.' Who's stickin' in the knife, kid?" he added softly. "Who's stickin' it in and turnin' it around?"

Pallafox shook his head sadly. "I can't tell you," he said. "I wish I could, but I can't."

Hardrock nodded. "All right, you can't tell me anything, but let me tell you. Like the old prizefighter said, you can run, but you can't hide."

Pallafox sighed. "I know," he said.

"'Cause no matter how hard you run," Hardrock added, "you're gonna keep hearin' footsteps—your own footsteps, echoin' back from where you started runnin'."

They were quiet for a moment. Then Hardrock asked, "Where you headin' next?"

Pallafox smiled. "I didn't have the slightest idea till half an hour ago. But now," he added, "I know. I'm going to New York, all right—but via Las Vegas."

"Vegas?" Hardrock scowled.

"To see a lady," Pallafox said.

Hardrock's big broad beefy face split with a warm grin. His body, tense till then, with his hands clasped in front of him, suddenly relaxed. "A woman," he said, relief in his voice. "I should have known. That's all it is, some damn broad."

"That's it," Pallafox agreed, wishing it were that simple, "just some damn broad."

That evening, they drove the 600 miles back to Phoe-

nix. Pallafox was flying on to Las Vegas that night,
Hardrock back to San Francisco. On the way, they de-
toured 50 miles off the main road to stop at Tombstone,
Arizona—Boot Hill, the O.K. Corral, Billy the Kid, the
Earps, the Clantons, and Big Nosed Kate. Chased indoors by a chill desert breeze, they leaned against the
bar of the Crystal Palace Saloon—a replica of the noto-
rious bar room where Wyatt Earp dealt Faro and William Bonney dealt death—quenching their thirst with
Coors and sarsaparilla, just as they had in the old days.

Almost a couple of thousand miles in little over a
day, Pallafox was thinking, but all worth it. It was a
detour that was leading him straight to Norma. It was
his obligation to her to tell her about the kidnapping; it
was his obligation to himself to find out if she was involved.

"Dammit," Hardrock roared suddenly, slamming his
open palm against the bar top, "I have got this dream, it
haunts me. I am driving down a road in the middle of
nowhere, and I see this Mexican kid outside a shack,
hurling a big brick at a tree. I jam on the brakes, I run
out—knowin' I've finally struck pay dirt, found another Catfish Hunter, Koufax, Seaver—another Pallafox. He can't even speak English, he's never seen a
baseball glove, but I sign him, and he wins thirty games
a season for ten years. And he is my discovery!"

They drained their glasses in silence, the detective
and aging scout, the pitcher and distraught father. Then
they stepped out into the quiet desert night, when suddenly a series of explosions thundered from a nearby
mine—the impact echoing like a Bunyanesque fastball
thudding against a Gargantuan mitt.

Hardrock smiled. "Maybe he's just beyond those
hills," he said.

Pallafox didn't smile. He didn't have a dream, he had
a nightmare. The explosions in the mine reminded him
too much of the sound of a shotgun blasting. For a moment, thinking of Kathy, he felt utter despair.

5

Early the next morning, Friday, Jenny and Rick board-
ed the plane that would ferry them from Oakland to New
York, where the Series would resume on Saturday at
Patriot Stadium.

Now, two hours airborne, Rick was succumbing to
that sleepy, dazed semicoma—a kind of resigned paral-
ysis—that overcomes transcontinental travelers who
know that in a few days they'll be making the same tiresome journey back again. So he leaned back. He spent
his time plotting defensive chess moves. He was the
king under attack; Phil Hanson was a phalanx of ruth-
less rooks, angry bishops, all bent on checkmating him.

Rick was exhausted. Jenny was exhilarated. She had
only spent two days in Oakland, but such exciting ones
that it had seemed like a week. All her life, she thought,
she had been a bystander, doomed to watch and listen,
but not to participate. Now, suddenly, fate had cast her
headlong into the vortex of events that would ultimately
affect the outcome of the World Series itself. She had
been thrust into a world brimming with money, over-
flowing with glamour. She still felt like a bystander, but
now one who had been jostled by the expensive limo of
an Arabian sheik. It was better to become involved ac-
cidentally than not be involved at all.

The memories were her priceless mementos—freshly
hewed and glittering. Last night's party at Wally Kelly's
was the most dazzling. Maybe it was the wine she had
drunk. Maybe that was what gave it, even in retrospect,
such an exotic aura. But no, it was more than the wine.
It was the essential strangeness of the party—Kelly a
Mad Hatter escorting her, Alice, through his Looking

Glass menagerie. The highlight of the evening, of course, had been appropriately bizarre.

"What did you think of Alvin Allen?" she asked Rick, tapping him on the shoulder till he opened his eyes and blinked at her.

Rick yawned, stretched stiffly, his stocky body straining against the narrow seat. "The hypnotist?" he said.

"I couldn't believe it when he snapped his fingers and put Spider into a trance. That was cruel of Kelly," she added firmly. "He shouldn't have embarrassed Spider that way."

Rick glanced at her. Her mouth was set in a grim line. That was like her. He took his moral stands on "issues"—race prejudice, economic injustice. . . . Jenny got upset over nuances and she judged strangers by how they measured up on her scale of dos and don'ts. Still, she was probably right, he admitted to himself. Most of the time Kelly had struck him as being merely brash; last night he had crossed that line separating aggressiveness from aggression.

It was about two in the morning. The silver punch bowls had been drained, leaving a soggy mass of sliced fruits. The buffet tables, set behind the house, were buried now beneath stacks of paper plates and half-eaten hamburger rolls, and the guests were riding the smooth crest of a champagne high, when Wally Kelly strode to the center of the garden and demanded their attention.

"Friends and enemies," he had called out in his booming baritone, "every court must have its jester, and I am proud to say I have a pair. You all must have heard of Alvin Allen," and he bowed mockingly toward the thin man at his side—in his sixties, but wearing tapered jeans and a sport shirt with a plunging neckline, and two-inch heels. "Like Lamont Cranston, whom those of you forty and over will remember as 'The Shadow,' this insignificant-looking creature," and Kelly mussed Allen's carefully combed brown hair, "has the power of clouding men's minds. Once upon a time, of course, he was squandering his talents in country fairs and squalid dives. Then his act struck it rich in Vegas. He gave up show business. He became a healer, a modern Mesmer, relieving the symptoms of those who were sick, and, at the same time, their silver. His clients currently include a host of Hollywood stars, whom he has treated from every infirmity from nail biting to narcolepsy. And tonight, he's agreed to provide us with a small demonstration of his powers. Or is it," Wally added wickedly, "a demonstration of his small powers? Ladies and gentlemen, my dear friend," and he squeezed Allen's narrow shoulders, "Alvin Allen."

Allen stood alone for a moment, nervously puffing a cigarette. Then his face brightened. "You know," he said, in a gravelly voice, "a doctor I once knew told me Wally's medical literature is the best he'd ever read, considering that it didn't contain one single scientific fact."

A ripple of laughter swept over the guests.

"And another doctor told me that Wally came to see him one day. He had a new product he wanted to sell, to help the crippled and handicapped. 'But, Wally,' said my friend the doctor, 'do they really *need* rubber crutches???' "

This time the laughter convulsed Allen's audience—all, Rick noticed, except Wally O. Kelly, who was glaring at Allen angrily. "That'll be enough, Alvin," Kelly commanded. "Just put the trained dog through its paces."

"Anyway," Allen said, regarding Wally with a wry smile, then turning away, "Wally, with, as usual, more wit than charm, has asked me to entertain you folks with a simple demonstration of my art. Hypnosis." He coughed once, then again, dropping his cigarette and grinding it out beneath the toe of his polished boot. "Spider," he called, "would you be kind enough to come up here?" The Golds' pitcher slapped hands with a few friends, left the attractive blonde who had been clinging to his arm (the one, Rick recalled, named Selma, who had planted herself on his lap at Pallafox's party before the first Series game), and approached the hypnotist. "Spider is one of my clients—or, as I like to call them, my patients," Allen announced.

"Right," Spider said. "Alvin here's been working real hard with me. He's helping me lose weight. Y'know—taking all those twenty-dollar bills that were weighing down my wallet, dig?"

Everyone broke out laughing again, and no one was laughing harder than Spider himself—till Alvin Allen raised two fingers in front of Spider's face, and snapped them together. Suddenly, Spider's head began to loll side to side. "That," said Alvin Allen, "is hypnosis."

He led Spider by the arm to the buffet tables, in the center of the semicircle of crowding spectators. Then he said, "Spider, sit down on that chair," pointing to a white stool set next to a table.

Spider walked over to the chair. He sat down.

"Now, Spider," Allen continued, speaking quietly but firmly, "we are all alone in this garden, just you and me, isn't that right?"

"That's right, we're all alone," Spider replied, his voice beginning to drone a little.

"I want you to catch this orange I'm going to throw," Allen said.

He picked up a handful of soggy orange strips from a punch bowl and tossed them at Spider. The pieces, compressed together, flew apart in the air. Spider managed to catch several strips with one hand.

"Now, remember," Allen cautioned. "There's nobody here right now but you and me. Got that? No one but you and me."

Spider nodded his head mechanically. "Nobody but you and me," he repeated.

Allen pointed at Ray Fowler, standing at the edge of the crowd. Gesturing with his index finger, he motioned to Fowler to approach the buffet table. Allen pulled over another stool. Fowler sat down on it, facing Spider, about ten feet away.

"Who's sitting in that chair?" Allen asked Spider, pointing right at Ray Fowler.

Spider stared blankly at the newsman. "Ain't nobody here but us, you know that, man," Spider said, irritation in his voice.

"That's right," Allen responded, slapping his forehead as if he had forgotten.

Then Allen took some pieces of fruit from the punch bowl. He handed them to Ray Fowler. He motioned as if he were tossing something at Spider, then nodded toward Fowler. Fowler threw the strips of soggy fruit. Four or five hit Spider squarely in the face. Juice trickled down his face onto his shirt. He sat there, staring at Allen, an uncomprehending look on his face.

"You see," Allen told his audience, "Spider cannot admit that Ray Fowler has thrown the fruit at him, because invisible men do not throw fruit while sitting on empty chairs. How do you feel, Spider?" he asked.

"Who you talking to, man?" Spider said. Then: "Fine—fine, man, though maybe just a little too hot." Spider wiped fruit punch from his forehead, as if it were sweat.

Now, as Jenny recalled the embarrassing demonstration, it had already begun to take on the fuzzy shimmer of a mirage, the crazy-quilt illogic of a nightmare. "I've never seen anything like it," she said, shaking her head in awe. "I've never seen anyone act so cruelly as Kelly did toward Spider."

"I don't know," Rick said. "Spider seems like a pretty loose guy. When Allen brought him out of it, he seemed to think it was just one incredibly big joke."

"It was a good scene for you, at least," Jenny added. "I mean, for your article."

"I'm not going to use that party," Rick replied. "Spider may not be embarrassed, but I damn well am embarrassed for him."

Jenny smiled, and Rick knew he had just tipped her scales of dos and don'ts in his favor.

By midmorning, all the people and paraphernalia connected with the World Series had begun moving East in an airborne gypsy caravan. The Golds and Patriots would play two games in New York before returning to the coast on Monday, to play game five on Tuesday.

Just as the team equipment managers were packing their players' favorite bats—three or four for each player—in aluminum trunks, and the TV technicians were coiling their thick cables, Norma Windsor, in Las Vegas, was parking her compact car in the lot behind the Shazaam Casino.

She got out of the car and stared for a moment at the outlandishly large neon sign that floated above the casino's roof—a smiling Aladdin rubbing his miraculous lamp; then the genie would leap up, his arms loaded with gold coins, before the sequence started again with the smiling Aladdin.

Norma entered through the door marked Employees Only. Once inside, she removed her large oval sunglasses; after two weeks working the nightshift, she'd found the early-morning glare painful. She negotiated a maze of twisting corridors, used her key to open the doors of the small executive elevator, and rode up to the third floor. She padded down the plushly carpeted corridor till she reached Harry Walters's office.

"Norma," he exclaimed, rising from behind an enormous desk and approaching her, "I'm so glad you got my message."

"Is it something about Kathy?" she said. "Something wrong with her?"

"No," Harry replied. He leaned forward to kiss her, but his lips only brushed her left cheek as he casually turned her face. "Kathy is fine, don't worry about her, she's just fine."

"When can I see her?" Norma asked, anxiety in her voice.

"You know what I told you," Harry said. "No one should see her for a while, not even you, not till we get this thing all ironed out."

"But . . . is she eating . . . is she unhappy . . . oh, Harry, I don't know . . . this whole thing . . . it *scares* me."

Harry moved as if to put his arm around her shoulders, comfortingly, but Norma pulled away. "You said you had to see me before I went to work this morning," she said, rubbing tears from her eyes with her long, slim fingers.

"Pallafox is coming here," Harry said.

"My God, you didn't tell him anything!"

"No, of course not," Harry replied, twisting the diamond on his finger nervously. "I just told him you'd meet him here, at nine A.M., which," he added, consulting his watch, "is about ten minutes from now."

"See him? I can't see him," she cried out. "What would I say to him?"

"You have to see him," Harry replied carefully. "If you don't, he's going to be very suspicious. And we can't afford that, not right now, can we?" Harry added, putting his hand on Norma's arm.

Again, she moved away from him. "All right, I'll talk to him," she replied, biting her lip.

"Don't give anything away," Harry warned.

"Don't worry," she said, "I won't."

Harry leaned forward, aiming a kiss at her mouth. For the second time that morning, Norma averted her face, so that his lips brushed sandpapery across her left cheek. Harry pretended he hadn't noticed. "I'll be downstairs," he said. "I'll tell Billy to put someone at your table till you finish with Pallafox."

Harry left the room. Norma sat down on the big brassy couch that faced the window in the wall. She adjusted the collar of the white silk blouse, tailored to emphasize the thrust of her breasts. She smoothed the wrinkles out of her red silk slacks, cut to accentuate the breadth of her hips and to flare out around her calves because Harry thought her legs a trifle too thin.

Outside, she could see the Amazing Astronauticas' tightrope wires crisscrossing at eye level, hooked onto three tall poles the Astronauticas shinnied up at the start of each performance. Below was the broad safety net, sagging in the middle, as if supporting some invisible burden. And turning away, she saw herself in the wall mirror behind Harry's desk—the short blonde hair, the layers of makeup she had applied to keep her pale skin from looking sickly in the brash light of the casino. Pallafox, she mused, would find her appearance very different. In the days when they were lovers, she had let her hair grow down past her shoulders. There had been no mask of mascara, no clinging slacks or snug silk blouses.

Well, she reflected bitterly, the Norma Windsor of baggy peasant skirts and uncoiffed hair and unpainted skin hadn't been able to compete in the marketplace. Las Vegas had taught her how to turn sleek and sexy.

Norma sighed. She wasn't looking forward to this encounter, not at all. She knew he would demand an explanation for her transformation. And Norman dreaded providing that explanation. As much as possible, she avoided explaining it even to herself.

There had been the month of indecision after she left college, which she'd spent at her father's apartment in Manhattan—the father she called "John." Like Pallafox, her psychiatrist father also advised her to have an abortion—the Supreme Court having legalized the act, in 1973, for women who were in their first three months of pregnancy. The more he badgered her, the more adamant she became. To hell with the Supreme Court! She wouldn't let him do to her baby what he had tried to do to her. She *would* give her baby a chance to live, she *would* carve out a career for herself.

She left New York. She returned to California, living at first with her mother and stepfather in San Diego. Kathy was born in January 1974. Soon after, Norma took a job as an airline stewardess, while her mother helped out with the baby-sitting. Three months later, she was assigned to the New York–Las Vegas run. She rented a small house in Las Vegas, sharing with three other stewardesses, one of whom was always around to take care of Kathy while Norma was at work. Her roommates, lured by the beckoning whirr of one-arm bandits, the bright lights of downtown that promised adventure, were soon spending time prowling the casinos. But as much as they coaxed, Norma refused to join them. For all she saw of Las Vegas, they used to kid her, she might just as well have been living in Des Moines.

From time to time, though, Norma would—as was the custom among single stewardesses—date some first-class passenger she had met on the plane—avoiding the boisterous types for starched, impeccably attired men who, she soon learned, were often hotel and casino executives. She avoided the younger ones, chatting only with those old enough to be her father. That way, she told herself, she could stay out of compromising situations.

Then, one day she met Harry Walters on a flight from New York. Walters seemed wise, he seemed worldly, yet, at the same time, shy and somehow vulnerable. He was an older man, in his late fifties, courteous and concerned for her welfare. She liked him. And he seemed intrigued with her.

He was sympathetic to her status as an unmarried mother—a fact, she had found, that lowered her in the esteem of other men she met. He began escorting her around Las Vegas, bringing her to the Shazaam Casino as his guest, letting her play the various games with house chips. He seemed astonished at her quick grasp, her instinct for the nuances of cards—her ability to retain numbers in her head with almost photographic recall. It wasn't long before he offered her a job—at a salary five times what she earned as a stewardess, plus a cut of the table take, and tips. Norma weighed the pros and cons. Dollars were the decisive factor. It would allow her to put money away for Kathy's education, and, at the same time, permit her to spend far more time with her daughter than she had been able to.

That was three years ago. Since then, she had managed to make her compromise with The Strip. A schizophrenic compromise, perhaps, but one that worked. At the casino, she thought of herself as an actress hired to play the role of a cool, alluring vamp. Outside the casino, she lived simply, in the little white house in a quiet suburb, the house with the child's swing—still these long days now—in the backyard. She would date once in a while, but restricted her friendships to men like Harry Walters—men with power and prestige, but who treated her kindly, who had their choice of almost any woman in Vegas, yet chose to be with her, despite the fact that she would sleep only with a man she loved. Despite the fact she hadn't loved a man since Pallafox.

Pallafox wouldn't understand. He was a big-league ballplayer. Anyone who ran a craps table in a Vegas casino was by definition a whore, an unfit mother.

The door opened. Pallafox entered. He looked at Norma—the shimmering red slacks, the white silk blouse hugging her breasts; the short blonde hair trimmed in bangs over the forehead, the blue eyes that still looked the same, except for the deepening shadows beneath that even makeup couldn't hide. She was smoking a cigarette. He noticed that, despite the calm of her beautiful face, her hands were shaking.

Norma looked at him—the fiery red hair still raging in wild growth, creeping over his ears, tumbling over his forehead . . . the eyes . . . brown . . . turned hard as the button eyes of that toy panda Kathy always slept with. He was gripping a pair of sunglasses.

There was silence for a moment, as they warily surveyed each other. Then Pallafox said, softly, "Hello."

"Hello," she replied, just as quietly.

"You've changed your hairstyle. You used to wear it long," he said.

"You've changed your life-style," she said. "I can't open a newspaper without seeing your face."

Pallafox walked over to an armchair opposite Norma's couch and sat down, crossing his legs, turning his sunglasses over and over in his hands. "I'm sorry we've had to go through all this hassle over Kathy," he said.

Norma tensed. "What is that supposed to mean?" she asked.

Pallafox raised his eyebrows quizzically. "I mean the custody fight, what else?" he said.

Norma relaxed. "Yes, the custody fight . . . I guess you were only trying to do what you thought was right."

"I couldn't see her growing up here," he said, waving his hand at the frantic activity outside the window in the wall behind him, where, high above the tables, the Amazing Astronauticas were cavorting on high wires and trapezes. "I just couldn't see my daughter growing up in this kind of environment," he added, "surrounded by gamblers and hookers, and mafiosi and incurable losers."

"You'd rather she grew up living the life of a ball-player's daughter," she retorted, "with her father gone playing winter ball in Puerto Rico during the off-season, and on the road half the regular season. You'd rather she grew up among cheap groupies, in front of TV cameras—surrounded by the same gamblers and mafiosi and losers."

"The big leagues aren't like that, dammit," he replied hotly.

"And neither," she replied icily, "is Las Vegas."

There was silence again, till Norma ended it. "Look," she said, "we're not twenty-year-olds sitting in the snack bar before a philosophy class. I have to get to work. Harry said you wanted to see me. Why did you come? Not," she added bitterly, "to see the mother of your child, because you damn well fixed it so Kathy doesn't have a mother."

Pallafox shook his head despairingly. "Not me," he said, "my lawyer. My lawyer said that till the adoption proceedings were finalized, you couldn't see Kathy. It's only temporary. Christ, do you think I really want to deprive the kid of her mother?"

"I don't know what to think," Norma replied. "Except that for three years you didn't give a damn, while I was struggling to put food in Kathy's mouth and make a home for her. Then, suddenly, someone serves me with a summons. One month later, my daughter is gone."

"How could I find you all those years? How could I have helped you?" Pallafox said. "You made sure I couldn't find you."

"Damn right," Norma said. "You had your choice, me or the big leagues. You made your choice, I made mine. Anyway," she added, "this isn't going to get us anywhere. What is it you want with me?"

Pallafox stared at her. She did look different; despite the years, he had pictured her face the way it had looked when she was nineteen—the soft look her eyes had then, the innocence, the enthusiasm for living. What did he want with her? To tell her that Kathy was gone. To share his loss, his terror, with someone aside from the reporter, Holman, or the editor from *Action*

Sports, Jenny Cohn—someone who would feel the way he felt. Yet, he couldn't bring himself to tell Norma, not yet, at least, while her bitterness was a barrier between them. If he told her now about Kathy, he realized, instead of feeling just the loss, he would feel the guilt over losing Kathy, too. To tell Norma, he decided, he would have to know more about her, he would have to learn to trust her again.

"Look," he said, "I wanted to find out what happened to you, from the time you left college till you turned up here."

"You want to trace the decline and fall of Norma Windsor?" she said, her tone ironic. "Well, I'll tell you."

Norma outlined for Pallafox the sequence of events that had turned her from cheerleader into craps dealer. She was careful not to romanticize, not edit unflattering details. By the time she was finished, one thing, at least, was evident to Pallafox. Her transformation had been dictated by necessity. Kathy's welfare had always been uppermost in her mind.

He had been an ass, he admitted to himself. Through her chance meeting with Harry Walters, Norma had stumbled onto a way to support herself and Kathy. She was no more a part of the Las Vegas scene than he was the stereotyped major-league ballplayer, the Artie Gibbons who lived for broads and boozing. In fact, he thought to himself, they hadn't drifted that far apart, after all.

"I'm sorry," he told her, this time with a kind of humbled honesty that penetrated Norma's defenses and stirred up her own emotions.

"I think you mean it," she said.

"I do," he said. "I've been selfish about Kathy, and not very fair with you. I couldn't believe you could be . . . well . . . *you*—and survive in this kind of life."

Norma smiled. "And I couldn't believe you could have so much success without turning into a hairy-chested superegotist."

For a few seconds they sat watching each other with a mutual warmth. Then Pallafox's face grew somber.

He wanted to tell Norma about Kathy, but was afraid to. What if she insisted on telling the police? Or, worse yet—what if she was directly involved? He decided to test her with an outright lie, scanning her reaction.

"Kathy's doing fine," he said. "She's up with my parents, in Fargo, having one helluva time—out with the dogs, taking little walks with my old man, going on fishing trips. My mother just spoils her silly," he added, with false gusto. "You know Mom. She always wanted a little girl."

"I'm glad," Norma said. "I want Kathy to be happy."

Pallafox gazed at her. There was something in her voice when she replied—he couldn't put his finger on the emotion. It could have been a quiet gloating. It could have been a vengeful, mocking smile hidden behind her smooth, unconcerned mouth. Or, it could have been his own overworked imagination. "Do you know something I should know?" he said to her suddenly.

"What are you talking about?" Norma responded, bristling.

"Kathy," he said softly, "has been kidnapped."

"My God," Norma replied quietly.

Pallafox scrutinized her face—cool, beautiful, her long, graceful fingers lying still—not fluttering, not tense, but perfectly composed and relaxed. For a moment, he suspected . . . but no, he thought; he was projecting his own anxiety and guilt onto her. She didn't know anything; how could she? Thank God, he decided, he didn't tell her about the death threat in the kidnap note.

The New York fans swarming toward Patriot Stadium, for the third game of the World Series, were different from the crowd in Oakland. They used elbows educated in rush-hour subway jousts to ward each other off. They kept their wallets in a front pocket, knowing that among the happy-faced Patriot fans were scores of pickpockets. They kept to the beaten trail—avoiding less traveled streets where stragglers could be picked off one by one and mugged.

The sky was gray, overcast. A few blocks beyond the

stadium the burned-out tenements of the South Bronx
loomed, barren and menacing. But inside, exultation
reigned. For the second year in a row, World Series had
come to New York, and New Yorkers were welcoming it
as only they knew how. With cheers for their heroes,
scraping over throats parched by years of disappointment. With hisses for the Golds that sounded like seventy
thousand cobras poised to strike.

Rick was standing behind the batting cage, his face
pressed against the wire mesh, watching the Patriots
take batting practice. This was one of the moments he
loved best: being down on the field before a Series
game, mingling with other reporters and the ballplayers, while the masses of fans stayed penned up behind
the metal railings—envious, but without privilege.

Ray Fowler was hovering by his shoulder, with the
collar of his sport jacket turned up against the wind.
"This is one helluva stadium," he was telling an Oakland writer, "but the city is never gonna get a penny out
of it."

The stadium had been renovated recently, in a classic
municipal boondoggle engineered by the Patriots'
owner, Fred Hartwood. By threatening to pull the Patriots out of New York, Hartwood had cowed the city
into refurbishing the stadium to the tune of $100 mil-
lion. His public-relations ploy had been to dangle his
civic mindedness as bait: the plan included a few million for renovating the surrounding ghetto, too. Later,
though, during the city's budget crunch, those few million had been lopped off to pay for decorating the "circle suites" purchased by corporate powerhouses and
multimillionaires.

"The city's tax break is too low," Fowler explained,
"and so is the rent. The city can't rent the stadium without Hartwood's permission—and he's very particular
about who tramples his infield. You've got a different
situation with Wally Kelly in Oakland," he concluded.

"Right," said the reporter. "Wally's taxes are high,
and so is his rental, so the city makes a profit and he
usually takes a bath. Still, there are rumors he's actually

going to make a profit this year. With the new stadium he's got there, fans have been turning out in droves."

"A profit?" Fowler exclaimed. "Unheard of. No owner wants to make a profit. If he makes a profit on his baseball club, what's the point in owning one? These guys like Hartwood and Kelly don't buy ball clubs to make money, but to *lose* it. If the tax laws didn't allow them to write off their losses from baseball against their profits from their main businesses, you couldn't give any major-league franchise away in any damn sport."

"I'm telling you," the Oakland reporter insisted. "This year, Wally may have a big problem. He may actually make so much money he can't cook the books enough to hide all of it."

"Well," Fowler replied, "I'll believe it when I see it. I suspect Wally would rather stick his profit in a furnace and burn it before he stopped using his ball club as a tax shelter."

Rick turned away, shoving past reporters clustering in foul territory around the playing field. He entered the Golds' dugout and moved through the dungeon-damp tunnel that led to the visitors' clubhouse.

The Golds were still optimistic today, even though they had managed only a split in the first two Series games. If they could salvage only a single victory out of the two games to be played in New York, they would return home with a chance to lock up the Series with a pair of consecutive wins. The Golds' tape recorders were blaring funky music. The hair dryers built into the walls were cuddling carefree heads.

In the center of a knot of reporters, Rick found Spider Johnson—a new Spider, revived by his crucial win two days ago, a part of the team again, projecting the old magnetism, the old self-confidence.

"He's over there," Spider shouted, nodding at the trainer's room, where Pallafox was bathing his left elbow in the ritual ice bucket.

Rick waited until Joe Idella, the trainer, left the room. "Where did you go yesterday?" he asked.

Pallafox, lying flat on his back on the trainer's table,

barely opened his eyes as he answered, "To Vegas, to
see Norma."

"What did you learn?" Rick asked breathlessly.

Pallafox opened his eyes wide. He stared at Rick
thoughtfully. "About Kathy? Nothing. About myself? A
helluva lot."

"But does she know anything about your daughter?"

"If she did," Pallafox sighed, "I'd know that Kathy
was at least safe. But she doesn't. She loves the kid. She
could never have written that note."

"You still love her," Rick said quietly.

Pallafox closed his eyes, immersing his elbow among
the soothing ice packs again. He recalled his meeting
with Norma, her reaction to the news that Kathy had
been kidnapped. She had wanted to know what he intended to do—the thought that he would be forced to
lose in the Series seemed to disturb her, he realized, almost as much as Kathy's disappearance, which she had
taken rather well. Too well?

Finally, it had been time to leave, to catch the plane
to New York. He stood up, they shook hands, their fingers touching, perhaps an instant too long.

"One thing," he said. "It doesn't matter now, I
guess—but exactly why did you disappear so completely, so suddenly out of my life? Was it just my sign-
ing with the Golds?"

Norma, still holding his hand, shook her head no.

"Then it was my asking you to get an abortion," he
said.

She looked at him, her eyes searching his, for what,
he didn't know. Then she said, "You remember what I
told you the first time we met, about my parents, when
they were first married—how my father, John, wanted
to let some butcher plunge a rusty wire hanger into me?
Well," she added, in a numb voice, "I wanted to have
your baby. But I didn't want the baby to grow up as I
did. I didn't want my baby to grow up calling her father
'Jim.' "

Upstairs, in the press box, just before the game
started, Rick was joined by Jenny, who'd arrived out of

breath and excited. "How's Phil taking all this?" he asked her. She had spent the morning on a mission of mercy—trying to con the wrath out of Phil Hanson's vengeful heart.

"Never mind Phil," she said, pulling his elbow to get him away from the file of newsmen who were trudging in. "While I was at the office, I got a call from Alvin Allen."

"The hypnotist? What did he want?" Rick asked.

"He wanted you," she replied, "but since you weren't in, they put the call through to me. Anyway, he says he just has to see you when the Series returns to Oakland on Tuesday. He said he had a session with Spider yesterday, and learned something that's troubled him ever since. He said he made sure Spider wouldn't remember what he had revealed by giving him a posthypnotic suggestion. I tried to get something more, but he said he wouldn't talk over the phone. Except that it had to do with the World Series, and with Pallafox, and with Wally Kelly." Jenny paused. "He sounded scared."

6

Alvin Allen *was* scared. He was sitting in the den of his
nine-room apartment in a plush suburb of San Francisco. If he looked left from his lounger, he could see,
through the broad plate-glass windows, the Golden Gate
Bridge, sprawling artfully across the Bay. On the wall in
front of him, he could see trophies and photos. The trophies were culled from his youth, when entering talent
contests as a magician had been his passion. The photos
were a more recent record, revealing his rise from
small-time vaudevillian to hypnotist to the stars. There
were forty or fifty of them—he had never bothered to
count them—color shots of Hollywood celebrities and
big-league athletes, draping their arms around Alvin Allen's shoulders. There were no captions identifying the
different celebrities. Theirs were faces that everyone
recognized immediately, or else they wouldn't have been
worthy of Alvin Allen's den wall.

But right now Allen wasn't enjoying either the spectacular view, or the spectacle of himself in the company
of the famous. He wasn't enjoying anything at all. He
was staring at the large TV screen, where the Golds and
Patriots were playing the third game of the World Series, and thinking hard about Spider Johnson, about his
session with the Golds' pitcher the day before.

As usual, when Spider arrived Allen had escorted
him into his office, seated him on a chair, then sat
down across from him. They had chatted briefly, then
Allen said, "Today, what I want to do is explore the
emotions you felt the other day while you were pitching.
I want you to live through that experience again, in the
most minute detail possible. I want to dredge that expe-

rience up, keep it from sinking into your unconscious."

"What's the point?" Spider asked. "I don't see why I need more help. I won, didn't I? I pitched good, didn't I?"

Allen didn't say anything, but Spider's conviction that he was "cured" he interpreted as a positive sign. That, after all, was what his "treatment" was all about: making his patients believe they were little engines that *could*.

"I think you're right," Allen replied after a pause. "But it's not enough for your conscious mind to know that. Your unconscious mind has to be convinced, too. What I'll be doing now, and in the next few sessions, when you come back from New York, is reinforcing— making sure your unconscious knows that your performance the other day was no fluke. Remember what I told you when we began: picture your unconscious mind as a man floating in a liquid medium, in a dark, empty room, cut off from all direct experience of the world outside. Before he gets an accurate picture of what's happening, it must be repeated a hundred times over."

"And the more it's got to be repeated," Spider said, "the longer the treatment, and the more money I gotta pay. That's the only message I'm getting right now," he added.

Allen sighed. He glanced at his watch. He had no time today for repartee. He snapped his fingers once in front of Spider's face, just as he had at Kelly's party. And just as it had at Kelly's party, Spider's head lolled suddenly sideways as he fell into a deep trance.

Allen started leading Spider back, regressing him hypnotically to the beginning of the World Series, in order to bring him up to his successful pitching performance in the second game. They had been talking for almost an hour, when, without warning or preamble, Spider started mumbling a phrase that immediately caught Allen's avaricious ear. Allen quickly turned on his tape recorder, as Spider said, "Walter's got a half million riding on the Series, and millions more with the big boys."

"What's that about?" Allen asked carefully.

"It's Walter's double-cross," Allen heard him say, in a dreamy voice. "Walter's got a half million on the Series and the big boys have millions more."

Allen had heard enough; perhaps, in fact, too much. Quickly he cued Spider onto another subject. It didn't take a genius, he thought, to figure out that Walter was Walter O. Kelly, and that the half million and millions and double-cross had some connection with the World Series. He didn't want to hear anymore. He didn't want to absorb a lethal dose.

Now, a day later, he was glancing at the TV screen, where the Golds were winning behind the pitching of the left-hander, Freddy White, beating the Patriots, 7–3, at the end of eight innings. Most of all, he didn't want to know what Spider had meant about the "double-cross."

But all last night, and today, the thought had haunted him. Something was going on. That's why he had telephoned the reporter he had met at Wally's party, Rick Holman. It was a piece of news he thought *Action Sports* might be interested in. The kind of tasty tidbit the publisher might trade for an article about Alvin Allen— his astounding success rate with pro athletes—an article which would undoubtedly produce more celebrity-studded photos on his den wall.

The Golds' lead held up in that third game of the World Series. They won by the final score of 7–3. Now, the next day, Sunday, Jim Pallafox stood in the visitors' bull pen at Patriot Stadium, warming up to pitch the fourth game. The pain in his heart from Kathy's loss was compounded today by a piece of information he had picked up in the locker room, while dressing. Some of his teammates had been talking about today's surprising betting line. The Patriots were favored despite the fact that Pallafox's opponent was an aging vet who had won only thirteen games all season. When they noticed that Pallafox was listening, they lowered their voices to a whisper. It made him feel even worse.

Lightly tossing the ball back and forth with Marcus Hayes, the catcher, Pallafox was considering the implications of that startling set of odds—3 to 2, in favor of the New Yorkers. True, the home field gave the Patriots an advantage. Their skills were tailored to their natural grass turf, just as the Golds' were suited to artificial turf. The Patriots' lineup was loaded with sluggers, who hit the ball hard, and usually in the air. The right-field fence was close in and beckoningly low. The Golds' lineup, on the other hand, had the kind of slappers and speedsters whose choppy hits skidded briskly across Astroturf, giving them singles in Oakland that would be easy outs in New York.

Yet the advantage inherent in Patriot Stadium wasn't sufficient explanation, he realized. Even allowing for that home-field edge, his performance this year had been so far superior to that of the Patriot pitcher, Rollie Harris, that the Golds should have been decided favorites. Perhaps, Pallafox reflected, the oddsmakers in Vegas knew something that he didn't—or something he wouldn't want them to know. One thing was sure. The World Series was the biggest betting event of them all—bigger even than the Super Bowl, since more than one game is required to complete it. The odds on each specific game, involving a turnover of millions of dollars, had been calculated on evidence more reliable than a hunch.

As Pallafox continued to throw, harder and harder now, the public address announcer began orchestrating the World Series' pregame ritual. First the visiting team lined up along the third-base line, each man stepping forward when his name was called, then the home team did the same along the first-base line, receiving, naturally, a much heartier welcome. Only the starting pitchers were absent, engaged in too serious an endeavor, the crowd would realize, to take time off to doff their caps. Then, the national anthem began to blare. During the regular season, the singer might be a player's wife with ambitions toward becoming a professional songbird, or, just as often, a player's mistress. At the last World Series the Golds had participated in, four years ago, Wally Kelly had inflicted upon his fans the contralto gurgling of the reigning Miss California, a tall, willowy blonde who had been Wally's frequent companion that season. But today, no amateur would suffice. A leading baritone from the Metropolitan Opera was bellowing out the "Oh, say can you see . . . ," adding one more ounce of fuel to an already fired-up crowd. Before the anthem was half sung, the crowd had begun to roar, drowning the baritone out under a solid cataract of sound.

Pallafox tucked his glove under his arm. He walked out of the bull-pen area and toward the Oakland dugout. All his life he had been waiting to pitch in Patriot Stadium. It was every ballplayer's dream, as it was the dream of every basketball player to perform in Madison Square Garden, no matter how cynical, or satiated with fame, he might pretend to be. The plaques to Gehrig and DiMaggio and Ruth . . . a mound straddled by Don Larsen, Vic Raschi . . . this was Mecca, Jerusalem, pure heaven.

But not today, he thought bitterly, flopping down on the dugout bench, far away from his teammates. Today, it was sheer, living hell.

Pallafox had spoken to Rick that morning, and learned about Allen's telephone call. He knew Jenny was already headed back to Oakland to confer with Alvin Allen in person. Pallafox had been tempted to go right up to Spider and ask him, till Rick had convinced him that Spider wouldn't be able to recollect that information, since Allen had given him a posthypnotic suggestion, burying the data deep in Spider's unconscious.

Strangely enough, till now the thought of who might be behind the scheme to fix the World Series hadn't occurred to Pallafox at all. He had been too preoccupied, worrying about Kathy, and his own dilemma: should he throw games? And if so, how to lose intentionally.

Now, Allen's mysterious phone call that seemed to connect Wally Kelly and himself with some shady World Series deal—plus the fact of today's inexplicable betting line—had both Pallafox's curiosity and suspicions aroused.

That it could be Wally Kelly just didn't make sense.

If anyone had everything to lose by a Golds' defeat and nothing to gain, it was the ball club's owner. A maverick he might be, an eccentric. But not a kidnapper. And he was too ardent a baseball fan to sacrifice the game's most cherished event on the altar of greed, or revenge—or any other motive Pallafox could think of.

There was another possibility, of course: Norma. Kathy's disappearance might really be part of a desperate scheme to regain custody. Yet, there were those threats . . . and gut instinct told him she would never tolerate such viciousness. Anyway, had the whole thing been a kidnapping-for-custody caper, there would have been no need for threats at all. He sensed that the threats were the cake, not the frosting.

He was still thinking about these troubling pros and cons as he took his place in the dugout to watch his teammates' futile attempts to solve the style of the Patriots' knuckleballing pitcher, Rollie Harris. Then, he himself was on the mound, still thinking—about Kelly, about Spider, about Norma, always about Kathy—when he should have been thinking about Patriot batters, about their fat bats connecting with his fastball, spraying sharp line drives around the stadium in a frenzied flurry. By the end of the first inning, Pallafox was losing, 3–0.

In the first half of the second inning, the Golds scored once, reducing the Patriots' lead to two runs. But the three hits off Harris had been scratch singles, owing more to good fortune than finesse. Harris's knuckler was waffling all over the plate. When Harris had his control, and he had it today, he was almost impossible to hit.

So, beginning in the bottom of the second inning, Pallafox quit worrying about the problems that were plaguing him. He faced one dilemma squarely. He had to lose to save his daughter's life. He had to quell the schizophrenia that had been gripping him—having to lose when he had always been a winner, when winning had ranked, throughout his life as an athlete, second only to Godliness. He decided to concentrate hard, to aim his pitches carefully, to give the Patriots pitches

they could hit. Goddamn it, if he was going to lose intentionally, he was going to get far behind fast; he
would force Oswalski to take him out of the game for a
relief pitcher—or force Kelly to force Oswalski.

The first Patriot batter he faced in the bottom of the
second was the shortstop, Jim Hinton. Hinton, Pallafox
knew, was a curveball hitter. He could hit the curve for
high average, but could be handcuffed by the fastball,
inside and low. Pallafox had struck him out twice in the
first Series game on low, hard fastballs. So the first
pitch he gave Hinton was a curveball, one that broke no
sharper than a Little Leaguer's and hung over the plate
belt high like a harvest moon. Hinton smacked it for a
double down the third-base line.

Pallafox proceeded methodically down the batting order, pitching each Patriot according to his needs. Gabriel, the slugger, he awarded a fat hard one. The power
hitter parked it over the right-field fence. Andy Worley,
the left fielder, couldn't, according to the scouting report, hit the inside pitch. He didn't have to. Pallafox
wasted one pitch in the dirt, then aimed his second pitch
to intersect with the fat tip of Worley's bat. Muldoon,
too, got the only pitch he could hit, a slider. Pallafox
gift wrapped a shoulder-high fastball that streaked
down the middle of Joe Rasmussen's power alley; Rasmussen lofted his ball over the same fence Gabriel had
cleared. At that point, Pallafox decided he had done
enough damage for one inning. The National League rule
forcing the pitcher to take his turns at bat was in effect
this year. He was due up at bat the next inning. He had
given Oswalski/Kelly the perfect opportunity to pinch-
hit for him, without embarrassing anybody. With grim
self-satisfaction he forced the next three batters to
ground out, ending the inning. The Patriots had scored
four runs, giving them an imposing 7–1 lead.

He sat in the dugout, watching his teammates flail at
Rollie Harris's erratically fluttering knuckleball. The
sweat was pouring off him, though the temperature was
in the mid-fifties. Well, he thought, he had done it; for
the first time in his life, he had deliberately thrown
pitches to be hit and hit hard. Strangely enough, he

didn't feel angry, he didn't feel sick. He just felt empty, completely empty.

Suddenly, someone was tugging at his sleeve. "It's your ups," Oswalski said, pointing to the bat rack.

"But I thought . . ." Pallafox uttered, astonished that, after his dismal performance the previous inning, he was being asked to stay in the game.

"You thought Wally was going to bail you out," Oswalski said.

Pallafox reared back. "What's that supposed to mean?" he said, with an anger born out of guilt.

"I mean," said the manager, chewing nervously on the stub of his cigar, "you and me both know that you just don't have the kind of consistency you were throwin' with right up till the end of the season. Believe me, kid, if it was up to me, you'd be takin' your shower. Everybody has a bad day. This is yours. But Wally says let the kid pitch, so—the kid is gonna pitch. So," Oswalski added, "show 'em what kind of stuff you're made of, kid. Go out. Forget last inning. Get your head together. Stop aimin' the ball. Just throw the ball."

"Maybe that's it," Pallafox said, pretending he was mulling over Oswalski's advice. He was really thinking about Wally's refusal to pull him again, even after he had given so inept a performance. "Maybe I was just aiming the ball too much."

"That's it, kid," Oswalski encouraged. "Go out there. Forget that we're behind. Even if we don't take this one, we got more chances. Show 'em who you are, for the next time you face 'em. Let 'em know what kind of stuff you're made of."

Pallafox grabbed a bat off the rack. He strode to the plate. He swung wildly at three consecutive pitches, ending the inning. The problem is, he thought, as he walked out to the mound, Oswalski didn't understand that what the Patriots had seen of him last inning was not the preliminaries but the main event.

He pitched adequately after that—adequately enough, that is, to serve his own purpose. When, in the sixth inning, Artie Gibbons blasted Harris's knuckler for a solo homer, making the score 7-2, New York,

Pallafox rewarded the Patriots' leadoff hitter in the bottom of the sixth with his own home run, preserving the Patriots' six-run lead.

After that, there was no need to pursue the game of tit for tat. In the late innings, the Golds found Rollie Harris's knuckleball more baffling than ever. The game ended in an 8–2 Patriots' victory.

Afterward, in the Golds' locker room, Pallafox—still sweaty, still carrying his glove on his right hand—stormed into Oswalski's office. "Why the hell didn't Kelly lift me when he saw my stuff wasn't there?" he demanded. "What's he trying to do, embarrass me?"

Reporters were filing in, lured toward Oswalski's office by the shrill sound of Pallafox's voice.

"Don't ask me," Oswalski commented, turning his back on Pallafox. "I'm just the manager. Ask the man who owns you," he added, jerking his thumb back over his shoulder, "and for that matter, me, too."

"Why didn't Oswalski pull you out of the game?" Wally Kelly shouted, striding into the locker room and posing theatrically amid a circle of reporters. "I'll tell you why, because I told him not to, that's why.

"First of all, Jim," he continued, his voice becoming softer, more reasonable now, "I wanted to show the world I had confidence in you. After all, it wasn't your fault you lost the first game. Willie Richardson's error lost it for you. Now," he added, his voice beginning to rise, "you're pitching your second game of the World Series. Your nerves seem frayed. You're losing. Well, I want to show the world I still have faith in you, because if I don't have faith in you, then the Patriots are going to think you're a sham, and there goes the whole damn Series.

"And besides showing them I still have faith in you," he continued, his voice climbing toward a calculated hysteria now, "I wanted to remind you of something. You got a fat bonus. You are right now bitching that you deserve to be the highest paid pitcher in baseball. Well," Wally was actually screaming now, "you had better start pitching well, or I am going to *embarrass you into pitching well, you hear me?*"

Pallafox threw his glove down on the floor. He stalked toward the other end of the locker room, fuming. It was typical of Wally, he thought—or maybe not. Maybe it was a carefully engineered ploy. For if Wally *was* behind Kathy's kidnapping, this was exactly the public outrage he might perpetrate to justify keeping him on the mound through a string of losing appearances. The man was as devious, Pallafox decided, as he could be charming. The question was: *how* devious.

It was still early afternoon in San Francisco, when Alvin Allen clicked off the TV, poured himself another triple Scotch, and sat down at his mahogany captain's desk, his portable cassette recorder in front of him. Time after time he had played, then rewound and played again, the tape he had made with Spider two days ago, the one with the disturbing half-mumbled comments about Wally Kelly, a double-cross, and millions of dollars.

Perhaps, he was thinking, instead of calling that reporter, he should have gone straight to the police. After all, if there were some double-dealing going on during the World Series, the police should know, shouldn't they? They should, he admitted. Still, three considerations held him back:

First, what evidence did he have? The ramblings of a semicomatose ballplayer? Statements open to half a dozen interpretations?

Second, if there were some dirty business afoot, he was very sure he didn't want to become soiled. He had worked too long in Las Vegas not to know that if, as ridiculous as the idea was, the Golds' owner was risking his millions on the Series' outcome, someone else would be risking the deadliest kind of muscle.

Third, and not by any means least important, he craved exposure in *Action Sports,* whose interest he knew he had suddenly kindled with his telephone call yesterday. He could barter the information, preserving his anonymity, in exchange for celebrity, later, in a feature article detailing his accomplishments.

So Alvin Allen simply sat in his office, staring at the

orange sun hovering outside his window, inducing in himself the kind of semihypnotic trance he recommended for clients troubled by decisions they couldn't face.

Then the doorbell rang, startling him. His doorbell rarely rang unless preceded by a call from the doorman sixteen stories below.

Allen stood up, putting Spider's cassette back in its box and securing it in one of his seven metal file cabinets. Then he walked toward the front door, pausing in front of the full-length mirror in the hall to gingerly pat his freshly trimmed brown hair into place. Before opening the door, he peered through the peephole. He found himself staring into the robust, neatly goateed face of a man sporting a black homburg hat at a jaunty angle. The man was smiling to himself, as if someone had told him a clever story in the elevator, and he was having a hard time swallowing his laughter. "Who is it?" Allen called through the door.

"Mr. Allen?" the man's voice boomed brightly. "I'm Harold Cameron, of the NBC-TV programming division. May I have a word with you?"

Allen was relieved. Early Friday morning, he had placed a call to Cameron, having been advised by his agent that NBC might be willing to consider him for a guest appearance on the "Tonight" show. Cameron wasn't in, however. His secretary had promised Allen that Cameron would "contact" him this morning. Allen had never imagined that Cameron would contact him in person.

He opened the door. "What can I do for you?" he said, as the man with the homburg pushed his broad shoulders through the doorway and strolled into the room.

As Allen shut the door behind him, the man said, "Well, for a start, Mr. Allen, you can die—and die slowly."

The sun was beginning to pale now, promising more warmth than it could deliver. Jenny wasn't sure whether it was jet lag, or tension, but she was feeling the chill that comes with overtiredness. She was glad that, on leaving the hotel room, she had decided to take a sweater.

She gave her name to the doorman, who guarded the entrance from behind a counter in the lavishly appointed lobby, a small, pinched-face little man, with a mustache sparse as cat whiskers. He ran his finger down a list, until he came to her name. Then he rang Allen's apartment. No answer. He rang again. Finally, he put the receiver down. "Well, he isn't answering, but I know he's up there."

"How do you know?" Jenny asked.

" 'Cause I let one of his friends in a couple of hours ago," the doorman replied.

"A friend?" Jenny said. "Not a client?"

"A friend," the doorman replied. "The guy told me he wanted to surprise Mr. Allen. Then he surprised *me*, with this." The doorman pulled a crumpled ten-dollar bill out of his coat pocket. "The guy's gotta be up there," he added, " 'cause he didn't come through here on his way out."

"Maybe you missed him," Jenny said. Dammit, had she rushed three thousand air miles only to find Allen out?

"Miss him? Are you kidding? Could I miss a ten-ton truck if someone drove it through my lobby? Not on your life. This guy was like two Raiders' defensive tackles glued together. This guy was King Kong."

"Well, either he climbed down the outside wall, with Mr. Allen on his back," Jenny replied dryly, "or else they're still up there."

The doorman shrugged. "I guess so. I guess he just doesn't want to take any calls."

"Well," said Jenny, "why don't I just go on up and wait till he's through? I'm sure he won't mind my interrupting. I came all the way from New York this afternoon, just to see him."

The doorman shrugged again. "I don't know. You see," he added, "I got these orders. It's a big risk if I break 'em. I could lose my job."

All of a sudden, Jenny got the point. She reached

deep into the large shoulder bag she was carrying and produced a ten-dollar bill.

He nodded toward the elevator. "Apartment sixteen D," he said, winking. "If he asks, just tell him I wasn't around. Tell him there was a sign that said, Doorman back in five minutes."

Jenny rode the elevator up toward the sixteenth floor. She felt very alive and very happy. Ridiculously enough, this was the first time she ever had had to bribe her way in to see someone. Instead of making her feel guilty, the act made her feel, somehow, like a true professional, a Woodward or Bernstein on the track of something big.

The elation fled when she pressed the buzzer and got no response. She rang again. Then she did something else she had never done in her life. Without first having been invited in, she turned the knob of someone's apartment door. And, even stranger, the knob spun freely in her hand. The door opened, revealing a hallway bathed with shafts of light from the picture windows in the living room.

"Mr. Allen?" Jenny called out, stepping in, but careful not to close the door behind her.

No one answered. She moved forward, then paused before the gallery of photos mounted ostentatiously on one wall of the den: the beaming, beatified face of Alvin Allen, in sheer bliss among a flock of celebrities. Then, she became aware of a whirring noise, a soft purring from a corridor that led left off the living room. "Mr. Allen," she called out again bravely, "it's Jenny Cohn of *Action Sports*."

She passed two darkened doorways. The whirring sound grew slightly louder as she advanced. Finally, she located the source—a room on her right, whose door was half closed. She knocked once, gingerly, then gently swung the door open. On a mahogany captain's desk was a portable cassette recorder. That's where the whirring noise was coming from. Then she became aware of the chaos—books tumbled from their shelves, file cabinets upended, their contents strewn over the floor in a random mess.

Out of an ingrained sense of propriety, she moved to shut off that wasteful flow of electricity powering the recorder. But just as she was leaning over to shut off the machine, she saw him: he was lying in back of the desk, his face contorted horribly, his body twisted at a gruesome angle. She kept staring, at Alvin Allen, nearly floating in his own blood. An astonished scream battered at the wall of incredulity blocking her throat, till, with a terrifying gush, the dam broke, her voice spilled out in a frenzy of fear.

Then she was running out of the office, banging into walls, knocking over an umbrella stand, in her haste to escape that horrifying sight. . . . Until, just as suddenly, an unanticipated calm took hold of her. She stopped at the front door. She struggled to overcome her revulsion. In an instant, it was finished. She had regained control of herself. That hard, pragmatic side of her had taken over.

He was dead, she told herself, then added, as her grandmother had whenever a relative died: but life is for the living. And the one whose life was at stake now was Pallafox's daughter. Before she notified the police, she had to hear that tape. Until they knew who was behind the kidnapping, she felt obligated to keep the secret from the police.

She had to force herself to walk back into that office. Once there, she carefully blotted out from her mind what was lying on the other side of that desk. The first thing she did was turn on the recorder and rewind the cassette she had found on it. She was relieved when she pushed the playback button and heard voices speaking—doubly relieved when none of the voices turned out to be Spider's. Now she was convinced that the killer—and she didn't doubt for a second that Allen had been killed in connection with the information he had given her on the telephone yesterday—had not found whatever it was he had been looking for. If the killer had found the last cassette Allen had made with Spider—and it was evident that Allen habitually recorded sessions with his patients—he would have either taken it, or erased it. The fact that the last tape he played was the "wrong" tape, not Spider's tape, made her feel confident that the killer or killers hadn't found what they were looking for. She began to search for that vital recording.

The cassettes had been filed each in its own box, inside seven large metal file cabinets. The problem, she learned while fishing among the tapes strewn on the floor, and the ones thrown about within the file drawers, was that none of the boxes bore a name. Allen, to protect the privacy of his patients, had some system of filing his cassettes other than alphabetical, by name of patient.

At first she scanned the cassettes themselves, to see if they contained a clue to how they were cataloged. Then she peered at the boxes again—but found nothing like a system. The boxes bore only their factory-stamped trademarks and brand names. The only item that wasn't printed on by the manufacturer was the blue-stamped price, obviously put on by the retailer.

She was about to replace the box she held in her hand in a file cabinet, when suddenly a detail struck her. Those prices stamped onto the boxes . . . they differed, by a few cents, perhaps, but still they differed; no two boxes had exactly the same price. She went quickly to Allen's desk, approaching it from the front and reaching across to open drawers, studiously keeping her eyes on the wall in front of her to avoid the twisted body sprawled below. After a few minutes, she had found what she was looking for—a stamper and a blue ink pad. Quickly, she went back to the boxes of cassettes on the floor. She picked them all up. She began filing them in the drawers of the metal cabinets.

The prices climbed from $5.95 to an even $7.00. A clever filing system, she thought to herself, clever enough, at least, to have foiled the murderer's search. Having filed every tape in its appropriate place, Jenny then removed those cassettes stamped $6.90 through $7.00 and stuck them into her shoulder bag. These, she guessed, would have to include all the tapes Allen could have possibly made during the past few days. Then

Jenny walked out into the living room. She dialed the telephone number of the San Francisco police.

The following day, Monday, was a travel day, as the two teams and their entourages packed their Gucci bags, snapped fresh pints of Jack Daniel's into their hip flasks, and slipped gold chains around their necks, from which coke spoons would dangle aggressively, and prepared to depart from New York City to resume their partying three thousand miles to the west.

Some of the press were privileged to fly on team charters, courtesy of Wally Kelly or Fred Hartwood. Rick had not been invited. Nor would he have accepted an invitation had one been offered. It was difficult enough, he often said, to remain objective when you were eating an owner's food and drinking his liquor, without having him pay for your transportation between cities as well. He preferred to ride commercial flights. It had the added advantage of allowing him to travel alone, a condition he cherished at this particular moment. He needed time to collect his thoughts. Jenny had telephoned him late last night. She had told him that Alvin Allen had been murdered.

Try as he might, he was still unable to make any sense out of it all. The notion that Wally Kelly might somehow be involved struck him as both indecent and improbable. What would Kelly—a millionaire juggernaut salesman, a flamboyant showman who had had everything money could buy in life but fame, and who had acquired fame by purchasing a pro baseball franchise—have to gain by getting entangled in so sleazy and dangerous an undertaking as a World Series fix and a kidnapping?

When he arrived in San Francisco, Rick drove directly to the police station, identified himself, and was led to a large room with three or four desks. He found Jenny seated beside one of them, describing the circumstances in which she had found Alvin Allen, while a uniformed officer typed out a report.

"What's happening?" he said to her, arching his eyebrows slightly as their eyes made contact to ask silently,

Have you found out anything new? Jenny shook her head no, almost imperceptibly.

Rick sat down and listened to Jenny's tale. When she had concluded and signed her statement, the police officer departed, and another man entered. He was large, beefy, with deep bags beneath red-rimmed eyes, thick leathery skin dappled with freckles. He extended his hand first to Jenny, then to Rick.

"Hi," he said. "I'm gonna be handlin' this case from here on out. My name is Levon Harrison. But," he added, in that deep Texas drawl, "you can just call me by the name they used to call me when I was pitchin' ball. Call me 'Hardrock.'"

Rick reached out and grasped the large, thick hand that was being proffered to him. Then, suddenly, he took a step back. He said, "Hey, I know that name. You scout for the Golds once in a while, don't you? In fact," he added, "you're the scout who followed Jim Pallafox at UCLA."

"Part-time only," Hardrock said, a broad grin splitting his face. "Rest of the time I spend scoutin' prospects for the prison league. Now, about this here Alvin Allen who you found yesterday," he added, turning to Jenny. "I was scroungin' around Allen's office last night, and came up with this." He held up a small metal box full of index cards. "Seems to be Allen's client list, and quite a list it is. 'Specially," he continued, "to someone who follows big-league sports. Why, I even found the name of Pallafox's roommate, Spider Johnson, in here."

Jenny and Rick exchanged a quick, worried glance, while Hardrock turned his back toward them and loped over to a chair behind the desk vacated by the uniformed typist. "Now, miss," he said to Jenny, "would you just mind tellin' me what you were doin' at Allen's place yesterday?"

"It's all down in the report," Jenny said.

"I know, I know," Hardrock said apologetically. "But I didn't quite understand why you'd be seein' a hypnotist treatin' Spider, if the piece you're doin' really is about Jimmy Pallafox, see?"

"I asked her to see him," Rick said. "While I was covering Pallafox out in New York, Jenny was supposed to come back here to get information on Pallafox. We'd met Allen at a party Wally Kelly gave last Thursday, after the Series opener. The idea of the piece is to come up with some sort of solution as to why Pallafox doesn't like to reveal much of his private life. Since Allen said he'd heard some good anecdotes from Spider, ones he could tell us, I asked Jenny to come back to San Francisco early and talk to him."

"It's true, though," Hardrock said pleasantly, "that Allen had called you a couple of days ago in New York, isn't it? I got that from the phone company."

He'd done his homework, Rick thought. "He called and spoke to Jenny," Rick said. "He repeated he had some dynamite anecdotes. That's why she flew out early." Rick was lying, and he knew he was lying, but he couldn't reveal anything that might lead Harrison to the kidnapping. Not, at least, until he spoke to Pallafox and cleared it.

Hardrock nodded, that friendly smile never leaving his jowly face. "Well, let's get on to somethin' else," he said. "Somethin' that's been troublin' me, that maybe Jenny here can shed some light on, or maybe she can't. It's clear to any fool, even this one, that whoever killed Allen was lookin' for somethin'. And it seems he may have found what he was lookin' for."

"How do you know that?" Jenny asked, curiosity getting the better of caution.

" 'Cause," Hardrock replied, his eyes twinkling merrily, but his voice turning a little harder now, "there were about ten or eleven missin' tapes that should have been in that office."

"How do you know that?" Jenny asked.

"Well, see, a little horse sense, that's all," Hardrock answered. "You know those metal file separators that come in those seven standing file cabinets in his office? Well, when I put all them cassettes in order, accordin' to the prices marked on 'em, they filled six drawers real tight. But the last drawer, with the highest prices—so probably the most recent tapes—had space for 'bout ten or eleven more boxes of cassettes, between the last cassette and the metal file separator. Seems likely that Allen wouldn't have fixed the file separator so far to the front if it hadn't been holdin' somethin' up.

"I figure that the killer took a bunch. So," he added, "what I'm doin' now is checkin' to see who Allen saw the last few days, who he might have put on tape. You wouldn't know if Spider Johnson was one of those people, now, would you?" he asked.

Jenny and Rick were quiet for a moment. Then Rick said, "Y'know, I think he did see Spider recently. He mentioned that over the phone to you, didn't he, Jenny?"

Jenny looked at Rick, then said to Hardrock: "Come to think of it, he did mention it, in passing."

"Well," said Hardrock, squinting up at Jenny, "did he by any chance mention anything Spider said to him that was important enough to get himself killed over?"

"No," Jenny replied quickly. "He didn't say anything at all. We weren't doing a piece on Spider, anyway," she added, bristling, "so why should he tell us anything except anecdotes about Pallafox?"

Hardrock raised his hand like a traffic cop. "No offense meant, miss, no offense. Just thought he might have mentioned somethin', somethin' that might have been troublin' him. Guess we'll have to come up with those missin' tapes to find out."

Later, Jenny and Rick caught a cab back to their hotel in San Francisco. "Christ," Rick said, as they sat in the back seat, staring blankly at the rush-hour traffic, "we're in trouble. We've lied to a cop!"

"Well, just remember," Jenny cautioned, "whatever trouble we're in, Pallafox's daughter is in worse trouble. Somebody's threatening to kill her."

Talk about trouble, she was thinking. Rick didn't know half of it. Not only had they told those little white lies, she had left herself, literally, holding the bag—full of the ten tapes that the San Francisco police were currently scouring the city for. What a bind. If she told the detective she had taken the tapes, then she would have had to reveal why she had taken the tapes—and he would have learned, prematurely, about the kidnapping. They couldn't risk telling the police about it now. They had to follow the kidnappers' instructions to the letter.

And now, she had put herself in double jeopardy, because she couldn't tell Rick about the tapes, either. If she did, then Rick would become an accessory. And one thing she didn't want to do was implicate him. She felt too much for him to do that.

My God, she thought suddenly, as the full impact of her situation struck her for the first time, what was she *doing!* In a week, she had become an accessory to a murder, a very convincing liar—and a common thief besides.

Jenny should have felt terrified. But she didn't. Instead, she felt—well, she had to admit it, damn excited.

"Hey," Rick said, "what are you smiling about? I didn't think we, or anybody else in the world right now, had anything left to smile about."

"Oh, I was just thinking," she replied.

"About how you'd like to be back in Brooklyn, how you wished you'd never heard of Jim Pallafox?" Rick said.

"Nope," Jenny said, smiling ever more broadly now. "Not on your ever-lovin' life."

7

Pallafox greeted Rick at the door and ushered him into a den lined with trophies—American Legion championships, Little League pennants, cups commemorating college titles and high-school heroics. Rick sat down on a sofa. Pallafox pulled over a floor cushion and sat down, pulling his long muscular legs up to his chest. "I'm worried, man," he told Rick darkly.

"We're not getting any closer to recovering your daughter, I know," Rick said sympathetically.

"I don't mean I'm just worried about Kathy. Losing, I think I can keep her safe, at least for a while," Pallafox replied. "I mean Spider. He came back on the plane this morning with the rest of us. Then he split. I haven't seen hide nor hair of him since. And then," he added, "this afternoon I got a call from Hardrock Harrison . . . he was looking for Spider . . . he said Alvin Allen, that hypnotist of Spider's, had been murdered."

Rick filled Pallafox in on all the details—how Jenny had found the body, how Hardrock Harrison had interrogated them at the station house, how they had deliberately misled him.

"Don't let Hardrock's folksy twang fool you," Pallafox warned. "He was born with a nose for trouble. And this time," Pallafox added, "I think he's picked up the scent of a rat."

"What makes you say that?" Rick asked.

"He called me himself. He could have had some flunky call me. You know, we go a long way back together," Pallafox added. "Maybe I gave him too many clues when I saw him in El Paso. Maybe he'll somehow connect me and Spider and Allen . . . and get his foot caught in the door they're keeping Kathy behind."

"What makes you so sure Allen's death has something to do with the kidnapping?" Rick asked.

"It doesn't sound like a coincidence to me that Allen was killed right after he called your office telling Jenny he had important information, something Spider said while he was under hypnosis, something involving Wally and a lot of money, and a double-cross."

"As a matter of fact," Rick admitted, "it doesn't sound like a coincidence to me, either."

"And now," Pallafox added, "Spider disappears. I called Willie Richardson; I called all the chicks of his I could get ahold of—no one's seen him all day. He cut practice, and that's not like Spider. Not when he pitched so well his last time out. He wouldn't blow his chances with Wally, cutting practice during the Series."

"So," Rick summed up, "you think Allen was killed because he found out something—something from Spider, about Wally Kelly—and that that something has to do with Kathy's kidnapping, too."

"Maybe it's crazy," Pallafox replied. "I don't know. "Maybe I'm just trying to spin gold out of straw."

"A single straw," Rick said, "named Wally Kelly."

"According to what we've heard, he did bet five hundred thousand on the Golds to lose," Pallafox replied. "And the way he's been pitching me, it doesn't seem he's trying too hard to win, either. You know that he's given Oswalski standing orders I'm not to come out of a game, no matter how badly I'm throwing?"

"I heard. But he says that's only to make you pitch up to par," Rick replied. "Don't forget, *you* know you're not going to win, but Wally just sees his star pitcher suddenly turning into a flop. He can't believe it's going to last."

"Maybe, maybe," Pallafox said. "But somebody's got Kathy, and Wally and his five-hundred-thousand-dollar bet are the only link we have right now."

"And the only person who can tell us what Wally really said is Spider."

"And Spider's gone," Pallafox said. He stared stonily

at the wall for a moment, then leaped up. "Goddammit," he said, "we are going to find Spider right now, no matter how long it takes."

"Wait one second," Rick cautioned. "I have an idea, something you should do first."

"What's that?"

"When you saw Norma, you didn't tell her about the kidnap note."

"Yeh, I told her about the note," Pallafox replied.

"But, I remember," Rick insisted. "You told me you didn't tell her about the 'die slowly' part."

"I didn't want to scare her."

"Call her now," Rick said. "Tell her about that part, too."

"Why now?" Pallafox asked. "What's the point? If she doesn't know anything about it, it'd scare the hell out of her. What good's that gonna do? Besides," and he paused, as if the thought he was about to voice was painful to him, "if she does know, then it's gonna be no surprise to her."

"Look," Rick said, "have you heard of those cases—there've been a lot of them lately—where one parent gets custody of a kid, then the other one 'kidnaps' the kid to another state? There's often nothing the first parent can do, 'cause the second state will award custody to the parent who did the kidnapping."

"Oh, I thought of that, believe me, I thought of it," Pallafox replied. "But I told you, Norma would never even consider making such a sadistic threat against Kathy. I knew that before. Now that I've seen her I'm convinced."

"But," Rick replied, "who says she knows the kidnap note contained that threat?"

"You mean . . . ?"

"I mean, maybe she is in on it. Maybe she thinks she's just getting custody of the kid, when really they're using her and Kathy to fix the Series."

Pallafox considered that for a moment. "All right," he said at last, "I'll call her. Wait here."

He went into another room. Rick heard him dial. He heard him say, "Norma, this is Jim. Can you talk?

There's something I have to tell you." Then Pallafox's voice dropped to a near whisper and Rick could no longer make out what he was saying. After only a few minutes, however, he did hear Pallafox slam the phone down on the hook. The pitcher stalked back into the room.

"How did she react?" Rick asked.

Pallafox had a perplexed look on his face. He replied, "See, I told you I shouldn't call her. She got completely hysterical. She doesn't know a damn thing about anything, just that her kid is missing. And now she's terrified."

"She said that to you?"

"No, not exactly," Pallafox replied, irritably. "She couldn't talk. She was sobbing too hard."

"Then maybe she knows more than you think she does," Rick countered.

"What's that supposed to mean?" Pallafox said.

"Maybe she's suddenly gotten a clue. To the fact that there's more to the kidnapping of her kid than she realized—if, that is, I'm right in my guess that she might have helped arrange it as a way to get Kathy."

"Enough of this Sam Spade, supersleuth bullshit," Pallafox snapped. "Let's go look for Willie Richardson. We better hope he can lead us to Spider."

As soon as Norma put down the telephone she went looking for Harry Walters. She found him in his office, overlooking the twenty-four tables below, engrossed in the paperwork that represented the millions of dollars invested by the nameless "businessmen" who shared in the casino's profits. Harry's silent partners, Norma knew, were silent not out of modesty, but out of necessity.

Usually, Norma kept, in Harry's phrase, her "nose clean," ignoring rumors that the casino's money was tainted by the thick, grasping fingers of mobsters. What you don't know, Harry had warned her when she first started working at the Shazaam, can't kill you. Now, however, those dimly perceived gangsters rumored to be bankrolling the Shazaam were vivid in her mind. The words, "die slowly," were eating away at her like a cancer.

Harry looked up when she entered. "Norma," he exclaimed, pushing back his chair and coming forward to greet her, "what a pleasant surprise. I didn't expect to see you till this evening. I hope nothing's wrong—you're not going to cancel our date are you?" he asked. "I've so much looked forward to escorting you to the party at LeGrand's house."

"Harry," she said urgently, "I got a telephone call from Pallafox."

He threw up his hands in despair. "Norma, not that business again," he said, but not in an unkind voice.

"He told me what was in the kidnap note, Harry," she replied, dabbing at tears that were starting to fill her eyes. "He told me it said if he didn't do what he was told, Kathy would 'die slowly.' You didn't tell me that was going to be in the note, Harry," she added. "I never would have allowed you to send a note like that. The idea of it . . . it's got me terrified, Harry, just the thought of it."

"Now, Norma," Harry said, putting his arm around her narrow shoulders and guiding her to a couch, "don't make a mountain out of a molehill. You're being silly. You're overreacting."

"Then he was telling the truth," she cried, sobbing outright now. "Why did you do it, Harry? You told me, when you suggested the idea, that I was within my legal rights to take Kathy away from him, that parents in divorce proceedings do it all the time. You told me that telling him to lose in the World Series was a false trail, leading him away from me, so I could get time to get custody of Kathy under Nevada law. You told me we had to keep Kathy hidden till then. And I went along with everything. But you didn't tell me you'd threatened to kill her, Harry. I don't see the purpose of that. Unless," she added, "what you're really after is not getting Kathy for me, but using her against Jim, to make him lose those Series games."

Harry sat down beside her, patting her knee paternally. "I simply didn't want to worry you needlessly," he told her, his voice smooth. "The World Series had nothing to do with this. The reason we included that silly warning was to convince him the note's authentic; if there had been no serious threat, he undoubtedly would have been convinced of the obvious—that you had Kathy. We never thought he'd go out and try to lose games," he added.

"You said 'we.' Just who is 'we'?"

"I've told you," Harry replied, "some friends who owe me a few favors, debts I called in so that I, in turn, could do a favor for you."

Norma wiped the tears away with the back of her hand. She sighed. "I'm sorry, Harry. I do appreciate what you're doing for me. It's just that, well, if only I could *see* Kathy. Just see her once. . . ."

Harry placed his index finger over her mouth, in a gently shushing gesture. "That would be very, very foolish," he told her. "For all we know, Pallafox doesn't believe our World Series fix story for a moment. For all we know, he has private eyes trailing you constantly, just waiting for the chance to snatch Kathy back. We wouldn't want to lead Pallafox to Kathy now, would we? After my friends and I have gone to so much trouble to assist you?"

"I *am* grateful," Norma said. "Believe me, Harry, I realize how much you've done for me, and for Kathy, too."

Harry stood up. He smiled. "Then trust me," he said. "And don't let any more tears stain that pretty face of yours. Kathy's safe," he added. "No one can get to her."

Not, he thought to himself bitterly, even me.

Rick and Pallafox met Willie Richardson at the Golden Circle Club, a garishly decorated discotheque on a back street off Jack London Square, in the heart of Oakland. As usual, Willie had a coven of svelte sex-witches in tow. As usual, Rick noticed, none of them was his wife Doris.

"You ain't caught up with that dude yet?" Willie said, in one of those rare moments when the combo beneath the flashing stage lights was taking a break. "I can't figure that, y'know? He told me on the plane he had to do some bullshit errand for Wally, and that he'd meet me here tonight. That's why I got myself surrounded by *three* ladies instead of my usual ever-lovin' two," he added, nodding from side to side, his glance encompassing the three women—two tall, one short, but all buxom and black and glittering with jewelry bestowed by one or another of the ballplayers they routinely serviced.

"Look," said Pallafox, "we don't have time for fun and games. We have to find Spider. Fast."

Willie's cynical smirk dissolved. "What's happening, man?" he asked Pallafox. "You think some of those Vegas boys got a little tired of waiting for their bread?"

"I don't know what to think," Pallafox replied. "You heard that Alvin Allen, that hypnotist Wally sent him to—he got his head beaten in yesterday?"

Willie whistled under his breath. He turned to the women. "Go buy yourselves another drink," he told them. "Tell Jerry to put it on my tab, y'hear?"

"But, Willie," one of them began, "I don't want no drink right now. I'm feelin' . . ."

Willie cut her off in midcomplaint. "Now, you just do what I tell you," he hissed. Mumbling irritably, the women strutted off through the crowd toward the brass-banistered bar on the other side of the club.

"This sounds bad, man," Willie said to Pallafox. "I think I better forgo the pleasure of immediate gratification, if you dig what I'm saying. I mean, let's see if we can sniff up Spider's trail."

Twenty minutes later, Pallafox and Rick and Willie were sitting in Willie's Cadillac, parked along a side street not two blocks away from their point of departure. "I can't figure it, man," said Willie. "He wasn't at the New Cotton Club getting drunk. He wasn't at Fat Freddie's getting high. He wasn't at Mamma Masseur's getting fucked. Ellen ain't seen him all night. Genevieve says he was supposed to be with Ellen, Doris says he's supposed to be with me and he hasn't called my place, and Wally's chauffeur says the dude never showed up there, and for a good reason. Wally never asked him to do no errand in the first place. I just can't figure it, man. Except that maybe he's fooling us all. Maybe, by now, he's back home at your place, humpin' some fox he hunted down, while we're busting our asses all over town."

"I've called him about ten times," said Pallafox; "you know that. And every time, no answer."

Willie thought a moment more. "Well," he said, "Ain't nothing left but to cruise, and keep asking."

Willie put on the lights, turned the key, and the Cadillac's powerful engine began to hum. He guided the car into traffic, then turned off the main street, slowly negotiating a maze of byways which even Pallafox, who had spent a great deal of time with Spider, didn't recognize. Periodically, Willie would pull over to the curb and hail some passerby. After the usual jive preliminaries, he would say, "Hey, turkey, you seen mah man Spider, tonight?" The answer inevitably was, "No, broth, I ain't seen that dude nowhere. Why, you got some fox fo' him I can pet while you lookin'?"

Pallafox, Rick could see, was getting more irritable by the moment. Rick was right. They had been cruising for three-quarters of an hour now, and still no sign of Spider. This futile search was unnerving Pallafox: Willie's predictable patter every time he pulled over to interrogate someone he recognized; the dank, depressing neighborhood they were cruising through. Clapboard houses, much like Pallafox's own, but with no promising scaffolding outside, no hint of better times to come. Streets littered with garbage, as if this ghetto were a random city dump, its inhabitants no better than sewer rats.

"Let's go to my place," Pallafox finally snapped. "I just can't take any more of this."

Just then, though, Willie was slowing down, pulling to the curb in front of two "ladies" dressed in extrashort skirts, loitering at a busy corner, pretending to be engaged in deep conversation, but eyeing every car and pedestrian that passed. This time, Willie got out of the car and struck up a conversation. Pallafox could see the women gesticulating, then pointing down the street. All of a sudden his hopes brightened. "Hey," he said to Rick, "maybe we've struck paydirt."

Willie climbed back into the car. "I got something out of those two whores," he said, shifting the car into gear and roaring off down the street.

"They've seen Spider?" Pallafox asked.

"Not Spider," Willie said, "but Spider's wheels."

"Did they tell you exactly where they saw his car?"

"Where do you think I'm headin', man?" Willie said, careening around a corner, taking two lefts, then a right, before pulling up before a flashy fire-red Corvette convertible. "That's why I'm against banning street-walkers," he said. "See, those two old pussies are so hard up they gotta prowl the mean alleys and byways. And if they didn't have to, we never would have caught up with ol' devious Spider."

"Wait a minute," Pallafox said, staring at the three-story brownstone on the quiet, tree-lined street—a cut above the other neighborhoods they'd been combing. "I think I've been here once. Who's pad is this?"

"Selma's," said Willie. "Don't know why I didn't think of her before, 'cept that she's white. I was thinking black tonight. I guess ol' Spider and me was tuned into different channels. He was after some blonde pussy, that was all the mystery."

"Selma—that was the girl at the party, the one Spider laid on me—literally—to keep me away from you," Rick said. The memory set off a tingling sensation, resurrecting the feel of Selma on his lap, the way the pink Chinese lantern reflected off her blonde hair, the scent of her seductive musk perfume.

Willie found a space for his long black sedan. When Rick started fumbling with the door lock, Willie told him, "Don't bother, man, I don't have to lock up." He pulled Rick around to the back of the car, and showed him the license plate that spelled Willie. "Nobody rips off Willie Richardson around here," he said proudly.

By that time, Pallafox was halfway up the steps to the apartment house. Rick had to sprint to catch up with him. They walked up three flights, then halted in front of apartment 3B, the one Willie identified as Selma's. Willie rang the bell once, then again. There was no answer. "Hey, Spider, man," Willie began to shout, banging his large fist against the wooden door. "It's me, man, Willie. Open up."

Still no response.

"Maybe they left," Rick said.

"They're here someplace," Pallafox said. "If they'd left, it would have been in Spider's Corvette. He wouldn't have passed up a chance to show off Selma. It's warm enough to put the top down tonight."

"Spider, you sneaky motha," Willie boomed again. "I got Pallafox here and he says he's gotta rap with you, man!"

Again, the answer was silence.

Then Willie turned to Pallafox. "You say this is really important, man?" he said.

"I mean it—life or death," Pallafox replied grimly.

Willie shrugged. He reached into his pocket. "Well, I hope you do mean it, Jim boy, 'cause if it ain't, Spider's never gonna forgive me." Willie pulled out a set of keys and selected a thin, jagged silver one.

"What are you doing?" said Pallafox. "How'd you get a police passkey?"

"This ain't no *police* key," Willie whispered, "this is a *Selma* key. Y'see, Spider don't know it, but I been seeing her myself. Spider would hit the roof if he found out, man, so you better be right about this being a matter of life or death."

Willie unlocked the door, shoving it open. They stood there, at the threshold, gaping in horror. Finally, Willie said, in a weak voice, "I guess you weren't bullshitting me, man." They stared helplessly at the body, splayed grotesquely across the living-room floor, as rubbery in violent death as a marionette whose strings had been severed, then dropped from a great height.

Before Rick had departed from the hotel that evening, Jenny had been complaining of headaches and nausea and drowsiness. Rick, she reflected as soon as he left, would have been astonished by her miraculous recovery. The best description of her "illness," she mused wryly, was a form of tapeworm—not the kind of wriggly critter that bores into your intestines, but the plastic ribbony breed that comes in a cassette, and worms its way into your mind.

Moments after he had departed, she was taking her oversized shoulder bag down from the shelf in the closet, and dumping its contents over one of the room's elegant twin beds. And moments after that, she had snapped the first cassette into her small recorder.

There were ten tapes in all. The first one she put on dealt with the problems of an actor, whose voice was vaguely familiar but whose face escaped her. Allen was careful, on this tape and the others, never to use even a first name when talking to his patients.

At first, she was caught up in the secret pleasure of a voyeur—listening to the repressed fears and hopes of people she didn't know. Then, gradually, by tape five, the thrill began to wear thin. She found herself daydreaming, as she now, mechanically, snapped on another tape, listening, pressing the Fast Forward button, then Stop, backward and onward. Her daydreams were about Rick. How, in the heat of the chase, the defensive armor they each wore was beginning to melt, then fuse, joining them in a way that she somehow felt would endure after the chase had ended.

There was no denying that their relationship had transcended the limitations they had both set for it during their years together at *Action Sports*. Somehow, he had begun to see her as an equal. He sought out her judgments on things, which pleased her. He no longer found them a threat to his own masculinity, which pleased her even more. More, a kind of intimacy had grown up between them. Their shared secret had become a pipeline for other shared intimacies, though none physical yet.

Physical intimacy. Yes. She thought about that for a moment. Yes. She wanted him to sleep with her, she wanted to feel him close to her, not to leave her at night, to be one with her. And suddenly an awful yearning started gnawing inside, a desperate longing that startled her. My God, she said to herself, I think I love him.

She shook her head, fought down, bit tight onto the idea and put it in the little box where she had learned to hide her emotions. Then, mentally, she sat on the lid till the longing stopped. She put tape number six onto the recorder.

As soon as she depressed the Start button, every thought but one was driven from her mind. The voice was Spider's. She lay down on the bed, propping her head up on her fist, and listened, harder and more closely than she had ever listened to anything in her entire life.

She heard Allen, chatting casually with Spider at first. "You pitched one helluva game the other day," he said. "I just can't get over the progress you've made. I'm really thrilled."

"He's got me penciled in to pitch another game, too," Spider responded brightly, his enthusiasm almost infectious.

"Who's 'he'? The manager?" Allen said.

"Nope. 'He,' the owner," Spider said.

They both laughed—and then Jenny heard a snapping noise—the breaking of a dry twig, or fingers being rubbed together, bone against bone. The laughter died immediately. There was total silence, except for the sound of breathing, which became heavier and heavier, as Allen said, "You're drifting back. Entirely relaxed, right?"

"I feel fine," Spider answered, his voice radically altered now, the vivaciousness gone, replaced by a sort of somnambulistic drone. "I feel fine, real fine, man."

Allen then guided Spider back to the previous Wednesday, eliciting his feelings before the second World Series game, the one he pitched and won. Allen drew out of Spider his emotions before that game—the fear, the lack of self-confidence, then the tension, almost unbearable, when he stepped onto the mound and tossed his warm-up pitches. And finally, he took Spider on a grand tour of his own memories of the game,

—reinforcing, at every possible moment, Spider's overall feelings of success, while smoothing over any minor failures.

As the pitcher, guided by Allen, droned on and on, gabbing drowsily about called third strikes and sliders that sliced home plate and close calls that went his way for a change, Jenny grew more and more impatient. She hadn't risked her neck merely to listen to a washed-up pitcher gloat for fifty-five minutes over his triumphs— the whole painstaking recounting of which was to her a monumental proof of insecurities no hypnotist could truly eliminate. She was hoping and praying and listening for something more, something that would have caused Allen, whom Rick scarcely knew, to call him in New York with caution in his voice. Something, to put it bluntly, worth killing a man for.

She was nearing the end of the sixty-minute tape now. She lay on the bed, staring at the recorder, her hopes fading. And then, suddenly, in the midst of Spider's chatter about how he'd manhandled the Patriot hitters in the ninth inning, his voice became agitated.

"Walter's got a half million riding on the Series, and millions more with the big boys," Spider said.

"What's that about?" Allen asked, confusion coloring his voice.

"It's Walter's double-cross," Jenny heard Spider say in a dreamy voice. "Walter's got a half million on the Series and the big boys have millions more."

There was a clicking noise. The tape was empty after that, right till the end.

Jenny leaped up. She played the last thirty seconds of the tape again, to be sure she had heard what she thought she had heard. Then, she got off the bed. She walked over to an armchair. She sat down. She started thinking.

It was clear to her now: Wally Kelly had bet a large amount of money, either $500,000, or millions—what was the difference, anyway?—on the Oakland Golds to lose the World Series. And to make sure they would lose, he had kidnapped Pallafox's daughter, to hold her for ransom. Finally, she had tangible proof to back up her suspicion of Kelly—Spider, on the cassette, implicating Wally in no uncertain way.

At that moment, the telephone rang. Jenny rushed to answer it, sure that it was Rick and anxious to impart the startling information she had just learned. He *would* be surprised, she thought wryly, since he had no idea that she was the one who had taken the tapes from Allen's office.

She picked up the phone and gushed, "Hello, Rick . . ."

The voice on the other end of the line responded: "Listen, you're Jenny, right? This is Spider."

Jenny couldn't believe her ears. "Spider?" she said incredulously.

"That's right," he replied, his voice sounding muffled and indistinct, "Spider Johnson, and I'm in trouble. Where in hell is Pallafox?"

"Who?" Jenny said, straining to pick up the syllables of that half-muffled voice.

"Pallafox, I need Pallafox bad. I'm in big trouble," Spider whispered back.

"Why, he's out looking for you. I thought he and Rick would have found you long ago, but I guess they haven't," she added helplessly.

"Look," he whispered urgently, "I need help, right now. I need someone to talk to, someone I can confide in. And I need someone quick, y'hear?"

"You need the police?" Jenny asked. At this point, there was no sense in hiding anything from Hardrock Harrison. In fact, just before Spider had called, she had been thinking of calling the detective herself.

"No cops, no cops," Spider hissed. Then he added, "Please, you come on over here. I need your help and I need it *now*."

Jenny was caught up in the urgency of his plea. "I'll be right over," she said. "Just give me ten minutes to dress, and tell me where to go. In the meantime, sit tight. Don't panic."

The voice droned directions, then hung up. Quickly, Jenny threw on a skirt and blouse, not even bothering to hunt up a bra. Her hand was on the doorknob when

she remembered: She should leave Rick a note. Otherwise, if she didn't reach him with the news that she had
located Spider, when he returned to the hotel he might
worry terribly.

She wrote out a brief note—telling him she was going
to see Spider, giving him the address Spider had given
her. She also mentioned the tapes—telling him that the
one on the recorder was the one the police were searching the city for. Then she left the room. She sprinted
down the corridor toward the elevator, clutching in her
hand the address in Oakland Spider had dictated to her.
She was already hailing a cab when the phone in her
room began to ring.

The moment Rick and Pallafox found Spider, his
body broken in exactly the maniacal way as Alvin Allen's, he and Pallafox decided that Willie should depart.
After all, the last thing Willie needed during a World
Series was to become entangled in a scandal. Pallafox's
involvement was inescapable. Spider had been his
roommate.

As soon as Willie left, Rick headed straight for the
telephone.

"Hey," Pallafox said, rushing over and forcing the receiver back onto its cradle, "who the hell do you think
you're calling?"

"Look," Rick said, "this thing has gone too far. First
Alvin Allen, now Spider. These people aren't kidding
around. They're killers, don't you understand that?"

"And what about my daughter," Pallafox said, still
gripping Rick's arm, forcing the telephone receiver down.
"They're killers all right, and that means if the cops
get involved, they're gonna kill Kathy."

Rick backed away from the telephone, shaking his
head in confusion. "I didn't think of that," he said.
Then, "But, Christ, what are we supposed to do? Just
walk away? Suppose we were seen around here, suppose
the cops find out from the people Willie asked, or from
Willie himself, that we spent the night looking for Spider? They put us at the scene of the crime. It's not hard
to make a case that we also committed the crime. And

that," Rick added, "would suit whoever is masterminding this whole thing just fine."

"And I guess we owe something to Spider, too," Pallafox said quietly. "Okay," he added, "we're damned if we do and damned if we don't. So, I'll call Hardrock. But we don't have to tell him anything he doesn't ask, right?"

"Like what?"

"Look," Pallafox pleaded, "the Series'll be over in a couple of days. I'll have Kathy back; we'll cooperate fully."

It was time, Rick thought to himself. Time to tell Pallafox, time to unburden the gut feeling he'd had ever since he'd heard about the sickening way in which Alvin Allen had been disposed of. A feeling only compounded by the sight of Spider Johnson brutally beaten to death; even Rick, no expert, whose experience with violence had been limited to prime-time detective shows, could tell that the killer had gone out of his way to perform his task with the cold-blooded, calculating sadism of a confirmed psychopath.

"Goddamn it, Jimmy," he said evenly, "if they let Kathy go, it may be like this"—and he pointed at Spider's gory, mashed torso.

Pallafox gagged. He ran for the bathroom. Rick telephoned the San Francisco police. He asked for Hardrock Harrison.

It was shortly after 10:00 P.M., then, that Rick had put through his call to Jenny back at the hotel. He waited and waited, growing more impatient with each unanswered ring. Where the hell was she? Finally he put down the phone. He picked up a set of keys he had found on a coffee table.

"I'm going to borrow Spider's car," he told Pallafox, who had recovered from his attack of nausea and was slumped on a chair, staring morosely at the crumpled body of his roommate. "I'll have to get back to the hotel. I have to find Jenny. I'll call you as soon as I find her."

Pallafox didn't respond. He kept staring at Spider.

But he wasn't seeing Spider dead there on the floor. He was seeing little Kathy.

Rick drove the Corvette recklessly through side streets, spinning around corners, onto broad boulevards, the pressure pushing down from his mind, through his body, forcing his foot down harder and harder on the accelerator.

He made the trip from Oakland back to the San Francisco Shelby Hotel in a record fifteen minutes and screeched to a halt in a stall in the hotel garage. He sprinted for an elevator, hardly able to control his anxiety, as it inched silently toward Jenny's floor.

While the doors were still opening, Rick rushed out, ran down the hall. Without knocking, he grabbed at the doorknob, wrenched it to the right, and entered Jenny's room. He saw the note on the bed, and recognized the address: Pallafox's house. With foreboding in his heart, he picked up the phone and dialed Selma's number. Hardrock Harrison answered the telephone. Rick cut short all the civilities. He asked one crucial question: "Hardrock, how long would you estimate that Spider has been dead?"

"Well, I can't tell till the medical examiner gets here, and that'll be another quarter hour or so, but I would estimate at least eight to nine hours. Why?"

Rick's heart fell. He sat down heavily on the bed. "You remember Jenny Cohn? The one who found Alvin Allen's body? Well, she left me a note at our hotel. She said she got a call from Spider at a quarter to ten, asking her to meet him at Pallafox's house in a hurry."

There was silence at the other end of the line. Then Hardrock said, quietly, calmly: "What in hell are we waiting for?"

8

It was ten-thirty when Jenny's taxi pulled up in front of Pallafox's brownstone. Even in the dim light, she recognized the house from Rick's description. The flimsy scaffolding, clinging to the walls like a spiny skeleton, the unstained planks covering the steps that led up to the porch, the posts between the porch floor and ceiling that tilted like the mainmast of a storm-battered sailing ship.

Yet, she noticed, the house already looked far better than those around it. The grimy masonry, caked with the dirt of years of neglect, had been partially scraped clean. The window frames and gutter trimming had already been painted a dazzling white. Right now, she thought, the house looked like a woman getting dressed for a party: she was not ready yet, but she was going to be the belle of the ball.

Pallafox had purchased the house from the city of Oakland with just that purpose in mind, he had told Rick. The city had auctioned off this house and others like it for merely a token dollar on the strength of a promise that the new owners would renovate, and thus breathe a spark of life into this moribund ghetto.

Jenny paid the cabby and stood there in the street, watching the yellow vehicle drive off, its taillights receding into the distance. She felt apprehensive. The truth was, she had never in all her life stood alone on a ghetto street, in the dark. She suddenly longed for the brightly lit streets of her neighborhood in Brooklyn, the semi-detached redbrick garden apartments, with their neatly manicured hedges and geometric plots of grass. She felt alone. She felt vulnerable. She was frightened.

She overcame her fear. She walked up the path toward the steps, her eyes darting from side to side along the length of the deserted street. Up the plank-covered steps she went, her high heels rapping, she reflected, like ghost knuckles on a table at an eerie séance.

The house was dark. There were no lights showing at any of the windows. Jenny rang the doorbell, then waited. After what seemed an eternity, but could have been no longer than a minute or two, the door opened to reveal the silhouette of a thin black man, barely visible against a patch of light reaching the hall from some inner room. "Come on in," he said, nearly whispering, "I been waitin' for you."

"You're Spider," she said, hesitating at the threshold, trying to peer at the face which now had receded into shadows.

"That's right, that's right," the man said, impatience edging his voice. "Come on in, I ain't got all night."

There was something about his voice that troubled Jenny. She had, of course, only really been close to him once, at Wally Kelly's party. And her memories of that night mostly revolved around his slack-jawed performance under Alvin Allen's domination, his voice a drowsy parody of the droning somnambulist. She was still hesitating at the doorway, when, in the hall, she saw a figure step out, smile, and say, "Hi, please come in." It was Selma, the blonde girl who had accompanied Spider to Wally's party. Her warm, welcoming smile relieved Jenny of her fear. She was simply being paranoid, she thought, stepping into the hall, as the man closed the door and locked it behind her.

A second too late, she realized she had made a mistake. The moment the door closed, Selma's warm smile disappeared. The man clamped his hand on her arm and started shoving her into the living room. "You're hurting me," Jenny cried, shocked by the violence with which Spider was treating her.

"And this is only a preview of what you're gonna get if you don't cooperate," Spider hissed, twisting her arm up behind her and shoving her again.

She screamed, then felt his hand clap over her mouth,

and a vicious kick that sent her sprawling into the center of the darkened living room. Only a dim light filtered in from the streetlights outside.

"Walter knows all about those tapes," he said, as he threw her to the floor, pinning her there with his knee in the small of her back, holding her hands behind her while Selma, at his bidding, tied Jenny's hands tightly at the wrists with what felt like electrical wire. "I couldn't find 'em," he added, "but then we found out from that fucking doorman that you went up after our man. Putting two and two together, Walter figured out you got the tapes, the one with me giving away the big secret to that jerk, right?" He yanked on the wire binding her wrists. A flash of pain seared the length of both her arms. She screamed from the very pit of her stomach.

"Goddamn bitch," he cursed, then pulled harder on the wire, so it felt as though it were slicing through her skin, through her veins, lacerating her wrist bones. "You do that again, and I'll beat the livin' shit out of you, lady! Walter told me to go easy on you, but I'm gonna go just as easy as you let me."

Jenny stopped struggling. Now he was standing up, releasing the pressure at the small of her back, around her wrists. She felt so totally helpless, but fought to overcome the fear that was engulfing her—lying there, flat on her stomach, with her hands bound behind her back. "Walter who?" she said finally, trying to show him, through the forced calm of her voice, that she wasn't afraid. After all, this was a major-league baseball pitcher, Pallafox's roommate. She was sure he wouldn't really do anything more to harm her.

"Walter O. Kelly," he spat back. "Who else?"

So, Jenny thought, she had been right. Kelly had been behind Kathy's kidnapping, and the tape Spider made had been proof. Summoning her courage, she decided to get as much information as she could. "Where is Pallafox's daughter?" she said.

"Shut up, bitch," he replied, giving her a vicious kick in the side. "I'm gonna ask all the questions."

The worst part of it all, she thought, was being helpless in the power of someone who refuses even to look you in the eye. He kept standing to her side, or behind her. She hadn't really been able to get a good look at him yet.

"Okay," he said, "we know you got that cassette. Where is it, where you hiding it?"

"I don't know what you're talking about," she said. "I don't know anything about any cassette."

"Look," he said. "That tape is the only thing in the world linking Walter to two events he wants very much to stay away from, dig? The World Series fix, and the kidnapping of that goddamn kid. I told you, Walter told me to go easy. But he also told me to get that tape. Or else," he added, "what happened to Alvin Allen is gonna happen to me, dammit it!"

So that was it, Jenny thought. That was what had turned Spider so brutal. Fear that if he didn't recover the one piece of incriminating evidence against Wally Kelly he, too, would be eliminated.

"Hey, I know a lot about you," he said, his tone suddenly shifting from terror to seduction. "You're not like Selma here, right, Selma?"

The voluptuous blonde had taken a seat on a couch. Turning her head so that she lay on her left cheek, Jenny could just make her out in the semidark, the glowing tip of her cigarette flashing on and off like a lighthouse beacon, as she puffed, then exhaled, the smoke. Up to now, the girl had said nothing. In the back of her mind, Jenny still considered her protection. Spider wouldn't do anything to her while Selma was around, she'd reasoned. But now, when Spider had spoken to Selma, the girl had laughed in an ugly way, snipping the last straw Jenny had been grasping at.

"According to what we've heard," Selma said, her silky smooth voice taking on vicious overtones, "she comes from a very sheltered scene. Just a sheltered little girl from Brooklyn," Selma added. Then, "We got a way to deal with sheltered little girls, don't we, Spider?"

"Yeh," he replied. "She's gonna grow up real fast."

Jenny heard a noise behind her—a belt being unbuckled. But when she tried to turn around, he gave her another painful jab in the side. "Stay put, bitch," he ordered. "And for the last time, if you know what's good for you," he leaned over and dangled his belt in front of her face, "you better tell us exactly where that tape is at, y'hear?"

"It's in my hotel room," Jenny said suddenly. "Please, it's in my hotel room, on the tape recorder, on my bed, where I left it when I got the call to come here."

"And we're supposed to believe that one? Walter's gonna laugh when I tell him that one," he said to Selma. Then, to Jenny: "Don't you think we figured it might be there? You think we're that dumb? One of the reasons for getting you over *here*, was so some of Walter's people could search over *there*. If they'd a found something," he added, "they would have called. And I ain't heard no telephone ringing here, have you, Selma?"

"No sounds at all, except this bitch's lies," Selma replied, with that bubbly little laugh that, every time Selma uttered it, sent terror through Jenny.

"But it's true," Jenny pleaded, her eyes starting to tear, even though she knew, had heard, that the worst thing she could do in a situation like this was to show her captors she was afraid. "I did leave the tape there, I promise, I'm not lying. Why don't you call whoever's looking for it? Call my hotel room, let me speak to them. I'll tell them where to find it. I promise. I'll tell them. Exactly where to find it."

"Too late," he said. "It's too late for any more stall bullshit." Jenny heard him thrust something overhead. She arched her neck back slightly so that she could see, if not his face, at least what he was preparing to do. "Oh, my God," she moaned.

"Get her clothes off," he told Selma.

"What are you going to do?" Jenny said, sobbing outright now.

"Only what you deserve done to you," he said viciously.

Selma came over to Jenny. She looked down at her. She smiled. Then, slowly she began to peel off Jenny's clothes, till she was lying there, cold and naked—and on the verge of hysteria.

Meanwhile, he had disrobed, too—she couldn't see him, but she could see the pile of clothes that grew as he tossed onto it garment after garment.

"Please," Jenny whimpered, "I'll tell you anything, anything you want to know. But please don't do that to me, *please!*"

"Relax, honey," Selma said, as she bent down and brutally yanked Jenny's legs up under her, so that her knees were touching her belly, her face pressing into the carpet. "Relax and enjoy it," Selma added, fastening electrical wire around Jenny's thighs and around her knees, so that she was forced to lie facedown, her buttocks projecting up in the air. Then Jenny shuddered. Spider's naked body was leaning down onto hers.

"Now," he said, his voice purring from behind her ear, "are you going to tell me where that tape is?"

At that moment, a car door slammed. Spider pulled away. Selma ran to the window. "It's them, let's split."

Spider grabbed at the pile of clothing, pulling on his trousers as a key slid into the front door lock. "I bolted it from the inside," he said to Selma, who was already running down the hall toward the back door, with Spider sprinting half-dressed after her, as a window in the living room shattered and a hand reached in to release the window lock. Just as the back door slammed shut, the living room window sprang open. Hardrock Harrison splattered the glass from the casing with the butt of his gun, then pulled his large body through.

"They've gone out the back," Jenny screamed. "Get them, get them . . . please. . . ." She fainted.

After what seemed like an eternity, during which she was trapped in convoluted corridors, trying to escape from a coven of nightmare monsters, Jenny opened her eyes, blinked, shut them, then opened them again. Bright light from living room lamps blazed away, as if she were being orbited now by half a dozen dazzling suns. Gradually, though, she became accustomed to the glare. She became aware of the aches—around her wrists, the inside of her knees . . . She raised her hands in front of her face, saw the welts imbedded by the electrical tape, and started screaming.

"It's okay," a voice soothed her, "it's going to be okay, Jenny."

She looked around, and saw Rick, standing there, his hands dangling helplessly, his face a mask of emotion. Pallafox was there, too, hovering large and powerful, and seething with rage. In the background, she heard another voice, and noticed in a far corner the detective, the one named Hardrock Harrison, talking on a telephone. Suddenly, looking at these three men, she felt an overwhelming sense of shame. She conquered her resistance. She looked down at her own body, then relaxed a little. They had hidden her nakedness beneath a sheet.

Hardrock put down the phone. He walked over to them. "They'll be down here with an ambulance in five minutes," he said.

"She's awake now," Rick told him.

"It's gonna be all right, now, miss," Hardrock said, kneeling down and taking her small hand in his large one. "If you can, though, while we're waitin' for the ambulance, it would help if you told me just what happened here. Who did this to you?"

Jenny began to weep, her body shaking, shuddering uncontrollably. Rick kneeled down. He took her head in his arms, gently rocking back and forth, not saying a word, but simply holding her head to his chest, the way a parent does a frightened child.

Finally, Jenny's weeping subsided. She felt drained, then, gradually, the emptiness in her began to fill with another emotion. Anger. Rage. "It was Spider," she said bitterly. "Spider and that girlfriend of his, that Selma."

"All right," Hardrock said soothingly, "you just rest now. Don't talk anymore. The ambulance will be here any second now."

Jenny pulled away from Rick's cradling embrace. She sat up, holding the sheet around her body. "To hell with the ambulance," she said angrily. "I don't need any ambulance. I need a *gun*."

Jenny asked them to leave the room for a moment. When they did, she stood up, with the sheet wrapped around her body. Then she let the sheet fall to the floor.

She ran her hands down over her breasts, over her belly, past her buttocks. It was still *her* body, she thought to herself. She was something more precious to herself than any chance encounter could defile. And dammit, she reflected, it was a good body, too. A body that could withstand a brutal assault. Quickly, then, she dressed, and called her three rescuers back into the room. Pallafox came bearing a cup of coffee. Pushing the cup away, Jenny said, "I'll take something stronger."

Rick sat there, watching Jenny sip Scotch, detailing, while she drank, all the events leading up to the horrifying scenario just enacted in that very living room. Jenny told them about taking the tapes from Alvin Allen's office, about discovering the one with Spider on it earlier that evening at the hotel, about the incriminating comments Spider had uttered about Wally Kelly.

At that point, Pallafox interrupted her. It was his turn to talk, filling Hardrock in, with help, on all the details of his daughter's kidnapping, his efforts to lose in the World Series in order to protect Kathy's life.

"So," Hardrock said, "you weren't jokin' when you said a lady was behind your lousy pitchin' performance. I just never imagined the lady might be so damn young."

Then Jenny told them what had happened when she arrived at the house, how Spider had badgered her, and beat her, and finally ordered Selma to remove her clothes. "If you hadn't showed up when you did," she concluded, her voice clouding with emotion again, "he was going to do something awful to me."

"Poor Spider," Pallafox said, "poor, poor Spider."

Jenny looked at him in astonishment. "Poor *Spider?*" she spat angrily. "What about poor me? He was going to rape me, goddammit!"

"Not Spider," Hardrock said to her gently, "not Spider Johnson."

"What do you mean?" Jenny cried out.

"He means," Pallafox said quietly, "that this guy was an impostor. Spider Johnson had already been dead for hours."

*   *   *

At Jenny's insistence Hardrock sent the ambulance away empty. For an hour, police milled around the Pallafox house, fingerprinting, and taking down statements, and telephoning and issuing orders or following them. Throughout, Hardrock never mentioned to anyone outside the circle of Pallafox, Rick, and Jenny, the possible World Series fix or the kidnapping of Kathy. He had promised Pallafox, on the strength of their friendship, that he would keep those details from everyone but his immediate superiors, whose cooperation he felt sure he could count on.

Finally, they were free to return to Rick's and Jenny's hotel, where, they hoped, the tapes would still be waiting for them. They went in Hardrock's unmarked police car.

By the time they reached the bridge to San Francisco, the positions had hardened, with Pallafox and Jenny and Rick convinced that Wally Kelly was behind the double plot, at least the plot as it appeared to them: to fix the World Series, by kidnapping Kathy and thus forcing Pallafox to lose crucial games. Only Hardrock Harrison wasn't convinced.

"You see," Hardrock drawled in that lazy Texas way of his, "there's this here loose end. Why did Kelly bother lurin' Jenny to Pallafox's house, to get raped by that phony Spider?"

"He wanted the tape," Jenny answered.

Hardrock shook his head. "I don't think so," he said. "But let's let it lay till we get to the hotel; I think that we'll prove who's right, if no one's taken that tape."

They arrived at the San Francisco Shelby around midnight, pulled into the underground garage, and took the elevator up to the seventeenth floor.

"See what I mean?" Hardrock said, gesturing around Jenny's room.

"I don't see anything," said Pallafox. "Just a hotel room, with a tape recorder on the bed."

Jenny walked quickly to the bed. She lifted off the tape on the recorder. She glanced at it. "That's it," she said in astonishment. "That's the tape with Spider. I wrote his initials on it."

"Now, miss," Hardrock said, "you say Kelly got you over there and got this phony Spider to work you over 'cause they were lookin' for that tape, right? Well, then why didn't they send someone over here to ransack this room while you were gone. That was supposed to be happenin', right?" he added.

Jenny nodded yes.

"And think about this. I'll bet that while this guy was fussin' with you, his girlfriend, that Selma, didn't even bother lookin' through your pocketbook, while they had you tied up."

"I'm sure they must have," Jenny responded vaguely.

"I don't think so," Hardrock replied. " 'Cause when we found you, that big shoulder bag of yours was full of everything I guess you'd been carryin' in it. Now, if they'd been searchin' for somethin' as small as a cassette, she wouldn't have stuck her hand in, she would have turned the bag upside down on the livin' room floor, dropped everythin' out to really see what was inside."

"Okay, okay," Pallafox admitted. "So, what was the point of the whole scene at my house?"

"It was just a setup," said Hardrock. "The whole bit at your place was just melodrama—a set piece meant to confirm us in the conviction that Wally Kelly is behind the kidnappin' and the fix."

"But they were taking a big chance," Rick said. "It was very possible that the police would turn up Spider's body long before Jenny went to the house. You said he may have been dead for eight or nine hours when I spoke to you over the phone."

"Their first and only slip-up so far," said Hardrock. "Someone killed Spider too early. When the phony Spider arranged to meet Jenny, he thought the real Spider was still alive."

"Well, what was the point of the . . ." Rick couldn't formulate the word "rape." Even though he knew that nothing had really happened, he couldn't talk about it, not with Jenny sitting there, looking so angry, yet so vulnerable.

"The question is not *why* he tried to brutalize her," Hardrock interjected, "but *how*. What I mean is," he added, coughing, and turning away so he didn't have to meet Jenny's gaze, "why did he choose to . . . make the back-door play, so to speak?" He coughed in embarrassment again. "And I think the reason he did that was so Jenny, in that position, wouldn't be able to see his face. It's that simple. He wanted to scare the hell out of her, he wanted her to think he was Spider, and involved with Wally Kelly. But he didn't want her to see his face, 'cause if she did see it, up close, she'd realize he wasn't Spider after all. After that, they planned to let her go, have Spider killed. It would look like Wally Kelly had done it, or had it done, to prevent Spider from talkin' to us about what was on that tape—the tape the phony Spider was supposedly tryin' to get from Jenny."

"But if it wasn't Kelly behind all this, who was it?" Jenny asked.

"I didn't say it wasn't Kelly. I just said that scene didn't prove it *was* Kelly," Hardrock said. "Maybe we should listen to that tape."

"I've already told you, in the car, what was on there," Jenny said. "All Spider keeps saying is, 'Walter's got a half million riding on the Series, and millions more with the big boys'—and then some gobbledygook about a double-cross."

Suddenly Pallafox leaped up from his chair. "What did you say?" he demanded.

"Spider said something about a double-cross, that's all," Jenny replied.

"No," said Pallafox. "I mean, what did you say he kept calling Kelly?"

" 'Walter' . . . he kept saying it over and over, Walter's got this and Walter's got that."

"Give me that tape," Pallafox said, grabbing it out of Hardrock's hand and snapping it onto the recorder. "Where the hell is that part about the double-cross and the money, about Kelly?" he asked.

Jenny took the portable recorder from him. Watching the counter carefully, she jabbed the Fast Forward button, letting the cassette run, then pressed the Stop button. "Listen," she said, pressing Start.

They heard Spider's voice saying, "Walter's got a half million riding on the Series, and millions more with the big boys."

Then Alvin Allen, asking, "What's that about?"

Then Spider: "It's Walter's double-cross. Walter's got a half million on the Series and the big boys have millions more."

Then the clicking noise, then silence.

"That's wrong," said Pallafox.

"What's wrong?" asked Hardrock.

"Look," said Pallafox, "Spider never called Wally 'Walter'; he called him 'Wally,' like everyone else who knows Kelly real well."

"The phony Spider called him Walter, too," said Jenny. "God, he must have said it at least a dozen times."

"Let's hear that tape again," Hardrock said. "Now, Jimmy, I want you to listen real hard. Maybe the fake Spider's voice is on that tape. Maybe Allen was in on this scheme: He makes the tape with the fake Spider, lets Rick and Jenny know about it by telephone—then the fixers give him the double-cross, paying him off, early, and forever."

Hardrock rewound the tape and played back the sequence involving the double-cross and the millions of dollars.

"No, that's Spider's voice, all right," Pallafox said firmly. "Sorta slurred, but it's Spider, all right."

"Okay," Hardrock said, "maybe it is. Anyway, I can have our voiceprint experts check it out against other tapes Allen made . . ." He stopped in midsentence. "Hold on, now," he said. "I have an idea. Play that thing back one more time."

For the third time, the tape was rewound and Jenny pressed the Play button. For the third time, they listened to Spider droning on, over and over about Walter's double-cross, his half million, the millions more with the big boys. . . .

Jenny pushed the Stop button. Hardrock began pacing the room, his ruddy face tense, the eyes unusually narrow, his forehead furrowed with rare worry-lines. "Now, I do have an idea," Hardrock said. "It may be sorta crazy, but let's give it a try. Does Spider say, 'Walter's got a half million riding on the Series,' meaning 'Walter *has got* a half million,' or does he say, 'Walter's got a half million,' meaning some guy named *Walters* bet a half million!"

"Oh, my God," said Pallafox. "Walters. That's it."

"Harry Walters," said Rick. "That Vegas casino owner."

"Then that setup with Jenny . . ." Pallafox exclaimed.

". . . Yeh," Hardrock completed. "One thing they were tryin' to do was reinforce the idea that, on the tape, the real Spider was sayin' Walter, meaning Kelly, when he was really sayin' Walters, meanin' maybe this Harry Walters."

For another half hour, confusion reigned as they tried to reconstruct the kidnapping and Series' fix, and what the aim might be of both, meanwhile bemoaning their stupidity at not having spotted the deception long before. Once they had rearranged the pieces of the puzzle, so that the edges meshed perfectly, a further question remained. What was their next step?

Rick and Jenny and Pallafox insisted that Hardrock take action immediately. "You have to get Harry Walters, you have to rescue my daughter," Pallafox said.

"I don't think so," Hardrock replied. "I don't think we're anywhere close to tippin' our hand yet. I think we've got to play it right now as if we bit the bait. We've bought their con, we've got to make them think that. If Harry Walters is involved, then this really is big time, I guess. We blow the whistle on 'em too early, and little Kathy is gonna be in a whole lot of trouble."

"Christ," said Pallafox, despair in his voice, "then what do we do?"

"Well, Kathy is gonna be completely safe as long as the Golds look like they're gonna lose the Series, that's for sure."

"So, what's the next step?" Rick asked.

"I think I'm gonna have a little talk and see what Walter's involvement in all this is," Hardrock decided.

"You mean Harry Walters?" Jenny asked.

"No," Hardrock replied apologetically. "I mean Walter/Wally. I'm gonna have myself a little chat with Wally O. Kelly."

9

It was Tuesday, the morning of the fifth game of the World Series. For once, the chatter in the NBC hospitality tent was all about baseball. But not the game at hand, as crucial as it was to the Golds' effort to redress the balance in their favor against the Patriots. Instead, the talk centered around the headlines in the morning newspapers and the stories beneath them recounting the death, in the midst of this World Series, of a leading protagonist, the Golds' veteran starter, Spider Johnson.

His murder had shocked the entire sports world. And, at this moment, that sports world, the segment of it that counted as far as major-league baseball was concerned, was concentrated beneath the eight corners of this enormous tent. The theories about who killed Spider Johnson, and why he was murdered, tumbled out faster even than the paper cups, emptied of early morning liquor, into the gaily decorated wastebaskets.

"As far as I'm concerned, he was wiped out by some jealous lady he had two-timed," Ray Fowler was telling an attentive coterie of writers.

"If that was all it took," someone replied dryly, "three-quarters of these guys would be dead already."

"Well, if it wasn't jealousy," Fowler amended, "then it might have been his Vegas hassles."

Rick had been standing at the fringe of the group, with Jenny at his side. But when Fowler mentioned Las Vegas, he moved closer to the center of the circle, anticipating, waiting. "What kind of Vegas hassles?" he asked Fowler innocently.

"Well," Fowler said, enjoying the limelight, "it's no secret that Spider spent more time in Vegas than he should have, and lost more money there than he could afford."

"You mean," asked someone from a Chicago newspaper, "that he got taken care of 'cause he couldn't pay up?"

"Why not?" Fowler said. "It wouldn't be the first time."

"Maybe that's why the betting line has been a little odd all the way along," someone else offered.

"Spider used to hang out in Vegas at a joint called the Shazaam Casino," Fowler added with a yawn, "run, I think, by some ex-hood named Harry Walters. I'm thinking of having a little talk with this Mr. Harry Walters."

"But how does this murder fit in with the other one?" asked a short, fat man Rick recognized as a reporter for The Associated Press.

"What other one?" someone asked.

"Why, Alvin Allen, the guy they called the hypnotist to the stars. Our guy who covers the San Francisco police beat says that both Johnson and Allen were done in in the same style, probably by the same people or person."

"You're kidding," Fowler replied. "Now, that *is* an enticing morsel of information. Especially since we all know that Wally sent Spider to Allen in the first place, in order to get past his self-confidence problem."

Rick was troubled. If there was one thing they didn't need now, it was Ray Fowler snooping around—perhaps frightening Harry Walters, if indeed Walters was involved in the kidnapping and the fix. An edgy Walters might make some precipitous move, one that might put little Kathy in even further danger. Somehow, he had to lure Fowler off the right track. He had to drop some glittering piece of fool's gold, information that would keep Fowler running in circles. He decided to lay Wally Kelly as bait. According to Hardrock, Kelly was being set up as the patsy. So, any suspicion Rick could cast on Kelly now would only make the kidnappers feel more secure, more confident that their scheme was working.

"Did you hear about Wally and his wife?" he asked.

Fowler turned to him. "Just like you magazine guys to come up with something totally irrelevant," he said.

"Maybe it's irrelevant, maybe not," Rick replied. "But I remember, back in New York, I heard you telling someone how the rumor was that Wally was in danger of making a profit this year—a profit that would cost him a lot of trouble. He wouldn't be able to write off his franchise losses, if there weren't any, against his profits from the pharmaceutical firms."

"Well, what of it?" Fowler said, slightly irritated that someone else was trying to share center stage.

"Okay," Rick said, dropping his voice a decibel or two, to strengthen his grip on the reporters' attention, "remember what you told Jenny and me at Wally's party? That Mrs. K., or the soon-to-be ex-Mrs. K., has also heard that the Golds are extraordinarily profitable this year, and that she's demanding a five-hundred-thousand-dollar cash payment from Wally? According to you, before Wally would give her that five hundred thousand out of his profits, he'd burn the money first."

"I still don't see what the hell that has to do with the price of beans," Fowler replied testily.

"Just suppose," Rick said, "that Wally was so desperate to keep the money from her that he put in a call to some of his friends in Las Vegas. Just suppose," he added carefully, "that Wally put that five hundred thousand down on the Golds to lose."

There was stunned silence for a moment.

"That would be one helluva good explanation for that flaky betting line," one reporter said, his voice reflecting the astonishment that had rippled across all their faces.

"Are you suggesting," said Ray Fowler, indignation brimming in his voice, "that this Series is not on the up and up?"

"I don't know what to think," Rick said. "You're the expert. Maybe, instead of talking to this guy Harry Walters," he added, "someone should talk to Wally Kelly instead."

Fowler stared at Rick thoughtfully. "Maybe you just

have a point," he said, "though I still think Spider's death might have something to do with his debts in Vegas."

"It sounds like a possibility to me—about Wally Kelly," someone else countered.

Rick slipped away then, leaving his fellow journalists in hot debate, mired in a confusion of conflicting theories.

At that very moment, high above the Oakland Coliseum, the two subjects of the reporters' discussion were having a conversation of their own. Harry Walters and Wally O. Kelly were staring out the plate-glass window of the owner's stadium suite, each, for his own reasons, deeply troubled. Down below, the Golds were clustering behind the batting cage. A coach, protected by a screen that reached to his chest, was on the mound, tossing practice pitches to Artie Gibbons.

Wally was particularly disturbed. Usually, this pre-game ritual—watching *his* team take their warm-ups, from *his* suite, in *his* stadium—gave Wally an enormous thrill. Growing up poor in Chicago, as a youth he had spent hour after hour sweating in the midsummer sun and freezing in the late-season cold, condemned to the farthest reaches of the bleachers. Now, this former bleacher bum, as he liked to call himself, was privileged to own one of the forty stadium suites that ringed the Coliseum like brass knuckles on a fist—the symbol of his utter control over his franchise, and right now, over the hearts and minds of the millions of spectators who would watch the World Series in person or on TV.

Every time he sat down on one of the fifteen plush, soft leather seats in his enclosed stadium suite, he remembered the bite of hardwood slats, and the metal armrests that were always too hot or too cold. The temperature-control button evoked memories of sweltering days in August, frigid September afternoons. The bar behind him at one side of the room reminded him, every time his private bartender—on vacation today—poured another drink, of the warm beer and cold coffee in the old days. When he saw his French chef—also off today—skillfully preparing platters of his favorite delicacies in the small kitchen in back, he recalled the taste of semiraw hot dogs, stale peanuts.

Wally had no use for nostalgia, except when he could use it to put his own phenomenal rise to wealth in perspective. Another millionaire who had purchased a stadium suite at the Coliseum had furnished it with benches auctioned off while Patriot Stadium was being renovated. Wally had no patience for that kind of sentiment. "Only people who were born rich can afford the ultimate luxury of living like the poor," he was fond of saying. Wally's suite had been decorated by an interior designer he'd flown in from New York. "If you have wealth, flaunt it," Wally also liked to tell people. "My son, I hope, will be ashamed of being rich. It's my job to build a reputation for ostentatiousness he can rebel against."

But now, minutes before the fifth game of the World Series, sitting in his own suite, in his own stadium, watching his own team practice below, Wally was getting very little pleasure out of his power and wealth. It wasn't even the presence of Harry Walters that was making Wally feel so depressed, although Walters wasn't helping, either. The problem was, he'd had a talk with Detective Hardrock Harrison. Hardrock had told him there was a connection between the deaths of Alvin Allen and Spider Johnson. Then he had coaxed an admission out of Wally. Wally had admitted he placed a bet against his own team.

Now Wally turned to Harry. He gazed at the black hair, neat as the Astroturf below. Harry was staring straight ahead, his face vacant of all emotion. A face, Wally thought wryly, made for bluffing. "I don't know, Harry," he said coolly, "I just can't understand why all of a sudden you want to sit up here, instead of using the pair of tickets I gave you alongside first base. Is some friend of yours going to use those tickets? Otherwise, in all the years I've known you, I've never seen you so far away from the action."

"I don't need the scoreboard today. The only pitchers anywhere will be right here," Harry replied, flashing a set of capped white teeth. "Besides, like I told you, someone lifted my wallet this morning in the hotel lobby—it had to be, 'cause I had it when I left my room, but not when I got to the ball park. And," he added, "the tickets were in my wallet. That's why I telephoned you from the gate."

"I've told you, Harry," Wally said. "I can issue you passes for those seats."

"There's really no point to it," Walters replied. "I've got nobody to sit with down there today, anyway. And besides, it's bad luck to sit in a seat after you've lost the ticket. It's like ignoring a warning from God to stay away."

The conversation shifted, at Wally's careful prodding, to sports and gambling. Harry told Wally about his life-long love for baseball—for *betting* on baseball. How he started off wagering five dollars with local bookies when he was a kid back in Brooklyn. How, throughout his teens, he increased his bets, his sophistication at wagering on professional and amateur sports, and his earnings, too. He learned which pitchers had sore arms—paying off trainers to provide vital tips about particular players. Most of the time the "payoff" was merely a favor, or a free drink. Trainers withered in the shadows cast by the superegos of the stars they pampered; they were grateful to anyone who pampered them. From baseball, he added, he moved onto basketball.

"It was the days of the New York City powerhouse schools," he said. "We had guys on every college team who should have carried around candy-striped barbers' poles, they were shaving so many points. We had guys who should have been members of the sanitation union, they were dumping so many games. It was beautiful."

In the late fifties, when pro football began to dominate pro sports, Harry became a fan of that game as well. Baseball, he added, was merely a hobby with him now, strictly for amateurs. "You see," he said, "it didn't take long for people to figure out how football and basketball were better betting games than baseball. In football and basketball, you could have point spreads. In baseball, all you could do was give a guy a number of runs, or something like that. The only real bet in baseball," he concluded, "is the World Series."

"And that," Wally added, "as we all know, is the biggest bet of them all."

The stands below were filling up now. Far away, across the placid green sea of playing field, men with straw hats and Hawaiian shirts were trudging up the bleacher steps. And while bleacher-bound fans were moving up, another breed was moving down, in their carefully tailored casual clothes, expensive knit shirts, made-to-measure jeans—toward the box seats that hugged the field from the third-base bag all the way to first base, in a semicircle of privilege.

Still, there was no bastion of privilege so sanctified as this one, Wally thought, leaning forward a little so he could see the other end of the horseshoe of stadium suites that swept outward at eye level, on either side of his own. His gloating was interrupted by Harry Walters's voice, asking him, for the first time, "Out of curiosity, Wally, just why did you bet on the Golds to lose?"

"That's really none of your business," Wally snapped. Then, remembering his talk with Hardrock, Wally added, "Harry, if you must know, I did it purely out of spite."

Wally explained to Harry that the rumors he might have heard were true. "I'm too good a negotiator," he said, "too effective a salesman. When the stadium was remodeled for this season, the lease I negotiated was too shrewd. Attendance is up thirty percent this year— mainly on the strength of Pallafox as a gate attraction. Meanwhile, I got a much better—or worse, as it turns out—deal on my rental, leaving me with a windfall profit I really don't need. About five hundred thousand, I think, although my accountants haven't gone over the books yet. And unlike you, Harry, I'm not really into baseball to win money, but to lose it."

"You mean for your tax write-offs," Harry replied.

"Look," Wally said. "That's why we're in the business of owning franchises. It's fun, they're toy soldiers, living chessmen we can order from square to square. They're a chance to relive our frustrated boyhood fantasies. We're too old to become players, but we can sure as hell buy a team and become de facto managers. Still, the main reason why you buy a franchise, if you're smart and rich, is to lose money—through tax gimmicks like depreciating players' contracts and the like—losses which you can then write off against the real money-makers in your financial portfolio. This year, I needed a million-dollar loss to offset the profits from Kelly Pharmaceuticals. What the hell am I going to do with a five-hundred-thousand-dollar profit? Making that five hundred thousand on the Golds is going to cost me a million or two in taxes."

"I also heard something about your wife," Harry said. "She wants money, isn't that right? Plenty of money?"

"Okay," Wally admitted, "so the tax write-off was only one reason for that stupid bet. One reason was that I didn't want to declare a profit on the Golds, and two, I wanted to make sure that Juanita didn't get ahold of that real profit of five hundred thousand. I wouldn't mind just handing it over to the IRS, if it wouldn't cost me so much with Kelly Pharmaceuticals. But I'll be damned if I let that bitch get it. That's why, in a fit of anger, I decided to throw the damn money away on a bad bet. I figured I would undoubtedly lose. And if I won against odds so heavily in favor of the Golds, at that point the profit would be so large, I could keep the money. Juanita wouldn't know where the money went, and it would take the IRS years to unscramble my cooked books. If I did win, then I would have the money in cold cash."

They were silent for a moment, watching the Patriots taking batting practice, as reporters now swarmed out onto the field, their hands full of tape recorders and notepads. Then Wally turned to Harry and said, "Isn't your coming here a little foolish, Harry—and very dangerous? Pallafox has been pitching like a Little Leaguer, and two people have been murdered."

"Yeh, Jesus, what a helluva thing to have happen during a World Series. Spider Johnson getting wiped out."

"Have you heard a reason for it?" Wally asked, trying to keep his tone nonchalant and careless.

"Who knows?" Harry replied. "A guy goes to Vegas a lot. He has problems with his career. He starts throwing a lot of money onto the tables. He starts losing more money than he's got—or he's ever going to get. Somebody says pay up. He can't. They pay him off. Of course," Harry added quickly, "he didn't owe the Shazaam any money, 'cause, as everybody knows, I always let him play for free. I never charged him for a chip, 'cause, you know, I kind of loved the guy. In ten years, he'd won a lot of big-money ball games for me."

"And what about Alvin Allen? What have you heard about him?" Wally asked.

"Who? Oh, that hypnotist guy. How would I hear anything about him? He doesn't pitch. He doesn't play first base."

"Spider was one of his patients, Harry. Didn't you know that?"

"Never heard a thing," Harry said. "People in Vegas remember the guy, 'cause he used to do a very minor act there a number of years ago. A mind-reading act, they say. But this guy and Spider?" Harry shook his head. "That's news to me."

"Consider the coincidences, Harry," Wally said, turning away from the window that overlooked the playing field and inching closer to his guest. "Alvin Allen and Spider Johnson get murdered in the middle of the World Series. And now, for the first time in memory, you want to sit up here with me—flaunting your slimy past and malodorous present."

Harry smiled mirthlessly at Wally. "You invited me at the start of the Series," he replied calmly.

"Only because I thought you had the good sense to refuse my invitation. Something strange is going on around here," Kelly added. "You up here—a couple of corpses out there—something's going on. And," he added, "it has to do with Pallafox. If I didn't know better, I'd think Pallafox was *trying* to lose."

"The kid's probably just nervous, that's all," said Walters.

Wally turned away abruptly. He stood up, walked over to the glistening Formica-topped bar and poured himself a drink. "Anyway," he declared, "I've had just about enough of him."

"What do you mean?" Harry asked, his brow furrowing with worry lines.

"I mean, I might remove him from the pitching rotation," Kelly replied, mixing a drink for Harry, too, and handing it to him. "If the Series does go to seven games, I just might start someone else, maybe Rich Miller, in place of Pallafox."

"A lousy pitcher," said Walters.

"An honest pitcher," said Kelly.

"I wouldn't do that if I was you," Walters snapped.

"Thank God you're not me," Kelly retorted.

"You'd regret it," Walters told him.

"Are you threatening me? What do you care if Pallafox pitches or not?"

"I just want to see you make your bet," Walters said evenly. "You bet on the Golds to lose, I want to see you get satisfaction."

"Then, hell, I should go with Rich Miller," Wally replied. "You just said he was a lousy pitcher. People are starting to talk, Harry," he added. "They say this Series smells as bad as the one in 1919. They say some of that smell is rubbing off on me. And I think it's because I've been rubbing shoulders with you."

"Let Pallafox pitch," Walters replied. "Otherwise, you're going to smell worse, when people find out you bet five hundred thousand against your own ball club."

Wally slammed down his drink, spilling some on his expensively cut leather sport jacket. "What the hell is happening, Harry," he said fiercely. "Tell me what is really going on!"

Walters turned away from Kelly, his face an impenetrable mask. "Your team is losing again, Wally, that's what's happening." He nodded at the playing field, where, during their argument, the pregame rituals had been performed, with the Patriots now at bat in the top of the first inning. At that moment, the Golds players were following the path of a ball in flight, sailing high over the right-field wall and out of the ball park. A Patriot ballplayer was trotting slowly around the bases. "It's a home run," Harry exulted, raising his fist in triumph. "Hey," he added to Kelly, "you better stand up and look sad like everyone else, Wally. Or people are gonna think there is something strange going on, you know?"

"Get out of here, Harry, before I have you thrown out," Kelly roared.

Walters gave Kelly a disdainful last glance. "Just keep Pallafox pitching," he said menacingly, slamming the door behind him.

The moment the door to the outer hall closed, Hardrock Harrison stepped out of the walk-in closet behind the bar, mopping sweat from his brow with a white pocket handkerchief; his graying curly brown hair was drenched with perspiration. "Hell, that was worse than gettin' locked in a clubhouse sauna," he said, slipping on his sport jacket as an antidote to the cool air blowing out of recessed air-conditioning ducts, high on each wall of the suite. "It sure was close in there," he added.

"All right," Kelly said abruptly. "I've done everything you asked me to do. Now, will you please explain all this to me?"

Kelly and Hardrock sat down, and, while his Golds fell further and further behind the Patriots, Kelly listened, as Hardrock reviewed the events leading up to Spider's death—the kidnapping, the kidnap note, Pallafox's forced participation in a scheme to fix the outcome of the World Series. "It was worth hidin' in that stuffy closet," Hardrock said at last, " 'cause I got my suspicions of Harry Walters confirmed. He sure was tightenin' the screws on you."

"But what the hell do I have to do with all this?" Kelly bellowed finally, irritated as much by the detective's folksy, long-winded style as the fact that his Golds were now losing, in this fifth game, by a margin of 4–1, in the eighth inning.

"Well, Mr. Kelly," Hardrock said, "what I think is that you are bein' set up as the pigeon in all this. I think that when you called up Harry Walters to place that there bet of yours, he called up one of his mob partners. We've learned through some of our people out in Vegas that Harry there owes his partners quite a bit of money himself. Well, he had a way to settle that debt, see? He just suggested that they all get together and do just what you were doin'—place a bet on the Golds to lose. Millions of dollars on the Golds to lose. That was the 'double-cross' Spider kept talkin' about on that tape I mentioned—Harry Walters double-crossin' *you*.

"And just to make sure, they'd get Pallafox's daughter, 'cause if Pallafox lost every time out, your team was a goner."

"But the betting line would reflect it," Wally countered. "If there were a couple of million or more against a particular team, there'd be no betting line. Investors all over the country would run and hide."

"Well, see, that's just the point," Hardrock said, almost apologetically, as if he, a country-bred detective, a part-time Golds scout, was really rather hesitant about contradicting a big-city magnate like Wally O. Kelly. "These people are so big, so powerful, well—they have the muscle to pound the line into shape, if you get what I mean."

"I still don't see how all this would make me the fall guy," said Wally.

"Well," Hardrock continued, his voice growing ever-more apologetic as his insights became ever-more astute, "the idea is, after the Golds lose, Pallafox gets back his kid. And then he reveals, naturally, there's been a fix."

"And I," said Wally, "am revealed as the fixer."

"You did put up five hundred thousand against your own team," Hardrock replied. "You did keep Pallafox on the mound even when he was losing. Spider did mention a name that everybody would have thought was yours, over and over on that tape he made with Alvin Allen."

"I would have been a sitting duck," Kelly said glumly. "How could I have been so stupid?" Then he brightened. "Still, there's one loose end. If Pallafox reveals the fix after the World Series, then there's no payoff, right?"

"It doesn't matter what happens after the Series is over," Hardrock pointed out. "Pallafox wouldn't have opened his mouth till he got his daughter back. By that time, the guys behind this would have collected their money, they'd be sitting back laughing, waiting for the law to add up all the evidence and come up with an equation that equals Wally O. Kelly."

"Well, why didn't you arrest Walters right now, for godsake?" Kelly said.

"Now, just take it easy, take it easy, Mr. Kelly," Hardrock soothed. "Gettin' upset when the fence breaks doesn't put the cow back in the pasture, if you get what I mean. Harry Walters is just small potatoes. He isn't runnin' this show. Before I pull Walters in, before we work him over, we gotta know where the kid is, and what they plan to do to her. Which reminds me," he added, "I gotta make a call."

Wally Kelly watched the hulking torso of Detective Hardrock Harrison recede, out the door and down the long hall that led to the Golds' administrative offices. Then he turned back to the game. The Golds were losing, by their own honest effort today, but with a big assist from Pallafox overall. Christ, he didn't give a damn about the lousy $500,000. The idea that people might think he would stoop so low as to arrange for the World Series to be fixed bothered him much more. God, he loved baseball, he thought, had loved it all his life. Now, as ironical as it was absurd, his reputation as an owner, as a celebrity, was in the hands of a big, lumbering part-time scout, an ex-pitcher, a transplanted bumpkin named Hardrock Harrison. How the hell, thought Wally Kelly, was this good-natured old-timer, who seemed to know more about fastballs than fast talk, going to outwit the clever, moneyed maniacs who had kidnapped Pallafox's daughter—and conned the brilliant Wally O. Kelly himself?

That evening, at 6:00 P.M., Norma Windsor was standing in the bedroom of her small house in a quiet suburb of Las Vegas, applying makeup to her face. While she dabbed on the creamy substances—two tones for her eyelids, three shades on her lips, to obtain just the right glow—she could see, reflected in the mirror, the back window of the house, and beyond that the yard, with short, neat hedges, a waist-high white picket fence, and in the middle, the set of swings, painful mementos of a happier time. How little Kathy loved to sit on the swing and be pushed higher and higher, her laughter climbing and falling like the cry of a swooping gull. Norma paused now, watching the metal swing glinting in the fading Las Vegas sun. It seemed so forlorn, frozen in the emptiness of the small garden, with no tiny hands to nudge it into motion.

Norma finished applying her makeup. She moved her chair back a foot from the dresser. She tilted her face left, then right, so the waning shafts of sunlight struck her cheeks and eyes and forehead at different angles. Satisfied that every minor blemish had been concealed, and that her lips glistened with the layers of wet pink lipstick she knew Harry Walters would hunger after, she stood up and walked to her clothes closet. Opening it, she was about to remove a conservative blue suit, with a high collar, from its hanger, when the words of that detective who had called her that afternoon again rang in her ears: "Somehow, lady, you have got to get to see your daughter. You're the only one who can pull it off. How? Well, that's up to you to decide."

At first, she had dismissed his accusation, that kidnapping Kathy was merely part of a plot to fix the World Series. She had refused to believe that Harry Walters would endanger her daughter. She had refused to accept the notion that Kathy was in terrible danger, because then she would have to admit her own guilt for putting her daughter in jeopardy. Soon, though, she had stopped denying to Harrison that she knew anything about the kidnapping. She didn't admit what she did know, just stopped denying that she didn't. The evidence that Harrison had amassed—the deaths of Alvin Allen and Spider Johnson, Harry's threats to Wally Kelly—had shaken her conviction that it was all a scheme of Pallafox's to get Kathy back.

"I'll find out what I can," she had finished, still without admitting she knew there was anything in Las Vegas to find.

As soon as she had put down the telephone, however, she decided she must see Kathy. She also decided how to make Harry lead her to Kathy. That's why, right now, she was putting the conservative blue suit back into the closet and removing, instead, a frilly sheer silk blouse, a matching silk skirt that she rarely wore because it hugged her hips so tightly. She stepped into the skirt, tugging it up over her hips. She slipped on the blouse. Then she walked over to the full-length mirror behind the door to the hall. The skirt was all right, she decided, but the blouse, without a bra, was positively indecent. And that, she thought angrily, was exactly why she was not going to put on a bra.

She finished dressing at 7:00 P.M. She walked into the living room, opened a cabinet, and took down a bottle of Scotch. Then she went into the kitchen and poured herself a drink. Returning to the living room, she dimmed the lights, sat down on a couch, and waited. Harry was due any minute now. He had promised to pick her up at seven, but she knew he would be at least a half hour late. While she waited, she gazed vacantly around the room, till her eye caught the photograph on the piano: of herself, holding Kathy in front of her, Kathy's hair braided into pigtails. Kathy's fiery red hair, courtesy of Jim Pallafox.

Could Harry be part of a scheme to force the outcome of the World Series, by holding Kathy hostage and making Pallafox lose? It seemed incredible, but apparently that detective from the San Francisco police was convinced. Harry, with his courtly manner glued over a gutter roughness, a veneer of sophistication beneath which brutal scars sometimes showed. He was so kind to her, and to Kathy, for that matter, showering them with presents, taking the little girl on outings to the park and to movies. That was one side of Harry.

But, she had to admit to herself, there was another side, too. Rumors that sometimes reached her ears in half-overheard snatches of conversation gave evidence that Harry had a darker side, a side that his blackest moods only hinted at. There was the dealer who'd been caught cheating the house in team with a playing partner. He had vanished, as surely as if he'd been picked up by one of those gleaming silver discs cultists were always claiming to have seen somewhere in the desert sky. And there had been the black entertainer, in love with the famous white actress. For years he was a fixture at the Shazaam, till one day, just after word of his proposed marriage leaked out, Norma saw him being escorted from the hotel by two of Harry's heavyset gofers. Later, she had heard the singer had been driven out into the desert, ordered out of the car, and told that he had two choices. He could keep walking straight ahead, into that vast wasteland of parched gulches and sandstorms. Or he could get back in the car, return to the city—and marry a black woman within forty-eight hours. She hadn't believed the story when she'd first heard it. Then, a day later, from the stage of the main room at the Shazaam, the singer had interrupted his show to announce that he was marrying one of the black dancers in his troupe. Later she had actually seen the payroll voucher, permitting Harry to deduct $10,000 a week for sixteen weeks, to be paid to the black lady dancer. After sixteen weeks, during which the white actress had married a Hollywood producer, the black singer obtained a Reno divorce.

And those mysterious "partners" of Harry's—the ones who arrived in the dead of night in fleets of rented limos, with the blinds drawn over every window. Harry had told her once, in a rare moment when depression had penetrated his habitual cool, that despite the fact he was probably a millionaire, he still owed enormous debts. "The kind you can't pay off with money," was how he phrased it.

Despite his millions, of course, there had been one thing he hadn't been able to buy: her. She had resisted his every advance, not so much because she found him repulsive, but out of fear that giving herself to him would spoil their relationship. In his eyes, she would be cheapened. In her eyes, he would no longer suffice as the father figure she had come to cherish, a substitute for the father she had called "John."

Just then lights flickered across the living room window as an automobile pulled into the small driveway out front. Norma stood up, glancing at herself in a half mirror. The slick lipstick glistened . . . the nipples of her large breasts were a pair of dark, searching eyes, peering from behind the semisheer silk blouse. She pulled at the blouse, tucking it farther into the waist of her skirt, unbuttoning another button. She was the dealer now, carefully calculating the odds. Staring at herself as the doorbell rang, she kept telling herself what she had been taught to feel about the casino's money when she was behind the craps table, and customers were temporarily winning: Don't let your ego get involved.

She opened the door. Harry stepped in. He stood at the door for a moment, blinking incredulously. "I thought we were just going to have a pleasant little evening together," he said, when he had composed himself, "but apparently you're in the mood to go someplace spectacular."

"I'd rather *do* something spectacular," she said coolly, using the bright, bantering tone she had perfected with customers at the craps tables. Then she bent forward and kissed him full on the lips.

Harry stepped back. He was wearing a tailored blue denim suit, and his face had the ruddy, tanned surface of an avid yachtsman, though Harry had confided to her once, she remembered, that the mere sight of a sailboat made his stomach queasy. Overall, she decided, regarding him for the first time in this particular way, he was distinguished looking and attractive. If only, she thought, he didn't wear a damn tie day and night, she might even find him exciting. But that tie. His emblem of respectability. She wondered if he wore a tie in bed.

Harry had been gazing at her quizzically, not sure what to make of her sexy outfit, her bold kiss. Up to now, every time he'd tried to kiss her, she'd averted her face. Whatever was brewing in her mind, he decided, the most prudent policy—and perhaps the most profitable in terms of future pleasure—was to banter back, and see how far this verbal foreplay would lead them. "That spectacular thing you're in the mood for doing," he said lightly. "Can we do it outdoors, or is it strictly an indoors activity?"

"The Beatles had a song once," she replied, turning her back to him, strutting to the bar. "According to them, everyone should 'do it in the road.' " She began pouring drinks—a double Scotch for Harry, a black Russian for herself. "But I think it's a lot better in bed," she said, turning to face him, with a drink in each hand and a coy smile pulling at her lips.

Harry took a few steps forward. He reached for the glass. When he took his drink from her hand, he let his fingers rest against hers for a moment. She didn't pull her hand away. "What do you want from me, Norma?" he said softly.

She moved closer. She put her head on his shoulder. "I have to see Kathy, Harry," she whispered. Then she added, in the exact phrases Hardrock Harrison had told her to use, "I went to the doctor today. He gave me sleeping pills. If you don't take me to Kathy, Harry, I'm going to swallow them. And there's no way on earth you can stop me."

"I didn't realize you were that distraught," Harry said, his arms encircling her, almost involuntarily, as if trying desperately to resist mixing business with pleasure—a dictum he held very dear.

"The truth is, Harry," she said, making her voice sound very small, "I know about the Series, I know about the fix." She felt his arms stiffen. "But it's all right, Harry," she added quickly, with all the passion she could manufacture. "I know you wouldn't let anyone hurt Kathy, and I *want* that bastard Pallafox to lose. I want him humbled, Harry," she spat out, the fear that he would see through her lies providing an honest passion now. "I want him embarrassed. I want him to suffer, the way I suffered those early years. All I want to do is see Kathy for a moment. Not just for my sake, but for hers, too, Harry. Don't you see?"

"She's all right, believe me, Norma. I wouldn't let any harm come to her," Harry replied, stroking her hair.

"Then take me to her, please," Norma pleaded, burying her body into his. "Please, Harry, take me to her. You won't regret it."

"I love you, Norma," he blurted suddenly, clutching her with a passion she had never believed him capable of. "I want you. I can have any woman around. But I don't love them, and I love you, and you won't let me near you."

His words struck her dumb. She was grateful her head was buried on his chest, otherwise she wouldn't have been able to control the revulsion she was sure had passed over her face when he revealed his feelings. It took every ounce of strength, every iota of calculated calm she had acquired behind the gaming tables, to reply in a sugary-sweet voice: "Take me to Kathy, and then," she added softly, "take me to bed."

Harry stood there, his hands moving slowly down her back, then up again to her shoulders. He felt old suddenly, trapped in his own absurd puppy-love yearning. She didn't really want him, he knew that, and the knowledge was bitter. She would never want him. She was a mother, willing to barter even her body for a glimpse of her child. Then he became aware of her again, the inviting nakedness that the slick silk blouse and skirt hinted at so tantalizingly. So what if he was acting like a schoolboy—wanting her simply because she had been the only one who was unobtainable? Wasn't that reason enough? "If I take you to see her, and the wrong people find out where she is," he said dryly, "I guarantee you that you'll be dead within twenty-four hours."

"I won't tell, please, I promise," she said.

"I won't even find out about it," he added, his voice

even flatter than before. "If the police learn about that hiding place because of you, I'll be dead long before you will."

"Who are these people?" she cried suddenly. "What hold do they have over you, Harry?"

"I saw a movie once," he replied. "It was about some primitive tribe somewhere. When someone saved a warrior's life, the only way the one who was saved could pay off the debt was to die doing something for the one who had saved him. I belong to the same kind of society," he added.

They were silent for a moment, Harry holding Norma, Norma holding Harry. For the first time ever, she felt a tenderness for him. She had never realized before—they both were victims.

Then he said, "I'll take you to her. And then," he added, with a sigh, "I will take you."

They had been driving for about an hour, with the top of Harry's convertible down. Norma was thankful for that. He was driving so fast, the wind howled around their heads constantly, precluding the small talk that would have been so painful. Instead, each was lost in his own thoughts—or, in Norma's case, her own memories. The star-studded sky overhead . . . the whipping wind . . . Riding in Harry's convertible resurrected in her mind another night, in another convertible. The night she had met Pallafox, and, after a snack at that Mexican cantina near campus, they had driven for hours. She recalled the wind, how it carried her laughter aloft. How bittersweet that memory was. Who could have known then that their relationship was a rare blooming flower on the tip of a spiny cactus? Who could have known that her laughter that night foreshadowed this night, years later, full of pain and foreboding? Who could have conceived then that they would conceive Kathy, the bond that linked her destiny with Pallafox's, no matter how hard fate had worked to keep their lives from intersecting again?

* * *

At that very moment, in a house not far away in the desert, a large man was sitting on a wooden rocker, watching a TV set, on top of which lay a homburg hat. A little girl, with a dress that matched the color of her fiery red hair, was curled up on the floor beside him, watching, too. A while ago, he had removed her blindfold, so that she could watch television. Now, she was growing tired of looking at things she really didn't understand—police and bad men and blonde ladies, a lot of blonde ladies, firing guns, or being fired at, or being kissed. She was tired of asking questions that the man, Karl, didn't answer. He would only laugh when she asked him a question. At the beginning, when she had awakened that night in his car, she had laughed when he laughed, too. Then, after a while, she had stopped laughing. He didn't laugh the way her mother laughed, or Jim laughed. He didn't laugh like anyone laughed. He didn't laugh *funny*.

Kathy stood up. And then she forgot. The wires that attached her to Karl. The wires that were part of the game he said they were playing—although he never could explain how long the game would last, or what it was about.

"What's the matter?" Karl said, turning his face from the television set and staring at her.

"I want to go there," she said, pointing toward the back door.

Karl smiled. "Yes," he said, "it's time you had a walk."

He stood up. He took her hand. He led her to the back door, and out into the cool desert air. Karl bent down, so that Kathy could pick up a handful of pebbles. She threw them at a tree nearby, and laughed when a few happened to strike the trunk.

And then she saw it—a little brown kitten that had leaped out from behind the tree, startled by the noise the stones made. "Here, kitty," Kathy whispered, her voice delighted.

The kitten hesitated, its pupils glowing in the night like coals. Then, slowly, cautiously, it moved toward the little girl. It began rubbing up against her right leg. Kathy moved to bend down to pet it, when suddenly the large man grabbed her by the shoulder. "Don't do that," he barked at her, "don't move like that again. Remember these," he added, pointing to the wires that led from under the little girl's right sleeve. "Remember our game."

"But I want to touch him," Kathy pleaded, watching the kitten snuggling against her leg. "He's so pretty."

"I'll get him for you," Karl told her. He reached down to pick up the cat. But the kitten didn't want Karl to pick it up. It arched its back, it slashed at his hand with its paw. A thin line of blood appeared along his knuckles.

With an angry roar, Karl snatched up the cat, held it dangling in the air for a moment, then smashed it down on the ground, again and again.

Kathy looked at the kitten, lying still now. She was crying softly. It wasn't pretty anymore.

It was almost eight o'clock when they reached the house. A rambling pseudo-Spanish, stucco structure with a red slate roof and colored tiles bordering the doors that led to an inner courtyard. Once the house had undoubtedly held promise for someone—a pleasant and pretty retirement home, Norma guessed, as Harry guided the car past the front door and pulled up alongside a two-car garage. But the sandy soil stretching out on all sides toward the horizon, the silhouette of a concrete foundation for another house a hundred yards off, the gravelly surface of an unfinished road that led to nowhere in the desert, all bespoke broken plans, a deceptive real-estate sale. On one side of the house was a tangle of wheelbarrows and concrete mixers topped with carpenter's tools, all strangely new-looking, preserved from rust in the dry desert air.

They left the car, stepping out into the cool night air. Harry walked in front, Norma following, toward an arched doorway, then into the courtyard, where a large, unfinished swimming pool gaped like a thirst-stricken mouth. Entering a small hallway, Harry rapped twice with a brass door knocker, paused, then rapped once again.

There were heavy footsteps on the other side of the ornately carved wooden door, then the sound of the peephole sliding. The door opened. Harry entered first, Norma right behind him. For an instant, in the dim light in the hallway, all Norma saw was the towering figure of a man framed against the light that filtered from an inner room. His body, featureless in the semidark, looked as if a boulder had been placed on the chopped trunks of two redwoods. The only detail, in fact, that identified him as a man, and not some primitive totem erected by some long-dead disciples of god-giants, was the hat he was wearing: unmistakably, the rounded contours of a homburg.

"This is Karl," Harry said, and despite the smoothness in his voice, Norma could feel his fear.

Karl grunted noncommittally, then said, in a deep, chilling voice, "And this is the mother, I suppose?"

"I had to bring her," Harry said, a plea pushing at his calm. "There would have been trouble otherwise. All she wants to do is see the child. She won't make waves. She's on our side."

Karl grunted again. He stepped to the side, turned around, and began walking toward the room the light was coming from. It was then, and only then, that Norma noticed the tiny figure walking beside him. "Kathy," she cried, and would have rushed forward to embrace her daughter, except that Harry's hand caught her by the elbow, restraining her forcefully.

"Don't," was the urgent word he whispered. "Don't do anything to upset him."

It seemed like an endless journey, a forced march for Norma, down that long, dimly lit hall, but finally they reached a room in which peeling wooden furniture was scattered, its decrepitude revealed by the relentless light from a bare bulb hanging overhead. Karl stopped, he turned around, the little girl turning with him. Norma stared in horror, then fell back a step, only prevented from collapsing by Harry's strong arms supporting her.

Kathy was blindfolded. A swath of white tape cov-

ered her mouth. Recovering her senses, Norma tried to
break free of Harry's grip.

"It's all right, Karl," Harry said, pointing to the firm
grip Karl had on the little girl's hand. "Remove the tape
and the blindfold. Let the little girl be with her mother
for a moment. It will do them both good."

Karl didn't reply for a moment. He just kept staring
from under the homburg, his massive shoulders
hunched menacingly. Then, the rock-face split, cracking
into a cavernous smile. Karl laughed, but without an
iota of humor. "That," he declared in an emotionless,
metallic-sounding voice, "is impossible. You see?" he
added, laughing mirthlessly again, as he raised the hand
that had been holding little Kathy's.

"Oh, no," Norma screamed.

"My God," Harry uttered involuntarily.

"You see," said Karl, "these wires leading from under the little girl's sleeve are connected to a pack of
explosives tied around her waist, on one end, and to the
detonator in my right-hand pocket, on the other end.
Merely by depressing the button," he added, a horrifying glee coloring his voice, as he nodded his head at his
hand buried in his right pants pocket, "the entire package would explode with enough force to pulverize the
girl, myself, the two of you—and probably that nice
new convertible I saw you park outside, Harry."

"For godsake, man," Harry hissed, "no one told me
about this."

"It was felt that, in the circumstances, you might be
too tenderhearted, Harry," the massive man in the homburg replied. "And judging by your reaction," he added
calmly, "I think the decision to keep you in the dark
was the right one."

"But what are you going to do with her?" Norma
said, weeping openly now. She was managing to stand upright only by leaning on Harry for support. "What are
you going to do with my baby?"

"In one half hour," Karl replied, "your little daughter
and I will begin a journey. We will keep moving on this
journey until the World Series ends. If that means a seventh game, my orders are to escort your daughter to the

ball park. We will sit in Harry's seats, by the first-base line, so that we are highly visible to the father of your daughter." Karl laughed in anticipation. "While he pitches that seventh game, we will serve as a reminder of the penalty for winning."

"And if the Golds win—in the seventh game, or if they take the Series in six?" Harry asked, a desperation now in his own habitual monotone.

"Then," said Karl, "the little girl will die."

"But, dammit, man, you'll die, too," Harry retorted.

"A quicker, cleaner death than if I didn't complete the task they have assigned me to do," Karl replied in a matter-of-fact voice. "You've heard of my nickname?" he suddenly asked Norma brightly, with more than a hint of pride.

Norma was standing there, leaning on Harry, her face turned ashen beneath the makeup, her lips forming the oval of a scream that was trapped inside her constricted throat.

"Tell her, Harry," Karl said. "I'm sure it would amuse her."

Harry shook his head.

"I said tell her, Harry!" Karl roared, raising the little girl's right arm so that the wires connecting her to him tightened dangerously.

"Karl . . ." Harry said, his voice as empty as a somnambulist's. "They call him . . . Kamikaze Karl."

The name triggered something in Norma, something insane, some hormonal flow that dated back millions of years, to the time when mothers responded to a threat to their children by attacking a mighty predator with their bare hands. She lunged toward Karl. Harry grabbed her, spun her around. He shook her violently. "He means it," Harry shouted. "Get ahold of yourself, or Kathy is *dead*."

Norma fell against him. She started sobbing, violently. "Do something, Harry," she wailed. "Call him off. Make him stop, here, right now, please!"

"Karl is a machine programmed to self-destruct," Harry said quietly, helplessly. "The only people who can change his orders are the big guys—the guys that gave him those orders. And," he added, "they don't take orders from me. Or anyone else."

The car pulled to a halt, the driver's door slammed shut, the passenger door creaked open, and she felt someone tugging at her arm. She blinked, trying to shake the nightmare visions out of her head.

"We're home," Harry said.

Norma looked around, disoriented for a moment. "But this isn't my house . . ." she began.

"It's my place," Harry said. Then he added, "Remember our agreement?"

"But not now," she pleaded, "not after tonight. Anytime, Harry, but not now."

"I'm sorry, Norma," he said. "I didn't know we'd find her like that, believe me. But you did lay your cards on the table, and I did lay mine," he added. "We both took a risk—and now I have to collect what's rightfully mine."

Suddenly, she no longer cared. She let him half-carry, half-pull her into the garishly lit lobby, into the elevator, into the apartment. He led her into the bedroom. He placed her on the bed the way, she recalled with a sharp pang of pain, Kathy always placed her panda bear before she climbed in and said her prayers. In the mirrors covering the ceiling overhead, she watched him remove her clothing, first the blouse, then the skirt, then her underpants. She watched him remove his clothes, too, then leap on her, clawing at her soft hidden parts like a tiger.

10

On Wednesday, the morning of the sixth game of the World Series, Willie Richardson picked up Pallafox at 11:00 A.M. Pallafox tossed his knapsack onto the Cadillac's back seat. He slid onto the front seat. Willie shifted the auto into drive, and glided off.

"Take a look at that, man," he said, indicating the newspaper lying folded between them on the front seat.

Pallafox picked up the newspaper, thankful that Willie had given him an excuse to forgo the ritual small talk. Spider had been a kind of intermediary. Now that Spider was gone, the self-imposed segregation white and black ballplayers practiced was bound to intensify once again.

Pallafox scanned the newspaper—Willie had left it opened to the sports page. "What am I supposed to be reading, man?" he said to Willie.

"Try Ray Fowler's column," Willie said.

Pallafox found the writer's photo set above the column of print. He began to read. After a moment, he said to Willie, with false optimism in his voice, "Sounds good to me. Fowler picks Freddy White to outduel Ernie Parker. He picks us to win today, and even the series at three and three."

"Keep reading," Willie said, his eyes on the road and his voice strangely noncommittal.

Pallafox got the point. Near the end of the column, Fowler predicted a seventh and decisive game on Thursday. Then the writer added, "So, the Series will end, in my humble opinion, the way it should: with the two best teams in baseball clashing head to head, in one game that will settle who's champion. The only problem is, folks, that the Golds don't have a chance in that seventh game. The Patriots will be pitching Gary Humboldt —a man. The Golds will be pitching a green kid—Pallafox, who has already failed twice. Pallafox is no Sandy Koufax. Sandy Koufax wasn't a quitter.

"The question is: Is Wally Kelly too stubborn to pull Pallafox out of the rotation? Or does he have his own reasons for wanting Pallafox on the mound if there's a seventh game? Your move."

Pallafox put the newspaper down. He fought to quiet the rage that was building inside of him. Was Fowler putting two and two together—the two being Wally and himself? Did he know something—or was he merely implying that Wally might act selfishly, imperiously, keeping him on the mound, and not—as he had suspected at the first reading—criminally. "What do you think about Fowler's column?" he asked Willie, controlling his voice as well as he could.

"I guess he's saying Wally might have to stick with you, otherwise he's gonna look bad for having gone with you this far already," Willie said bluntly. Then he added, "Anyway, it's what the other guys think that counts, dig? I'm supposed to lay this on you: When we get out to the ball park they gonna hold a kangaroo court."

"Who are they going to put on trial?" Pallafox asked, although he knew the answer already.

"Among others—you. Artie Gibbons is really ticked off by the way you've been pitching."

Norma awoke in an empty bed, startled by the unfamiliar surroundings. Overhead, in the faint light that slipped past the slats of the venetian blinds, she saw her own face and body reflected in the ceiling mirrors.

She looked at the clock radio. It was late, 11:30. She would be late for work, she thought suddenly—then remembered whom she had slept with last night. The boss won't yell at me this time, she mused bitterly.

He had kept her awake for hours last night, pumping his loins against hers, turning her over on her stomach, later on her back again, as he explored her as thoroughly as a pathologist examining a murder victim. She put her hand up to her shoulder. She felt the tiny soft scabs of a row of bite marks. If not willing, she had been compliant, she recalled. Yet he had raped her anyway.

Norma stumbled out of the bed. She had to get away from that mirror, she thought wildly, she had to escape from the sight of her own body, made unclean by his pawings and his fluids and his cold, calculating acrobatics. She staggered across the carpet to the bathroom and lowered her head over the sink, gagging with a leftover nausea. But her stomach was empty. The nausea was buried in her soul. She looked up from the bathroom sink—and, God help her, found herself staring into another accusatory mirror, on the medicine cabinet. She cried aloud, helplessly, and flung open the cabinet door. She wanted to banish the sight of her own distraught face, her own despoiled body.

Then another impulse took hold of her. Her eyes began to scan the contents of the medicine cabinet—full of hair dyes and skin lotions and—painkillers. She spotted a thin vial full of tablets and grabbed it off the shelf. Yes, it said sleeping pills—there were at least twenty, she guessed. Enough.

She began to press down on the vial, to release the safety cap, when the doorbell rang. The chimes chilled her. Her hands went limp. The pills clattered noisily into the sink. He's come back, she thought frantically. He wants me again. She began to sob, while the finger on the doorbell became more and more insistent. She wouldn't die fast enough, she was thinking, her body bent over the gleaming enameled sink. He would have time to take her again and again, each throbbing thrust of him one more painful wound.

The front door creaked open. She scooped up a handful of tablets that had tumbled into the sink. She lifted them toward her mouth, shutting her eyes . . . when suddenly a hand caught her wrist from behind, fingers yanked her fist open, and the sleeping pills fell to the floor.

"Let me do it, please, Harry!" she screamed, keeping

her eyes tightly closed, reluctant to abandon the forgetful darkness she longed for so desperately. "Please, please, please."

"Calm down, miss," a voice behind her said, "there's a lot of good livin' ahead for you yet."

Norma's hysteria cooled to confusion. She opened her eyes and swiveled her body till she was staring into the face of a large, heavyset man wearing an outlandish cowboy hat. Suddenly her fear rushed back in a wave that threatened to swamp her with hysteria again. "Don't hurt me," she whimpered, "I don't want to be hurt anymore."

The big man placed a thick, beefy arm around her shoulder. "I'm from the San Francisco police," he said gently, flashing his shield, then guiding her out of the bathroom and back into the bedroom. "My name is Levon Harrison, but folks usually just call me Hardrock."

Hardrock Harrison—the scout who had followed Pallafox in college, the detective who had called her at her home yesterday, telling her it was absolutely imperative that she get Harry Walters to lead her to Kathy, who had convinced her that she should find out, if she didn't believe him, whether or not Kathy was in danger.

Norma stopped. She looked at Hardrock. "How did you get here?" she said.

Then, before Hardrock had time to utter a reply, Norma Windsor fainted.

She awoke in her own bed. She was fully dressed. The sun was pouring in her bedroom window. Glancing out, she saw the comforting, yet at the same time, poignant, set of swings in her picket-fenced backyard. As soon as he saw her stir, Hardrock Harrison handed her a glass of orange juice. "I'll answer that question you asked me back at Harry Walters' apartment," he said kindly. "You see, I was around since last night. I followed you and Walters out to that house you went to last night, then back to Walters' apartment. That house is where they're keepin' your daughter, isn't it?"

Norma propped her back against the headboard. She sipped at the cool juice, nodding her head yes.

"I figured that," Hardrock said, "and I figured that if

I could convince you to convince him to take you out there, I might find out enough about the circumstances out there to get your daughter free."

Between sobs, Norma told him about Karl, how he had turned Kathy into a walking bomb, with his finger on a detonator he kept in a trouser pocket.

"Which pocket did he keep his hand in?" Hardrock wanted to know.

"I can't remember," Norma said. "It was all so horrible, so frightening, I just can't remember little things like that."

"Well, I'll figure out somethin'," Hardrock said, standing up and moving toward the door.

"But how could you be sure that I didn't know what they had done to Kathy?" Norma asked him.

Hardrock stopped at the door. "I called Jimmy yesterday," Hardrock replied. "He told me he'd been out to see you. I kind of got from his voice that maybe he still . . . Well, maybe he still felt pretty strongly about you. I know Jimmy pretty well," he added. "It was hard for me to believe he could love someone who was playin' games with the life of that daughter of his. So I decided, well, maybe that Norma knows and doesn't know, at the same time. Maybe she knows the girl's been kidnapped, but not why. Maybe they told her they were goin' to get custody of the kid for her, that they were goin' to use this World Series—fix thing as a decoy. Then, when I called you, I heard real fear in your voice when I told you who I was and how I thought you better get Harry Walters to show you your daughter. And now, your tryin' to take your own life was the final proof. A lady who'd dangle her daughter's life as bait wouldn't be thinkin' about takin' her own."

Norma lay there, in bed, staring across the room at this big, unassuming man, dressed in blue jeans, with the thick, hairy arms hanging awkwardly from a checkered shirt, and the large, wide-brimmed hat in one hand. He looked like a bit player in a John Wayne epic, not a detective. "What should I do, what can I do?" she asked quietly, somehow comforted by his bucolic calm.

"Like the old song says," Hardrock replied, grinning

broadly, "just don't do nothin' till you hear from me. I'll come up with somethin'. I don't plan to strike out on this one."

He kept smiling at her, till finally, despite herself, Norma felt a smile easing onto her face, too. "Did he really sound like that?" she asked in a small voice.

"Did who sound like what?" Hardrock said, scratching his curly hair in confusion.

"Pallafox," she replied softly, looking up at him over the rim of her glass. "Did he sound as if he still loved me?"

"Does a steer have horns?" Hardrock asked.

Before the sixth game, a night game, the dugout in the Golds' Coliseum was cool, its weathered brown bench still damp from a late afternoon downpour. Up the steps, beyond the gravel warning track, the black Golds were getting last night's dope bleached out of their bloodstreams, the white Golds, last night's booze. The Golds were casual, they were loose, hoarding their energy from a sun that still glowed with a fierce intensity as it set.

They were casual, that is, until Artie Gibbons moved in to second base.

Gibbons had been in the outfield, doing extra calisthenics. He was a braggart and a loudmouth, Pallafox was thinking, sitting on the bench in the dugout, but there was no doubting either his dedication or his ability on the field. In the locker room, the blond, golden-boy slugger tended to bully his teammates with the threat of his fists. Outside, on the playing field, he bullied them with his performance.

Gibbons joined the other ballplayers, scooping up balls in the infield, keeping his face sober, keeping his eyes glued to the bat in coach Marv Wilson's hand, a ball in his right. His teammates chattered, laughed every time someone lost his cap chasing a pop fly, or stumbled over a pair of leaden feet, or concentrated more on his tale of last night's sexual conquest than on that ground ball he should have been snatching. But the only time Artie Gibbons spoke was when the public-address system suddenly began blaring the recorded voice of Jerry Vale, singing the national anthem.

"Come on, Jerry," Gibbons yelled brusquely, "cut the shit."

For a moment there was silence. Pallafox couldn't tell if Gibbons was only kidding or if he was irritated. Apparently, his teammates couldn't tell, either. The first baseman was still laughing when Gibbons dove for a ground ball, then unleashed a throw that nearly ripped the first baseman's glove off.

After that, the Golds kept up their banter, but now with rivulets of perspiration trickling down their necks. Their World Series fever had conquered their worldly cynicism.

Pallafox got up. He walked back into the clubhouse. The trainer, Joey Idella, was on the telephone, talking to some woman, Pallafox could tell. Idella knew much more about women than medicine anyway. Short, wiry-haired, Idella performed more effectively as a part-time pimp than as a healer of sore muscles. On the road, ballplayers would spot an attractive woman in the lobby of a hotel, say, or in a restaurant. Idella would be called over. He would be pointed at the target, then let loose. He would walk up to the young lady, tell her bluntly that so-and-so of the Oakland Golds wanted to meet her. More often than any outsider could have imagined, the approach paid off in an assignation that ended in bed. As for treating his ballplayers' aches and pains, Idella had a simple formula. "If you can lift your arm above your shoulder," he had once told Pallafox, "you ain't hurtin' bad enough to go on the disabled list."

Of course, Idella had never been a fan of his. Pallafox almost never made use of his very special salesmanship. That meant he was never in Idella's debt, paying off in free tickets or a superfluous screw. Pallafox had learned his lesson early in the season. Idella had brought a girl to his hotel room who was "just creamin' to meet you, Jimmy." Without any preliminaries, the girl had dropped to her knees, clawing at the zipper of his fly. Meanwhile, a few of his teammates continued playing cards at a coffee table not five feet away. Palla-

fox had rejected all such human sacrifices after that, pre-
ferring to meet women on his own, preferably women
who had nothing to do with baseball—women, in fact,
who held attitudes toward athletes much like Norma's.

The noise of his teammates, their spikes clattering
against the cool, concrete floor of the access tunnel
from the dugout, interrupted his thoughts. They came
in, grim-faced and sweating. This "kangaroo court"
wouldn't be one of those brash, boisterous affairs, he
thought. Although the purpose would still be to let off
steam, the kidding would undoubtedly be replaced by
controversy. Spider was dead; the heavily favored Golds
were facing elimination today; and he, their bright hope
for victory, had pitched like a novice, so far. The Golds'
pride was at stake. And, even more important, their
winners' shares.

Artie Gibbons was the last to enter the locker room.

"Hey," someone called out, "everyone's here. Let's
get this kangaroo court jive *on*."

"And here," called out another black ballplayer,
"come de judge!"

Willie Richardson strode to the center of the locker
room, smirking. The other Golds all pulled their stools
up in front of their lockers. "This court," Willie called
out, brandishing a battered brown gavel, which he proceeded to rap against the wall a couple of times, "is now
in session."

The kangaroo court had been something that had appalled Pallafox when he'd first joined the Golds at the
beginning of the season. He had been astonished to find
grown men playing what he considered a silly game,
meting out minor punishments, by a consensus of raised
hands, for piddling infractions. But as the season pro-
gressed, he had begun to realize its importance to the
morale of the ball club, especially to a club like the
Golds, whose members were better known for their fist-
fights than their friendships, whose only unifying forces
were a love for money and a hatred of their owner.
Periodically, when tensions were running the highest,
Oswalski would call the court into session. Anyone
could voice any grievance he had about a teammate. By

a show of hands, the defendant's guilt or innocence was decided. The judge, Willie Richardson, then devised some punishment to fit the crime.

"The first case on our agenda," Willie intoned, "is about Big Dog. Stand up, brother," Willie added, waving his gavel at the Golds' shortstop, Hector "Big Dog" Garcia.

"What did I do?" Garcia complained in his fractured English. "I don' do nothin' wrong this time."

"That bunt you laid down in the third inning yesterday," Willie said. "You popped that damn thing up, then didn't even bother to run it out."

"Maybe he was tired from the night before," someone called out. "Maybe Big Dog was doggin' it 'cause he'd overused his dog on that broad he picked up Sunday night."

Everyone broke out laughing. Although sportswriters usually provided the fans with an explanation of each player's nickname that bespoke of some talent at hitting or fielding, in fact almost every player's nickname had some sexual connotation. Hector Garcia had been awarded the title of Big Dog the first time the players had seen him step naked into the shower.

"Okay," Willie said, rapping the wall for order, "what's the verdict on ol' Big Dog doggin' it? How many say 'guilty'?" Every hand but one shot up in the air. "How many say innocent?" Only Garcia's hand was raised. "The verdict is guilty," Willie announced, rapping his gavel importantly. "This court sentences you to five extra laps at practice tomorrow."

"Hey, judge, how you like to get a piece of that broad that keep me awake all night?" Garcia called out.

"Make that three laps," Willie amended quickly, causing more laughter to bellow through the locker room.

Willie quieted them down, then said, "Next case on the agenda. Artie Gibbons here accuses Jim Pallafox of calling him a loudmouth and a braggart, and of threatening his life and limb in front of his teammates, at the start of a World Series they know they just gotta win to pay their taxman."

The room grew suddenly quiet.

"What you got to say for yourself, Pallafox?" Willie said.

Pallafox felt every eye turn toward him. He knew his argument with Gibbons wasn't the issue. His losing was the issue, when they had all depended on him to win. "I'm willing to apologize," he said carefully, "if Artie is, too."

Willie turned toward Gibbons.

"To hell with him," Gibbons spat, tousling his blond hair, shrugging his broad shoulders, in irritation. "I don't apologize to chicken shit."

Willie's face became a mask. "Now, what's that supposed to mean?" he asked.

"I mean the fucker don't want to win, that's what I mean," Gibbons replied evenly, his eyes boring into Pallafox's. "Don't ask me, ask Marcus Hayes over there. Ask him what kind of shit Pallafox has been throwin'."

"I've been throwing by the book," Pallafox called out.

"Yeh," Gibbons yelled back, "by the book, all right. Except that book the scouts compiled ain't supposed to be for you to pitch to their goddamned strengths, but to their goddamned weaknesses!"

"You mean, brother," Willie said quietly, "that you are accusing Pallafox here of *trying* to lose?"

"Ask Marcus, ask him what he thinks," Gibbons roared back.

Willie turned to the veteran black catcher. "What say, man?" he asked.

Hayes glanced at Willie, then at Gibbons, then, finally, at Pallafox. He cleared his throat—he was the Golds' quietest ballplayer, a man known for his actions, not his words. "Pallafox has made some mistakes," he replied.

"That ain't what I asked you, man," Gibbons said. "What I was askin' is do you think Pallafox is *tryin'* to make mistakes?"

Hayes opened his mouth to answer, but Willie cut him off. "Hey, man," he said fiercely, "next thing, you're gonna be telling the world I was trying to lose when I dropped that pop-up in center field in that first game, the one that scored the game winner. Is that where you're heading? Huh? Y'know, I think you just don't dig Pallafox. I think you just don't dig him 'cause he digs *us,* see?"

There was no mistaking who Willie's "us" referred to. Pallafox could see the scowls forming on every black ballplayer's face.

"Okay, that's it," Danny Oswalski called out. He had been standing at the back of the room, his arms folded across his chest. Now he lumbered forward, his portly frame quaking with rage. "I should have known this fucking thing wasn't going to work. I shoulda known you crapheads were too keyed up, too crazy in your heads to let off a little steam without blowing your boilers completely. Get out on that playing field. Get your asses out there, and play the goddamned game," he screamed, "instead of sitting in here and accusing each other like a bunch of goddamn spoiled prima donnas!"

The ballplayers turned away. The kangaroo court broke up into two- or three-man cells, discussing the accusations and counter accusations. After a few minutes, though, there was no one left in the room except Jim Pallafox—and Artie Gibbons. Gibbons picked up his extra pair of spikes. He strode past Pallafox, who kept his eyes firmly set on his locker. "I'm gonna be watchin' you next time," Gibbons said as he passed, "I'm gonna remember every fuckin' pitch you throw."

Hardrock Harrison was sitting at his desk. His office at the police precinct in central San Francisco was merely a cubicle, about ten feet by twelve, with a glass partition separating it from the main hall and the front desk beyond. It was an office befitting an official of much less stature—a lieutenant, perhaps, or even a sergeant. And, in fact, Hardrock could have been sitting instead in one of those plush offices down the hall, with a glossy desk with a Formica top, a leather swiveler, a coffee table, a couch—even a thick carpet that could make you feel you were walking on air. But he preferred the metal desk, the hard-backed chair instead. He called the plush offices down the hall "the reserved grandstand," and told anyone who asked he felt more comfortable "here, in the bleachers." As for thick, pile carpeting, Hardrock would inevitably point toward his lino, and say, "I'm not Jesus Christ, so I damn well don't expect to feel like I'm walking on water. To hell with the carpet. I'll take this instead."

Outside his glass partition, there was a flurry of activity. Two suspects in a bank holdup were being booked, while the news media fought for the best angles to film and interview them. Normally, such a commotion would have brought Hardrock out and running, rubbing his hands together and calling, "Hey, don't ask 'em if they can place bail, ask them if they can play *ball*." In the spare time he had left after police work and scouting for the Golds', Hardrock superintended the prison league at the state penitentiary.

But this evening, he didn't even look up. He kept staring at the paperback book he held in his hands, flipping pages rapidly, as he skimmed over the details of Wally O. Kelly's life. He did, however, keep one ear cocked toward the radio resting behind him on a bookshelf. The play-by-play account of the sixth game of the World Series.

"You wanted to see us?"

Hardrock looked up over his book. He lifted his reading glasses up onto his forehead. "Why, yes, I did," he said, shaking Jenny's hand first, then Rick's. "I thank you for comin' down to see me, when we all want to be out there at the ball park instead."

He motioned Rick and Jenny onto two hard-backed chairs.

"What's the score?" Rick asked, nodding toward the radio.

"One to zip," Hardrock replied. "New York."

"And the inning?" Jenny asked.

"Bottom of the third," Hardrock said. Then he removed his reading glasses from his forehead, placed them in a worn plastic case, and said, "The reason I asked you people to come down here is 'cause I got some news about Kathy. I really should be tellin' Jimmy himself, but, what with him maybe havin' to pitch tomorrow, if it goes to seven games, I thought I should ask your opinion first. How he might take it, and all."

Hardrock then proceeded to tell them what he had learned from Norma. How Kathy was being guarded by a professional killer named Karl Hauptman, nicknamed "Kamikaze Karl." How Kathy had been converted, literally, into a walking bomb. How Karl had been instructed to blow the child up, at the stadium, should there be a seventh game, and should Pallafox pitch and win.

Rick and Jenny were horrified. After hearing the terrifying details, they both agreed that Pallafox should be kept in the dark till the last possible moment. "The guy is nearing the breaking point already," Rick said. "This might just nudge him over the edge."

"And what about Norma Windsor?" Jenny asked.

"She's a tough lady," Hardrock replied, "just as tough a competitor as Jimmy. She's still out there, tryin' to keep track, if she can, of Karl's movements with the little girl. Harry Walters never thought it was gonna go this far, apparently. He never believed they would put the kid up as a time bomb or nothin', so he's kind of on her side, though he's scared as hell. Besides," he added, coughing a couple of times into his large hand in embarrassment, "that's another reason for keepin' Jimmy out of it for a while longer. You see," he added, "the only way Norma can stay on the right side of Harry is to keep sleepin' with him."

"Good God," Jenny said. "That's awful."

"She's a mother," Hardrock replied, compassion in his voice. "It wouldn't be the first time a mother's sacrificed herself for her child."

Then he pulled out his reading glasses, slid them onto the bridge of his nose. He picked up his book and began reading again.

Rick and Jenny looked at each other in astonishment.

"But aren't you going to *do* something?" Rick asked.

Hardrock looked up over his book. "I am doin' somethin', son," he replied, "somethin' very difficult for me. Tryin' to read this book and listen to the ball game at the same time."

"He means something else, some kind of action," Jenny said, exasperation slowly coloring her voice. "You just can't let that maniac wander around the country, with Kathy wired up to him, and his hand on a detonator!"

"Look, miss," he replied finally. "The Patriots came into the game tonight ahead, three games to two. If they win tonight, the Series is over. The guys behind this will have collected their money. We'll have time to figure out how to deal with Karl. If the Golds win, well, the Series goes on to the seventh game tomorrow. Now, at this point, I can't stop the Patriots or Golds from winnin' today, but I sure as hell can make sure no one goes out to intentionally lose tomorrow.

"We've got Karl in our sights right now," he added, "but if we try to take him, he'll blow the kid up. If New York wins, I'm pretty sure he'll hand her over to us. He doesn't know any of the higher-ups. It's just a job to Karl. Either way, whether he blows himself up, or gives himself up, it don't matter to Karl.

"Besides," he continued, "who's gonna prove, if the Patriots win tonight, that there ever was an attempt to fix the Series? Sure, there was a note. The kid was kidnapped. But who's gonna prove Norma didn't do it just to get custody of the daughter? Look at it this way," he added. "There's been five games played up till today. Jimmy says he was tryin' to lose the first and fourth, but the first was decided by Willie Richardson's error in center field, and in the fourth, Wally Kelly—out of sheer damn mulishness—left Pallafox in long after he should have been taken out.

"No," he added firmly, "there's nothin' we can do till we find out who wins tonight. That'll determine where we go from here."

"What's that you're reading?" Rick asked, still unable to believe Harrison could be sitting here, reading a paperback, while a little girl was walking around wired to a madman and the World Series was in the process of being fixed.

"It's one of these here quickie biographies, about the life of Wally Kelly—how he made his money, some of the crazy stunts he pulled off—things like that."

"Why are you reading about Wally Kelly?" Jenny said angrily, barely able to conceal her impatience anymore.

"Well," Hardrock replied, "it's obvious that Wally was supposed to be the fall guy in this here caper. I want to see if maybe I can come up with somethin' about him I can use—some way to use him, if I have to."

"You have us completely baffled," Rick said. "I just don't know what the hell you're planning to do about all this."

"Me neither," Hardrock replied, with a smile. "Y'see, I gotta prevent the fix from happening. If there is a seventh game, and the Golds lose, there'll be a payoff even if we can get to Karl and the little girl afterward. And if we blow the whistle on the fix beforehand, Karl blows up the little girl, I'm sure of that."

"He's really crazy enough to blow himself up, too?" Jenny asked, incredulously.

"That's why they call him 'Kamikaze Karl,' " Harrison replied. "He's about the craziest, and loyalest som'-bitch in his business. And his business," Hardrock added, "is killing folks for cash, on contract.

"But besides preventin' the fix," Hardrock continued, talking more to himself now than to Rick and Jenny, "I gotta get the kid away from Karl. And my best chance is when we've got him fenced in and sitting tight—right there during a game—that seventh game, if there is one. The only thing is, I haven't been able to figure out how, without risking little Kathy's life.

"You see," he added, still thinking aloud, using Rick and Jenny as sounding boards, "getting to little Kathy at the ball park is a two-part problem, too. First, I would have to figure out a way to clear the immediate area around Karl, without making him suspicious. There have to be people in the seats around him—or else he'd smell a trap. And those people can't be police—he'd spot them a mile away. In fact, I figure if there is a

seventh game, he'll show up a little late. He'll want to
see who's sittin' in the neighborhood of Harry's seats.

"Second, I would have to find a way to distract Karl.
I would have to find a way to get his hand out of his
pocket, off that detonator."

Rick was about to ask a question, when suddenly
Hardrock held his index finger to his lips, indicating silence. He cocked his ear toward the radio. The Golds,
losing one to nothing for six innings, were rallying.

"They got two on base, first and third, and one out,"
Hardrock said. "Now, my guess is the New York
pitcher, Colon, is gonna walk Artie Gibbons, to load
'em up. The Golds' next hitter is Garcia. He's got a little muscle pull, and they'll figure he can't run too fast,
so they got a good chance of doublin' him up."

The play-by-play proved Hardrock a minor prophet.
Artie Gibbons received an intentional walk, loading the
bases.

"There goes the Oakland big chance, out the window," Rick said glumly. "Garcia can't run, and he
doesn't have much power. The Golds are going to have
to get real lucky to get a run out of this inning."

"Don't be too sure of that, son," Hardrock replied,
turning to face the radio, watching it as if it were a television. In fact, Rick realized, Hardrock *was* seeing the
game. He had seen so many over his lifetime he could
visualize every detail just as surely as if he were sitting
right now in the Oakland Coliseum. "Y'see, they're
overshifting to the right. That gives Garcia one big
chance."

"But he's a lefty," Rick countered. "He always hits to
right field."

"That's cause Hector has a real quick bat. He gets
around on the ball real fast. But I saw him down in the
minors ten or eleven times before he came up to the big
leagues. He can go to the opposite field if he wants to,
right down that big hole they're gonna leave down the
third-base line."

"But he never wants to go the opposite way," Rick
argued, as the play-by-play announcer reported, over

the crowd's noisy roaring, that Garcia had taken the first pitch for a strike.

"He never *has to* go the opposite way," Hardrock countered. "He's got good line-drive power to right. But I think he's gonna try to do it now. It'll stun 'em. If he can put the ball down the third-base line, even with his bum leg, I'll bet you he can get a triple out of it."

Hardrock had hardly finished speaking when they heard the crack of a bat.

"That's it," Hardrock yelled, "he got good wood on that one, all right."

"It's a line drive . . ." the Oakland announcer was shouting, "down the third-base line . . . *fair* . . . one run scores . . . two runs . . . three . . . they're trying to cut off Garcia at third base . . . *safe* . . . Garcia slides in with a triple, and the Golds have taken the lead for the first time, three to one!"

Hardrock leaped up, elated. "I knew it," he yelled, pounding his desk joyfully. "I knew Big Dog was a helluva lot smarter then they give him credit for bein'."

They listened in silence then, as the next two innings passed routinely. Neither side was able to mount an offensive. The Golds' two-run margin proved decisive.

Then, as the Golds' pitcher recorded the final out of the first half of the ninth inning, sealing the victory for Oakland, and ensuring that a seventh game would be played, Hardrock did something that astonished both Rick and Jenny. He folded his hands piously in front of him on his desk. He bowed his head. "I want to thank you, Lord," he said quietly.

"For giving us the chance to get Kathy back for Pallafox, for giving us that seventh game," Rick cut in, winking on the sly to Jenny.

"I want to thank you, Lord," Hardrock continued soberly, as if he hadn't heard Rick, "both for givin' us the chance to get back Jimmy's little girl—and," he added, "for makin' the Golds come up with three runs today."

Rick looked at Jenny. He shook his head helplessly. "What, if I may ask," he said to Hardrock, "is the significance of 'three runs'?"

Hardrock looked up at them. A broad smile creased his fleshy, weather-beaten face. "Why, three is my lucky number," he replied. "Always has been." He opened a desk drawer. He got up from his desk and brought a slip of paper first to Rick, then to Jenny. "See," he said, "I got together this little precinct betting pool for the Series," waving the mimeographed sheet in front of their faces. "I got the Golds in seven games," he added, "but more important right now, I got the Golds for three runs today." He slapped his thick right thigh. He began to whoop, to holler. "Wahoo," Hardrock yelled, causing heads to turn out by the booking desk, "this old cowboy has made it to the *finals*."

11

Rick rolled over in his bed, in his room at the San Francisco Shelby Hotel, and hid his head under the pillow. Already the sun was filtering through the thin curtains, stabbing at his eyes, forcing his mind—still full of half-dreams and exotic fancies—to face the dawning of a new, and very special, day.

Without opening his eyes, he pulled at the pillow. It wouldn't budge. He jerked his body around—and felt the contours of another body. Then he remembered. He sat up. The World Series wasn't the only thing special about today. He was staring at Jenny, sleeping, her knees curled up against her chest, her brown hair tumbling over her cheek; Jenny, lying there beside him in his bed. Just then, in her sleep, she sighed. Her hand slid over the blanket to find his, resting on his palm as fragile and tentative as a butterfly alighting on a flower. She stopped sighing, her breathing became regular again. The dream crisis had passed.

They had returned to the hotel about six last evening, both exhausted after listening to Hardrock Harrison explore his alternatives for saving Kathy, while a radio spun a tale of the Golds' sixth-game victory, leading to the seventh and decisive game today. They had eaten dinner at the hotel—their last dinner together in San Francisco. Tomorrow, whether the Golds won or lost, they would be returning to New York, Jenny to her routine as managing editor of *Action Sports,* Rick to his rounds as a free-lance writer—assignments for various magazines, a book that he was writing and which was already overdue at his publishers. Rick had suggested to her that, for once, they splurge, and dine at the hotel's elegant Paris Room. "Phil Hanson can afford it," he had said, when what he had really wanted to say was: Let's give ourselves a dinner to remember us by. Neither one dared to voice the opinion, but both suspected that after they returned to New York, they would, as a matter of course, slip into their old roles, their old relationship. He would be the ex-managing editor, who had given her her start in the business. She would be his grateful protégée. The closeness they had come to feel for each other would turn out, in retrospect, to be a proof of the World Series' fleeting power to transform its participants' lives—but only for as long as the Series lasted.

So they had dined on lobster thermidor, choosing from the menu like spoiled kids—by the price list only. Rick had used the same tactic on the wine list, settling at last for a bottle of Dom Perignon. They had talked about Pallafox, and Kelly, and Hardrock Harrison—and about the seventh game, which had now become a matter of life and death. There was only one subject which they studiously avoided. Themselves.

Afterward, heady with champagne, they had walked through the lobby, crowded with men and women too fired up by the prospect of a seventh game to spend their last evening in San Francisco doing anything but talking about the Series. In the elevator, they had kept on talking, pretending that they weren't aware that their fingers were entangled. Rick had escorted her to her room. He kissed her, hurriedly, as if his lips lingering too long on hers might spark a fire in him he wouldn't be able to extinguish. Then he went to his own room. He changed. He tried watching television. He shut off the TV, stripped to his underwear, and lay on the bed, waiting for sleep to come.

An hour, perhaps two hours later, there was a knock on his door. He slipped into his robe, he turned on the lights. He opened the door and saw Jenny.

"Did I wake you?" she said, trying to hide her embarrassment behind a bouncy kind of bravado.

"No, I was just lying down, thinking," he said, ushering her in and closing the door. She was wearing faded jeans and a sweat shirt. He realized that he had never

seen her before in anything that didn't look as if it had
just come from Bloomingdales.

"I couldn't sleep," she said. "I haven't been able to
sleep much at all," she added, "since what happened
. . ." Her voice died to a whisper.

"Since . . . what happened at Pallafox's house, with
that phony Spider," he said. "I should have known," he
added. "I should have known that you were putting up a
front. I should have known the hurt would last longer
than that moment."

She sat down on a chair. She hid her head in her
hands.

Rick felt his mouth go dry. He felt tears collecting in
his eyes. He took her in his arms. "I love you," he said.

Then they had kissed.

Then they had made love.

The early afternoon was crisp and clear. The sky was
an endless blue lake, the sun a golden island. "It's a
damn good day for baseball, I'll tell you that," Hardrock Harrison was telling Rick, as they stood outside
the NBC tent, watching late stragglers scurry from the
parking lot, anxious to reach their seats before the pregame ceremonies started.

They had been waiting there for an hour already,
watching thousands of cars converge in a monumental
traffic jam, as far as the eye could see, and hundreds of
buses emptying tens of hundreds of passengers. San
Francisco had already seemed strangely deserted when
Rick had left the hotel that morning. It was more like a
Sunday than a Thursday. And in truth, the men,
women, and children marching shoulder to shoulder
down the broad concrete walks that led to the entrance
gates had resembled churchgoers more than sports fans.
Their bright, polished faces were already ecstatic in anticipation: their gods had descended from Olympus; the
conflict between Good and Evil would be resolved today, in this ultimate sporting event, in this open-air ca-
thedral.

"That's him," Hardrock said suddenly, gripping the
sleeve of Rick's jean jacket.

Rick followed Hardrock's gaze. He saw a massive man strolling toward them, a man who wore a homburg and a conservative pin-striped suit. "That must be Kathy," he exclaimed. A little girl with fiery red hair toddled along by the side of the man with the homburg hat. In her left hand, she held an ice-cream cone, melting fast in the brilliant sun. Her right hand was embedded in the man's huge left paw. His right hand was buried deep in the pocket of his pin-striped trousers.

"That's him, all right," Hardrock said. "That, my friend, is Kamikaze Karl."

"Where are your people?" Rick hissed. "Why don't they take him?"

"My people are all around," Hardrock replied, "and not just my people, but FBI people. A whole squad of them flew in this mornin' from Washington. Bomb experts, a hostage unit—the damn works."

"Well, why don't they *do* something?" Rick said, a plea that bordered on begging.

"They are doin' somethin'," Hardrock replied casually. "They're doin' what I told 'em to do, which, at this point in time, is absolutely nothin'."

Hardrock turned on his heels and entered the NBC tent. Rick followed reluctantly. All morning he had been trying to lure Hardrock away from the buffet tables, into the stadium. Wally Kelly had arranged for Hardrock to sit with Jenny and Rick up in the press box, a vantage point from which Hardrock could orchestrate whatever plan it was he had formulated. But now, watching Hardrock attack the buffet table with gusto, Rick's confidence in him was dissolving even more rapidly. He was in full regalia today—a Stetson hat, rawhide boots, a string tie. He seemed out of place among the champagne glasses, the pâté—the sleek women with hair piled up on their heads, the fashionably attired men whom the women were clinging to. It was impossible to believe that, however clever this old cowboy was at solving burglaries, however shrewd this old pitcher's insights were when it came to collaring bank robbers—he could come up with a scheme that would foil the best efforts of the big-time criminals who were, effectively, holding the World Series as a hostage.

"Well, seems I was right, not putting my men in the seats around Karl," Hardrock was saying, as he snapped open a can of beer and poured it down his throat. "Karl did come late—to check on who was in those seats nearby."

"You'll send your own men into the seats around Karl when the game begins," Rick said.

"No way," Hardrock replied. "Son, I had a pet mule once, back on the farm in Texas. He'd kick out with those hind legs of his every time you tried to hitch him up to somethin', but he was meek as a lamb when it came to feedin' time. What I mean is, Karl is crazy, but that doesn't mean he's dumb. I got to get my people in there without him realizing they're there, just like I had to sneak up behind that mule when he was eatin' every time I wanted to hitch him up. For a while," he added, sampling a tray of French pastries, "he's gonna be surrounded by just regular folks."

"But aren't you going to do *anything?*" Rick repeated.

"I already did," Hardrock replied, pulling out the book he had been reading in his office yesterday—the paperback biography of Wally Kelly. "I talked to Kelly, that's what I did. And I talked to Pallafox, too. I didn't need a book on Pallafox, thank the Lord," he added, " 'cause I know him as well as I know my own son, maybe better."

"You talked to Kelly and Pallafox about that book?" Rick asked incredulously.

"Here, son, try some of this stuff—what do they call it?" Hardrock said, deliberately changing the subject.

"Caviar," Rick replied, glumly.

"Not bad," Harrison said, licking his fingertips. "I've been tempted to try this stuff hundreds of times, but you know, I never quite had the guts to ask what it's made of. I'm a steak man myself," he added, "and this is some kind of freshwater fish, right?"

"Fish eggs," Rick said. "Raw fish eggs."

Hardrock's face turned white. He spit the caviar out

into a paper napkin. "I'd rather swallow chawin' to-
bacco," he announced.

The atmosphere in the Golds' locker room was thick
with tension. No tape recorders blaring funky soul music, no disco beat pounding off the walls like palpitating
hearts. The portable hair dryers weren't humming. The
Oakland Golds weren't bantering about women, or
bitching about the owner. The only sound was the creak
of locker doors, the clatter of metal spikes across the
locker room floor, the hollow echo of bats being tested
for hidden cracks. And when someone did break the
silence, it was to utter something blunt and professional.
"Remember the shadows," Oswalski was telling Pallafox. "After about four, five innings, when the sun starts
gettin' lower, there's gonna be a shadow over the batter's box. Once the batter's box is covered in the shade,
you can forget about your breakin' pitches. Just go with
your fastball. They'll lose it about five feet in front of
the plate, when it passes into the shadow."

Pallafox nodded. He bent down, and resumed lacing
his shoes. The whole scene reminded him of a movie
he'd seen recently on TV. A squadron of Marines, in
Korea, grim-faced and grimy, being sent out on a patrol. A patrol they knew they'd never survive. His teammates' faces looked like that—condemned men, sus-
pecting they were staring at defeat, but determined to
go down like professionals.

No one outside of Oswalski had spoken to him today.
But he knew he was on every ballplayer's mind. A little
while ago, while he was in the trainer's room soaking
his left elbow, he had overheard a snatch of conversation between Willie Richardson and Artie Gibbons. "I
was counting on that play-off money for a big trip to
gay Paree this winter," Willie was saying. "But looks
like it's gonna be beans and bacon instead. I've already
kissed that play-off money good-bye, man."

"The Sphinx don't have it here," he heard Gibbons
reply, punctuating his sentence with a loud thump. Pallafox recognized the sound. Gibbons was pounding his
chest—to say the pitcher lacked "heart," lacked guts.

He waited to hear if Willie would defend him. He didn't have to wait long.

"We're gonna have to call the Sphinx the Jinx if the man cops out in this game, too," Willie commented.

He couldn't blame them, he thought, kicking his heels down onto the concrete floor to settle his feet into the shoes. Later, maybe, they would change their minds, but right now they had no alternative but to judge him a quitter, or—even worse—a coward. Today would be the final proof. He would lose. He would lose, to gain a daughter, at the risk of his reputation. To hell with them, anyway, he decided. Kathy was worth a hundred Cy Young awards.

And then the thought that he had censored all morning crept back into his consciousness. Maybe Hardrock's plan would work, after all. Maybe it was just crazy enough to catch that killer off guard. He knew that, before every pitch he threw, before every sign he took from Marcus Hayes, he would be looking up at the press box, waiting for that sign from Hardrock Harrison. The signal for him to throw the most important pitch of his entire life.

"Hey, Pallafox," someone called out. "You got a visitor."

Pallafox looked up. It was that editor from *Action Sports,* Jenny Cohn. He hadn't seen her since the incident at his house, the phony rape by the phony Spider. And he didn't want to see her now, just because she reminded him that Spider was gone, that, at some level, he felt responsible for Spider's death.

He waved her away, shaking his head no; he didn't want to talk to anyone right now. "I have to see you," she called out across the locker room.

"Hey," someone called out. "I thought no female press was supposed to be in here while we're dressing. Get her out, huh?"

"You have to go," he called out to Jenny.

"I'm not going anywhere," she called back, stubbornly.

"Hey," the same ballplayer who had complained initially cried again, "somebody get this broad out of this locker room, will ya?"

Pallafox could see an argument brewing. With feelings running high anyway, it wouldn't take much of an excuse to turn this incident into an ugly confrontation. He got up and went over to Jenny. "Look, I don't want to talk to anyone right now," he said. "Will you please leave?"

"Someone's waiting outside to see you," Jenny said quietly.

"You've got Kathy?" he said quickly.

"No, they haven't recovered your daughter," she replied. "It's someone else, someone I think you should talk to. It might help."

Pallafox shrugged his shoulders. "Okay," he said, "but let's make it fast."

Jenny opened the door. Pallafox stepped out into the narrow hallway between the locker room and the outside corridor. Jenny kept right on going, past him, out the door, leaving him alone, facing Norma.

She looked different. She wasn't wearing any makeup, and her face looked paler than he had ever seen it. She was wearing a loose blouse, though, which he found instantly familiar.

They stared at each other for another long moment. Then Norma said, "Maybe I'll let my hair grow long again."

"Maybe," he said, "I'll go to law school in the off-season."

They didn't say anything else. They just embraced, and clung to each other for a very long time.

Jim Pallafox reared back on the mound and threw the first pitch of the seventh game of the World Series. When the home-plate umpire's arm shot up, signaling a strike, the crowd exploded as if Pallafox had just struck out the final Patriot batter of the contest.

The tension today was contagious. No quarter of the ball park could be quarantined against it. Even the press box was quiet today. The teletype machines were chattering, but not the journalists. They had dropped their pose of neutrality. The New York reporters were rooting for the Patriots shamelessly. The press from Oakland was just as fanatic in their support and encouragement for their Golds. Only Rick and Hardrock were strangely silent, although no less attentive than the others. Hardrock was staring at the field through a pair of binoculars.

"There they are," he said to Rick, passing him the binoculars, and pointing to a spot down below. "Right behind first base, the first row, directly in back of the Golds' dugout."

Rick saw them—the broad-backed man wearing the homburg, the little girl with red hair sitting quietly beside him. Harrison took the binoculars back and jammed them in front of his eyes again—just as Karl stood up, pulling the little girl up with him. He turned halfway around to hail a hot dog vendor. Rick watched him purchasing the hot dog, handing it to the little girl.

"That's it," Hardrock exclaimed under his breath. "I was hopin' we could check somehow. He still has the detonator in his right pocket, the way he did before. He took change out of his left pocket. He paid with his left hand. He kept his right hand in his pocket all the time."

By the start of the fourth inning, Norma was almost beside herself with worry. She and Jenny were sitting side by side, ten rows back from her daughter—ten rows, she was thinking, that might as well have been ten thousand miles, for all the help she could give, for all the good she could do. All through these early innings, she had been torn between the sight of Pallafox on the mound—almost effortlessly conning the Patriot hitters into swinging at pitches that were too high or too low, inside or outside, or simply too fast even for their finely honed reflexes—and the knowledge that Kathy was there, almost within arm's reach, her fate in the hands of that menacing man in the homburg, whose capacity for violence no one knew better than she herself. "What are the police waiting for?" she said to Jenny again and again. "Why don't they rescue my baby?"

"Have faith in Hardrock," Jenny said soothingly. "He has some kind of plan. I know it will work." In fact, she thought, she could sound so convincing because she herself did believe in him. Rick thought Hardrock was out of his league—he couldn't believe in someone who drawled out homespun homilies all day, who lacked that New York polish they had come to associate with success. But Jenny had begun to regard Hardrock differently. She had gained that respect during their meeting in his office, during the sixth game, yesterday. The detective might not seem very sophisticated, surely not the kind of smooth-talking tactician she had grown accustomed to seeing in movies and on television. One thing had impressed her, though—his prophetic description, when the Golds had two runners on base, with one out, of exactly how Big Dog Garcia would outwit the Patriots. Hardrock had even predicted that Garcia would end up with a triple. Garcia had. And the Golds had won the game. Perhaps she had been grasping at straws, but it had occurred to her afterward that underneath his country airs, the man had a keen nose for strategy. Furthermore, he knew more about the game of baseball than anyone she had ever met in her life. Was it possible for him to put the two together? Could he come up with a plan to rescue Kathy that made use of the one area in which he was undoubtedly more expert than the men who had planned the girl's kidnapping—his shrewd instinct for the potentialities of baseball? His insight into the value of a surprise move that might stun a smug opponent?

"Why don't they *do* something?" Norma pleaded, her knuckles white, her eyes red.

It was the bottom of the fourth inning now, with the top of the Golds batting order due to face Gary Humboldt, the Patriots' only twenty-game winner. It was Humboldt who should have pitched the first game of the Series, against Pallafox. But he had missed that game and his second turn, the fourth game, due to soreness in his ankle. A few days of rest had cured that minor ailment, and the right-hander was pitching today with the fire and finesse that had made him the American League's prime candidate for the Cy Young Award, for best pitcher this season.

Big Dog Garcia was the first hitter. He stepped into the batter's box. He was going to swing at the first pitch, no matter what. Humboldt had shown, over these first few innings, a tendency to lay in a fastball over the plate on his first throw to each batter, figuring the hitter would be under instructions to take the first pitch. Humboldt took his windup, he threw—Garcia got his fastball. He pulled it down the right-field line. By the time the Patriot right fielder had chased down the ball and uncorked his throw, Garcia was limping into second base, with a stand-up double.

The Oakland crowd, beset with so much frustration this Series—having watched their heavily favored Golds laboring to earn a split in the first six games—began to bellow a frenzied encouragement. And none was more vociferous or energetic than the Golds' owner himself. On Hardrock Harrison's instructions, Wally Kelly had abandoned his plush suite perched atop the stadium. He was sitting along the first-base line, near one end of the Golds' dugout, no more than fifteen or twenty seats away from the killer and his tiny captive. Beside him, looking uncomfortable, was Harry Walters. He was nervously twisting his large diamond ring, and saying, "I don't know what you're hinting at, Wally."

The beetle-browed Golds' owner leaned over to Walters. "I'm not hinting at anything, Harry," he said coolly. "I was just pointing out that now you know who got those tickets you claim were stolen out of your wallet the other day." Kelly nodded toward the man in the homburg and the little girl with the fiery red hair.

"Whoever ripped them off me must have sold them to the guy," Harry said, his voice now becoming as agitated as his hands. "And I still don't see why your owner's suite wasn't available today. I don't see why we had to come down here."

Wally grinned wickedly. "I told you, Harry," he said. "I got taken the way you did. Someone must have picked my pocket, because my key was gone. Security insisted we abandon the suite until they can change the lock. After all," he added, "we don't want the hoi polloi invading our sanctum of privilege, do we?"

At that moment, Willie Richardson, the second Golds' hitter of the inning, smacked a long ball that went foul of the left-field flagpole by inches. Wally stood up, a noisemaker in one hand, a Golds' pennant in the other. He began waving the pennant, flailing the noisemaker. "Give it to 'em, Willie," he was shouting as loud as he could. Out of the corner of his eye, he saw that thousands of other eyes in the stadium were upon him, including the all-seeing eyes of the handheld TV cameras wielded by technicians down on the field, near the Golds' dugout.

"You're going out of your way to make sure everyone knows you're here," Harry said, when Kelly sat down again.

"Every dog must have its day, Harry," Kelly replied.

"I like a different one," Harry said, lowering his voice, giving it a razor-sharp edge. "I like, 'dead dogs don't bite.' "

Wally made a reply, but Harry Walters never heard it. Kelly's voice was drowned by the roar of the crowd, as Willie Richardson blasted Gary Humboldt's second pitch into the gap between the left and center fielders. Willie reached second base, sliding in for a double. Big Dog Garcia, by that time, had managed to cross home plate. The Golds were leading, 1–0.

Wally Kelly leaped out of his seat. He pushed past customers. He clambered onto the top of the Golds' dugout. Using his pennant as a baton, he orchestrated the fifty thousand fans packed into the stadium in a chorus of "Go Golds, Go Golds, Go Golds."

Wally was enjoying himself immensely. He had always dreamed of being a star in a World Series. And Hardrock Harrison had chosen a perfect role for him— one he was going to play for all it was worth.

Pallafox held the Patriots hitless again through the fifth and sixth innings. In the bottom of the fifth, Artie Gibbons had touched Humboldt for a towering home run, giving the Golds a 2–0 lead that Pallafox seemed determined to hold—at least till Hardrock indicated otherwise.

"He's faster than all hell today," Rick was telling Hardrock, as they watched Pallafox deliver to the first Patriot batter of the seventh inning. "Do you realize he hasn't given up a hit yet?"

"Hey, cut that out," Ray Fowler called over. "You know that's bad luck, talking about no-hitters in the middle of the game."

Rick was about to reply that it was also bad manners to show superstition in the press box, when the Patriot batter hit a little squibbler back to Pallafox. Attempting to field it, Pallafox fell down, allowing the ball to scoot off his glove, and on through into center field. Willie Richardson picked the ball up and tossed it to second base, holding the runner on first.

"Well, there goes his no-hitter, at least," Ray Fowler chortled gleefully.

"Hey," said the Oakland reporter who was acting as official scorer that day, "that was an error. Any damn fool can see it was an error."

The New York writers began to grumble, but their moaning soon turned to elation when, pitching to the second Patriot hitter of the inning, Pallafox released a fastball that sailed high over the batter's head, permitting the runner on first base to advance to second.

"I suppose that was a base hit, too," the Oakland reporter acting as official scorer chirped.

"Naw, no hit, but we'll take it anyway," Fowler retorted. "Come on, you damn Irish ninny," he began yelling, as Sammy Muldoon stepped into the batter's box. "Get us a couple of goddamn runs!"

Rick had been caught up in the press-box bantering. He was surprised, then, when Harrison grabbed his arm. "Watch this," he whispered, pointing at Wally Kelly, who had left his seat near first base and was already sprinting past them, up the stairs that led to the public-address announcer's booth, another flight higher. Then Hardrock got up and ran out the press-box door, heading for the stairs that would take him down to the field level.

Ignoring the Authorized Personnel Only sign, Wally Kelly stormed into the public-address booth and demanded the microphone.

"Ladies and gentlemen," he told the fifty thousand fans who had turned out for the seventh game, "I suffer with you. It's sloppy errors like the two Pallafox just made that have brought us to this sorry state—a seventh game, when we should have won four straight. We should have blown these Patsies all the way back to New York City," he added, as the cheering turned into a fearsome roar.

At that particular moment, Hardrock Harrison leaped out of the right-field stands, and onto the field of play. He sprinted toward second base like an enraged bull, then veered off into center field, cutting right again like a football halfback dodging some invisible tackler, reaching the right-field barrier again, clambering over it and disappearing into the crowd.

"Get him out of here!" Kelly had begun screaming as soon as Hardrock's feet had touched the playing field. "Get that man!"

Spectators started scrambling over each other's backs, running this way and that, like twenty thousand Keystone Kops, as the emotion of the moment, and Kelly's imperious command, combined to set them off in a fury of senseless activity.

It took nearly twenty minutes before the stadium security guards and the Oakland uniformed police were able to get the crowd under control. By that time, Wally Kelly was back in his box seat near the Oakland dugout. Hardrock Harrison, puffing and panting while he made excuses to the assembled press corps for being in the men's room while all the action was going on, was sitting by Rick's side, his face flushed with exertion, but his eyes twinkling with amusement.

Rick looked down. Kamikaze Karl was still sitting directly behind first base. Little Kathy was still at his side.

"You failed," he said to Hardrock, despair filling his

voice. "You didn't get him. Your plan, whatever it was, didn't work."

"Never meant to get him, or the little girl," Hardrock replied pleasantly. "Look. Don't you notice somethin' different?"

Rick looked at Karl and Kathy again. Suddenly he realized: "Hey, those people all around them. They're not the same ones who were sitting there before."

"Pride of the FBI," said Hardrock. Hardrock lifted up the book he had brought with him that morning, that paperback biography of Wally Kelly. He gave it a big, wet kiss. "Karl never suspected a thing," he said. "Just another one of Wally Kelly's crazy stunts, like burning that bus in the outfield in Cleveland, like throwin' money all around the field before one game, then givin' selected fans ten minutes to scoop up as much as they could." He rapped the book on his knee. "This book is full of crazy stunts like that," he said.

One inning later, in the last half of the eighth, there was complete silence in the press box. Not only were the Golds still winning, 2–0, Jim Pallafox was still pitching feverishly. Karl hadn't made a slip yet. He hadn't taken his hand off that detonator. The agents surrounding him, forced to take every possible precaution, were still helpless. If they weren't able to make a move shortly, Hardrock would have to resort to his last option.

It was the top of the ninth inning now. The score was still 2–0, Golds. Pallafox was still pitching a no-hitter. Karl was still sitting behind first base, his massive torso dwarfing the little girl at his side.

It was as if everyone, as far as the eye could see, had suddenly been struck dumb, Pallafox thought. In the press box, in the lavish Stadium suites, in the grandstands, the bleachers—nearly every spectator in that stadium was edging forward on his chair, watching, with rapt attention, as he walked slowly out to the mound. He was three outs away from winning the World Series. He was three outs away from carving himself a secure niche in the Cooperstown Hall of Fame.

Pallafox reached the mound. He permitted himself to do what he had wanted to do all day. He looked over at first base, past the railing. He saw little Kathy, and felt a fist squeezing his heart. Then, he looked into Karl's face. The man removed his homburg. He tipped it in Pallafox's direction. Pallafox could see that he was laughing.

The press box was so quiet, Rick could hear Hardrock breathing, he could hear his own heart pounding. Pallafox was standing there, on the mound, his cap in his hand, running his other hand through his tousled red hair. Then the first Patriot batter stepped in. Pallafox reared back and sent a fastball whizzing by him for a called strike. Rick glanced over at Hardrock. Hardrock was staring at his stopwatch again, a look of satisfaction on his face. "Still ninety-three miles an hour," he said. "Jimmy hasn't lost a bit of zip."

Pallafox reared back and threw again. Another strike.

Then, suddenly, Hardrock Harrison stood up. He started waving a white handkerchief wildly from side to side in great sweeping arcs.

"Hey, cut out that crap, Hardrock," Fowler began to complain. "Scouts aren't supposed to be up here in the first place. What the hell are you doing? Waving to some broad you got stashed in the bleachers?"

Hardrock didn't answer. He just stood there, staring down at Pallafox, waving his handkerchief, a scowl souring his normally friendly face. Then Pallafox bent down. He began to tie his shoe. Hardrock sighed, in relief. He sat down. He said to Rick, "Signal, and response."

Pallafox was trying hard not to think. He was emptying his mind of everything that was irrelevant, and right now, that included the World Series, and Norma—and even Kathy. He was playing in an entirely different game now, with a new set of rules, ones devised by Hardrock Harrison. The stakes were ultimate. Nothing less than life or death. So, deliberately, he walked that first batter on four consecutive pitches. Then, with one man on, and no outs, in the top of that ninth inning, Gabriel, the American League home-run champion, stepped into the batter's box. Pallafox assumed the stance a left-hander takes when pitching from the stretch position, with a runner on first base. He stood with his back toward the third-base line, facing the runner at first. He whipped his body sideways, and threw his first pitch to Gabriel. Outside and low for a ball.

Marcus Hayes tossed the ball back to him. He shouted a word of encouragement. Pallafox resumed his stretch stance again. He looked at the runner on first, dancing off the base tantalizingly, then he looked at Gabriel—his shoulders hunched, his bat waving slightly behind his head. Pallafox lifted his arms up, holding the ball in his glove, then let them come to rest midway in front of his chest. He wheeled as if to fire toward home plate, but instead, blazed the ball toward first. The Patriot runner had to slide back into the bag headfirst to avoid getting picked off.

Pallafox took the toss back from the first baseman. He assumed his stretch position. Again, instead of pitching the ball toward home plate, he fired toward the base runner leaning off first. Again, the runner had to slide back to avoid being tagged out.

Pallafox straddled the mound again. He looked at Gabriel, then at the runner at first. This time he threw the ball toward home—fooling Gabriel, giving him a lot of motion behind a fat, floating change-of-pace. The Patriot slugger had nearly finished swinging by the time the ball crossed the plate.

One ball, one strike.

Pallafox's next pitch was a slider that sped toward Gabriel knee-high and outside, then suddenly broke across the plate. Gabriel took it for a called strike, making the count 1-and-2.

Pallafox threw over to first base again. And then a second time, before he delivered a pitch to Gabriel that was safely out of the strike zone: 2-and-2.

Again, before he threw his next pitch, Pallafox fired over to first base, sending the runner sprawling into the dirt in an effort to get back to the bag. Then he threw another ball to Gabriel, low and away, bringing the count to 3-and-2.

Now, he thought. Right now, as he straddled the mound and stared at Gabriel. He had established his pick-off move to first base, he had built up, painstakingly, the credibility of that maneuver. Now was the time for the single most important pitch of his life. On its accuracy, on its speed, depended his daughter's very life.

Jim Pallafox straddled the mound, sideways to the batter, facing first base. He could feel fifty thousand pairs of eyes boring into him. He could feel, from somewhere in the stands, Norma's burning desperation, he could feel his own heart pounding.

He raised his arms head high. He lowered them to his chest, with the ball concealed in his glove. He looked at Gabriel, then toward the runner at first base, then toward Gabriel again. Then he swung his right leg high in the air—but instead of pitching the ball toward the batter, he swiveled toward first base, as he had done so many times already this inning. But this time, instead of thudding against the first baseman's glove, the ball streaked by his shoulder—flying at ninety-three miles per hour, flying seventy-five feet, on a beeline toward Kamikaze Karl, seated behind the first-base bag in the first row of box seats.

For four-tenths of a second, the ball was a white flash of light, growing larger and larger in Karl's eyes, as instinctively, he raised both hands in front of his face, attempting to protect himself against the missile hurtling toward him. . . .

The moment he pulled his right hand out of his pocket, raising it to ward off the ball screaming toward his face, the agents Hardrock had planted all around him leaped from their seats. Scores of them pounced on the man with the homburg hat. They immobilized him. They gingerly removed the detonator from his pocket. They dismantled the wires leading to the little girl with the red hair. By the time the agents were leading Karl, with his hands cuffed behind his back, away from his seat, little Kathy was being enveloped by her mother's tight, loving embrace.

A few seats down, Wally Kelly and Harry Walters stood watching the commotion. Harry's face had turned ashen. "I've got one last bet to place with you, Harry," Wally said, as they watched a pair of agents approaching.

"What's that, Wally," Harry replied, his voice thin and dry, his eyes locked on the lawmen.

"I'll give you two-to-one, that you'll get twenty-to-life."

Few in the stadium had even noticed the furor that had taken place in the stands in back of first base. And the handful of spectators who did, soon forgot. The drama on the field was still unfolding with each pitch, as Pallafox fired a fastball past Gabriel, recording the first out of the inning.

He pitched masterfully after that, he was unstoppable. Marcus Hayes didn't even bother giving him signs. He knew that every pitch Pallafox threw would be a fastball. The Patriot hitters knew it, too. It didn't matter. Pallafox didn't give a damn. In just six pitches, the World Series was over. Jim Pallafox had struck out the side. The Oakland Golds were World Champions.

Bedlam broke loose. Fans began to pour over the metal railings, as the wall of tension that had penned them in their seats buckled, unleashing a tide of joyous, shouting Oaklanders onto the field. Pallafox began to run, too, toward the dugout, when his catcher, Marcus Hayes, caught up with him, and began pounding him on the back. "Hey, man," Hayes said, as they dodged the screaming fans, sprinting for the shelter of the dugout, "you were absolutely incredible out there, man. You know how many you struck out pitchin' the no-hitter? You struck out sixteen, man, you struck out sixteen!"

"Make that seventeen," Pallafox said, grinning.

Epilogue

Walter Kelly's victory celebration that night was one they would talk about in baseball circles for years. Suddenly, his massive mansion became too small to accommodate the celebrities of stage and screen, the corporate tycoons, the broadcasters, the ballplayers, who literally carpeted the garden, filled every one of the thirty rooms with heady chatter and the tinkling of champagne glasses.

Rick, at least, had been unable to find an oasis of quiet anywhere. Finally, he had settled for an upstairs den, where, with Jenny by his side, he was dialing Phil Hanson's home telephone number.

"Phil? This is Rick. And boy, as they say back in New York, do I have a scoop for you! Three scoops, in fact," he added, winking up at Jenny. "First of all, you've heard about the attempted fix, the kidnapping of Pallafox's daughter? It's headlines out there already? Well, good. 'Cause I have the exclusive on it. I started working on it back at the hotel; you'll have it in time to justify that blazing headline Jenny tells me you've been threatening to run on next issue's cover.

"But that's not all," he added. "I told you I've got three scoops, and I don't mean on an ice-cream cone. . . . Okay, I know you're busy. . . . I won't be funny. . . . The second scoop is, you're losing a managing editor. . . . The third scoop is, I'm gaining a wife."

Rick slammed down the phone; he was laughing. "He was still shouting when I hung up on him," he said, taking Jenny's hand. Then he glanced at his watch. "Nine P.M.," he said. "We should be getting back to our hotel. We've got a seven o'clock flight out of here tomorrow morning."

"Okay," she said softly. "Your place or mine?"

Jenny was smiling at him. Rick felt very, very happy. He wouldn't have to visit Tiffany's to see her smile set on a velvet pillow. He would see it every morning, on the pillow next to his.

"It's a toss-up," Wally Kelly was telling Ray Fowler, as they leaned against the bar in the living room. "As far as the police are concerned, I haven't done anything wrong. The bet was placed in Las Vegas, and there's nothing illegal about betting on the World Series there. Of course," he added, "the commissioner will make some kind of ridiculous fuss, saying it's bad for baseball when an owner bets against his own team, or some such drivel. But he's about as relevant as a dodo bird, and just about as smart, too," Kelly added, spotting someone in the far end of the room with an empty drink in his hand, and signaling to one of the waiters to fill it.

"But there's still the IRS," Fowler said, downing a Scotch and reaching for another. "Most of that money will go to them, won't it, since scuttlebutt says you made a profit on the Golds this year, and can't hide it."

"If they recover the five hundred thousand, it's either going to the government or the goddess," Kelly replied. "If the goddamned IRS doesn't take the money—preventing me, by the way, from writing off losses of my baseball club against the profits of my pharmaceuticals firm—my goddamn wife will. And worse yet, they'll probably hit me with income-tax evasion. Now, if only I had someone on my side, a cop, say, who would get up there and swear on my behalf—a character witness who could speak out and tell the world what a fine fellow I am, how much I cooperated . . ." Wally spotted Hardrock Harrison pushing his way past the guests, heading toward a table full of champagne glasses. Wally lit out after him.

For the first time this week, Hardrock Harrison was truly relaxing. The little girl was safe. Harry Walters was in custody; so were the phony Spider and that Selma. The FBI had taken charge of the case now, since the child had been transported across the state line, and the chances even looked good for collaring the mob brains who had engineered this whole damn caper. And that was just the half of it, he was thinking, patting the piece of crumpled paper in his pocket. Lady Luck had shined on him at last.

"Detective Harrison," someone purred into Hardrock's ear, "so glad you found time to come. You know, there's a little business I'd like to discuss with you . . . a consultancy with Kelly Pharmaceuticals that might be worth, say, five figures to you if we can work out a deal. . . ."

"Wally, old pal," Hardrock shouted. "Lookie here, ol' buddy," he whooped, draping one arm around Wally's shoulder, while he extracted the piece of crumpled paper from his pocket with the other. "Hell, buddy, I just won me a five-figure bet—on the precinct Series' pool."

Wally took the betting slip from Hardrock's hand. Despite himself, he couldn't keep from smiling. The sum was in five figures, all right: $118.35.

There was one quiet spot on Kelly's estate, alongside the water fountains in front of the house, majestically spouting towering blue geysers. Pallafox and Norma were sitting there on the grass. They were watching while little Kathy cavorted with the new toys Pallafox had bought her a few hours before. "Now, that was really crazy," Norma was saying, "buying her a bat, a ball, and a baseball glove. She's a little girl, silly," she added, putting her arm through his and snuggling closer.

"Better than a deck of cards," Pallafox replied, leaning down till he could smell the sweet scent of her hair—like spun threads of gold.

"Anyway," she said, "after we're married, you're not going to have much time to teach her how to play baseball. Not at first, at least."

"In the summers," he said. "I'll teach her in the summers. Girls are getting into the game now, too."

"You know," she said then, suggestively, "I've been thinking. Maybe I *should* let my hair grow out again."

"And maybe I should go to law school, right?" he said, smiling.

"A pitching career doesn't last forever," she replied softly.

"Almost nothing does," he agreed. "Except love." He bent his head. He kissed her, long and passionately.

Just then, Kathy came running toward them, her red hair flying, her body threatening to tumble down with each rocky step. "It broke," she was calling, waving the little glove in the air. "It broke," she repeated, pointing to the wrist flap, which had merely come unbuttoned. "Fix it," she demanded, thrusting the glove toward Pallafox. "Fix it, Jim."

"Kathy," Norma said quietly, her eyes meeting Pallafox's. "Don't ever, ever call your father 'Jim.'"

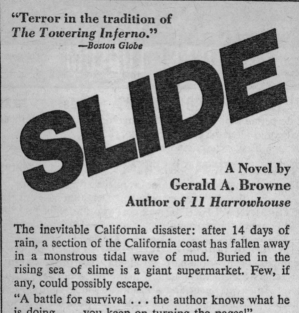

Dell Bestsellers

- [ ] **MAGIC** by William Goldman $1.95 (15141-4)
- [ ] **THE USERS** by Joyce Haber $2.25 (19264-1)
- [ ] **THE OTHER SIDE OF MIDNIGHT**
  by Sidney Sheldon $1.95 (16067-7)
- [ ] **THE HITE REPORT** by Shere Hite $2.75 (13690-3)
- [ ] **THE BOYS FROM BRAZIL** by Ira Levin $2.25 (10760-1)
- [ ] **GRAHAM: A DAY IN BILLY'S LIFE**
  by Gerald S. Strober $1.95 (12870-6)
- [ ] **THE GEMINI CONTENDERS** by Robert Ludlum $2.25 (12859-5)
- [ ] **SURGEON UNDER THE KNIFE**
  by William A. Nolen, M.D. $1.95 (18388-X)
- [ ] **LOVE'S WILDEST FIRES** by Christina Savage . $1.95 (12895-1)
- [ ] **SUFFER THE CHILDREN** by John Saul $1.95 (18293-X)
- [ ] **THE RHINEMANN EXCHANGE**
  by Robert Ludlum $1.95 (15079-5)
- [ ] **SLIDE** by Gerald A. Browne $1.95 (17701-4)
- [ ] **RICH FRIENDS** by Jacqueline Briskin $1.95 (17380-9)
- [ ] **MARATHON MAN** by William Goldman ... $1.95 (15502-9)
- [ ] **THRILL** by Barbara Petty $1.95 (15295-X)
- [ ] **THE LONG DARK NIGHT** by Joseph Hayes . $1.95 (14824-3)
- [ ] **IT CHANGED MY LIFE** by Betty Friedan ... $2.25 (13936-8)
- [ ] **THE NINTH MAN** by John Lee $1.95 (16425-7)
- [ ] **THE CHOIRBOYS** by Joseph Wambaugh ... $2.25 (11188-9)
- [ ] **SHOGUN** by James Clavell $2.75 (17800-2)
- [ ] **NAKOA'S WOMAN** by Gayle Rogers $1.95 (17568-2)
- [ ] **FOR US THE LIVING** by Antonia Van Loon . $1.95 (12673-8)

At your local bookstore or use this handy coupon for ordering: